Evelyn James

Evelyn James has always been fascinated by history and the work of writers such as Agatha Christie. She began writing the Clara Fitzgerald series one hot summer, when a friend challenged her to write her own historical murder mystery. Clara Fitzgerald has gone on to feature in over thirteen novels, with many more in the pipeline. Evelyn enjoys conjuring up new plots, dastardly villains and horrible crimes to keep her readers entertained and plans on doing so for as long as possible.

Other Books in
The Clara Fitzgerald Series

Murder in Mink

by

Evelyn James

A Clara Fitzgerald Mystery
Book 3

Red Raven Publications
2018

Chapter One

Clara had come to the conclusion that cars were a disagreeable way to travel, especially when they were open-topped and forced one to cling to one's hat. She also preferred to keep her eyes closed in case anything wandered into the road. A couple of miles back there had been an ambling farm labourer who had incurred the wrath of the driver of the car she was currently in, for having the audacity to walk along the road. The rudeness of it all had stunned Clara, but it seemed this was the way all 'car-people' drove and treated everyone else on the roads. She had to wonder how an inanimate vehicle could seem to bring out the worst in everyone.

Her brother Tommy sat beside the driver taking in every gear change and fast turning corner with the keen eye of the would-be car owner. Tommy had been left crippled by the war, but if only he had use of his legs the things he would do! He'd love a car, Clara mused, if only he would go see that damn doctor who said he might be able to help!

They turned a corner sharply and headed out of country lanes into a village. The driver, not a day over eighteen Clara was certain, honked his horn loudly as though everyone needed to know he was there. A few people moved aside, while others gave him an evil glare. Clara was trying to remember his name. Jimmy, or Timmy, something with a 'y' ending anyway. He had met them at the station under instructions from his employers the Campbells (Clara and Tommy's cousins) to escort them in the car to the Campbell country seat. Clara had feared as much, she had heard the Campbells were fond of modern things and would not be without at least two cars.

She closed her eyes again as they zigzagged down a narrow pathway between two old cottage walls. It surely did not seem big enough for a car, but the driver Jimmy/Timmy hardly dropped his speed.

It had all been so much bother since the letter had arrived the week before last. Clara had not given the Campbell family a thought in years, except for the traditional exchange of Christmas cards. Her grandfather had had a sister called Rosalie, who married Josiah Campbell, heir to a thriving coal mining concern. Rosalie had moved up North with Josiah and had two sons, while her brother had been more conservative and had a solitary child — Clara's father. Around 1900 Josiah Campbell had sensed trouble looming in the coal industry and had sold his mine for a ludicrous sum of money. He had been lucky, within years the coal market had collapsed, the war brought further calamity, prices fell, workers had to be laid off and instead of a golden goose, the average coal mine was now considered a white elephant.

Josiah Campbell never looked back. He invested his money, doubled it, then tripled it. There was talk of shady deals during the war, but nothing proven. When Josiah died in 1918, safe in the knowledge all his grandchildren (of which he had three) had survived the war, he was a millionaire many times over and his estate was tidily divided between his sons. Now, two years on, there was a wedding due, the eldest grandchild Andrew was to be married on Saturday and the occasion called for all branches of the family to be gathered - even distant cousins.

Needless to say Clara was a little anxious. Hogarth Campbell was the younger of Josiah's sons. He had kept in touch with Clara's father because they had once spent a summer together as boys. When Clara's parents had died there had been a gushing letter from Hogarth, bereft forever at the loss. She supposed the last time she had seen him and his wife Glorianna was at her parents' funeral. Then there were the children, Andrew, Penelope (Peg) and Susan. Clara had a vague memory of them hovering at the back of the funeral procession, Andrew still in uniform, home on leave, Peg and Susan dressed in matching black outfits looking little more than schoolgirls. They must be 18 and 20 now. Clara wondered if she would recognise them.

The car swept through a pair of stone gates ornamented with roaring lions and the driver pumped the accelerator and churned up gravel as they zoomed up the drive. Clara allowed herself a peek at the surroundings. Tall ornamental pine trees were dotted on either side of the lawn, there were chairs arranged beneath them and at one corner a croquet game had been laid out and then abandoned. The birds were singing in the treetops, but Clara noted there were no flowerbeds which disappointed her. April had turned into May and this was the season when many flowers found their form, it seemed strange such a grand garden was bereft of them.

The house loomed up in neo-classical style. The driver pulled them sharply around the curve of the drive, level with the front door. Clara hopped out before he had pulled on the hand-brake, she wasn't convinced he wouldn't start off again at any moment. A butler came down the front steps to greet her.

"Miss Fitzgerald?"

"Yes."

The butler raised a hand and two lads appeared to take the luggage from the car.

"My brother needs assistance."

The butler gave a knowing smile and personally went around the car, retrieved Tommy's wheelchair and helped the young man into it.

"Thanks, old boy." Tommy grunted as he was negotiated into his chair.

"My pleasure sir. May I ask you to both come through? I have been asked to bring you to the summer room where the family is awaiting your arrival."

Clara felt her nerves redouble. She was not one for worrying about appearances normally, but she had the strangest desire to make a good impression on her cousins. She automatically patted her hat and straightened out her skirt, she readjusted the waist which had ridden up from its fashionable position on her hips and almost gave away that she had a figure. The problem was she wasn't convinced it was enough.

"This way please." The butler politely coughed, halfway through dragging Tommy's chair up the steps.

Jimmy/Timmy the driver was rolling away in the car. There was no escape now. Clara braced herself and went to meet her long misplaced cousins.

Chapter Two

"Tommy, you look so well!" Glorianna Campbell swept across the carpet in extravagant high-heels and a dress Clara had recently seen in an advertisement for Harrods. She was not a day under forty, but she was the second wife and that gave her an excuse to wear dresses that would have looked more fitting on her step-daughters.

She approached with arms theatrically wide and embraced Tommy with faux sentiment, kissing his forehead and leaving a blotch of lipstick.

"Oh Clara, you look so nice! The longer bob suits you!"

Clara was equally embraced and treated to kisses on both cheeks. Glorianna's eyes gleamed a little too brightly.

"I am so delighted you could make it. I hate to think how long it has been since we last saw you. I said to Hogarth, we must not leave it so long again! Drinks?"

"Just a gin and tonic. Light on the gin." Clara said.

"Oh make it a cocktail!" Glorianna beamed, "Peg mixes the most splendid ones. Peg what is that new one you brought back from America last year? The Mississpi? The New York?"

"The Boston Belle." Peg had been languidly propped against the fireplace at the far side of the room, now she stood and came towards her step-mother.

Clara had to look at her twice. For certain the schoolgirl was gone; for a start Peg was dressed in trousers and her hair was cropped so short it barely touched the lobes of her ears. She was oddly androgynous in her get-up, there was not an ounce of femininity, from the way she stood to the flat shoes on her feet, yet also she was not precisely masculine.

"I'll mix it." Peg offered, flashing a smile at Clara and Tommy, "Glory never gets the quantities right."

"I thought our American friends had banned alcohol?" Tommy remarked.

"That they did. Prohibition began in January. I was there last October through December and missed the horrors of it all. I feel sorry for all those poor drunks. What will they do now?" Peg was grinning wickedly.

"I don't suppose you've seen Peg since she was a girl?" Glorianna gave a minor grimace, which might have been accidental.

Clara risked a glance at Tommy, who, of all of them, seemed unflustered by Peg's appearance.

"I say Peg, are you one of these modern women who can't stand men?" He asked with such simplicity that even Clara was convinced it was an unconscious faux-pas.

Glorianna tensed, the lines of her dress suddenly becoming straighter. Peg, however, laughed loudly.

"Don't be a fool Tommy. I can stand men as long as they don't expect me to marry them." She offered him a tumbler of clear liquid, "What about you?"

"Pretty much the same." Tommy grinned.

The tension in the situation defused as it seemed clear no one was taking offence. In fact, Clara had the distinct impression that Tommy had already developed a liking for Peg.

"So you've been to America?"

"Only briefly. I didn't like it. Too many gangsters running around willy-nilly with the law taking no notice. They do know how to make a cocktail though."

"The gangsters?"

"Americans!"

Clara took a cautious sip of her drink. It was quite sweet, with a bitter after-taste. Whatever alcohol was in it was cleverly masked, meaning it was probably hideously intoxicating.

"Hogarth? Are you coming to say hello Hogarth?" Glorianna was motioning to a large man to her right who had been standing in the background until the calamity over Peg had been dealt with.

Now he came forward, all joviality and good-humour.

"Darling Clara! Look at you! Why I remember you as that wee thing that pushed a dolly in a pram and refused to eat her carrots. Now you are all grown!"

Hogarth was over-weight, the sort of over-weight that worries doctors and has them prescribing liquid diets and exercise. He was capacious, with a flurried face and a slight hint of sweat brought on by hauling his massive girth about. But he was friendly and appealing. He embraced Clara and she smelt only soap and cologne. His eyes were merry and he seemed genuinely delighted by her presence.

"Your father would be so proud." He held her at arms' length to see her better and a tear dotted the corner of his eye, "Poor Gregory."

"Hogarth, don't upset yourself. This is a happy occasion." Glorianna patted his arm warmly, "You remember Andrew and Susan, don't you Clara?"

Almost eclipsed by Hogarth were his two final children. Andrew was tall and lean, complete opposite to his obese father. He also had a slightly haughty air and refrained from smiling as he shook Clara's hand. For a prospective bridegroom he looked rather under-whelmed. Susan was bubbly and much like her father, she clasped Clara's hand and kept saying how delighted she was by, well, everything. The wedding, them coming, the parties, the food, the dresses, just, everything. Clara suspected too long a time in her company could make you feel quite dizzy. With all the room announced, Glorianna returned to the practicalities of hostess.

"Now, you will want to go to your rooms and freshen up for dinner. We eat at seven, but cocktails at six. We are expecting uncle Eustace tonight. Do you remember him?"

Clara could not bring to mind the older Campbell brother, she didn't think he had come to her parents' funeral.

"Never mind, you'll meet him soon enough. We are rather informal for dinner. Oh, silly me, and dear Laura will be there. That's the bride-to-be."

Clara and Tommy were shown to their rooms (on the ground floor for Tommy's convenience) feeling a bit dazed by the whole experience of meeting the Campbells. Peg did the honours of showing them the way, pushing Tommy as though she had known him forever.

"What do you make of us then?" She asked.

Clara glanced up.

"Beg pardon?"

"Well, you're a female detective aren't you? Jolly good show, by the way. So you must look at that lot back there and have some thoughts."

Clara was not about to admit anything. Tommy was more forthcoming.

"Clara plays her cards close to her chest, but you're thinking something I take it Peg?"

"I'm thinking a lot, but I think it is because I've been in America so long. You see, over there you have to watch your step so much because you never know who the bad guy is, but there is always this unspoken tension and, well, I don't know. It seems to me that when I came home there was just the same feeling here."

"It's probably just the wedding." Clara replied, "Everyone gets nervous about these things."

"Yes, well you haven't been here long yet. Give it a while and you will see what I mean." Peg halted them before their rooms, "Something's not right among them.

Maybe someone's contemplating murder!"

Peg roared with laughter. Clara failed to see the amusement, over the last few months she had been embroiled in two murder cases, one recent, one historic, and there had been nothing funny about them.

"Well, I'll see you tonight, ta-ra!" Peg waved them off and left them to discover their rooms.

Clara pushed Tommy into his.

"I hope it's not true, that thing they say about policemen never having a holiday because their work always follows them." Tommy mused.

Clara looked at him curiously.

"Why?"

"Because it might be the same for private detectives."

"Oh don't be silly." Clara rolled her eyes, "We are at a wedding, what could be further from thoughts of murder? We only have to last the weekend and then we can be back home."

"Yes, you're right." Tommy shook off his sudden gloom, "Peg's a right one, isn't she?"

"I suspect she likes to shock people."

"I don't doubt it! At least she is a bit lively." Tommy surveyed his apartments, "Ever wonder what it would have been like if our grandfather had been the one with the fortune?"

Clara glanced at the green curtains and the hint in the air of fresh paint.

"I try not to. Life is far more complicated with money."

Chapter Three

Laura Pettibone had a little too much money and not quite enough common sense. She arrived at dinner dressed in a sequined slip of a dress that dripped down in folds across her unnaturally flat chest. Her pretty blond hair was bobbed with a kiss-curl teased out onto her forehead. She spun to show off her dress at Hogarth's request, making the old man roar with laughter and comment on what the world was coming to. Bubbly Susan greeted Laura like a long-lost sister. She could not hope to emulate her sparkle, she was far too homely, but she had done her best in green velvet and pearls.

Laura giggled and shook hands with everyone, until she reached her fiancé, who greeted her with a delicate kiss on the cheek. It was also the first time in the entire evening he had bothered to smile.

Clara observed Laura at a safe distance – her dazzle was slightly over-whelming – and wondered what had attracted this unlikely pair to each other. Andrew had to be a decade older than his bride and, at least from Clara's perspective, as well matched to Laura as a mouse to a cat. But when Laura appeared something within him changed. His shoulders relaxed, his manner loosened, he became almost human.

"What do you make of her?" Peg appeared with Tommy in tow, she had not left his side all evening, as if Tommy was some defence at the uncontained femininity all around them; even Glorianna had donned mascara.

"She wasn't what I expected." Clara admitted.

"All sparkle, no substance." Peg said bluntly.

"Does that matter?" Tommy grinned at them.

Peg shared a look with Clara.

"Typical male."

"I know."

"Wait until the first crisis and then where will all that glitter get you?" Peg shook her head, "I despair at the female race sometimes."

"There is room enough in this world for the sparklers and us dullards Peg." Clara smiled.

"You wait until you've talked with her for a bit!" Peg went to make herself another cocktail.

"You have a new friend." Clara smirked at Tommy as soon as the coast was clear.

"Peg's a good sort of chap to have around. You know she has a racing car?"

"Really?"

"Yes, up at Brooklands racing track. Andrew has one too. By the way, she won't admit it but she is woefully jealous of all this wedding lark."

That surprised Clara.

"I didn't think that would matter to her?"

"Apparently it does. Peg's rather a complicated thing altogether and anyway, beyond appearances, she is still a woman."

They were ushered in to dinner by the same butler who had greeted them on arrival. The early cocktails had gone to Clara's head and she felt a little queer as she took her place beside Andrew, almost dead opposite his bride-to-be.

"I'm so glad you could come to the wedding Clara." Laura gushed before they were barely seated, "When we first began planning the wedding I half-thought we would

11

have no guests. Daddy does not have many relatives who are alive or anything less than positively ancient and he doesn't have any friends. I'm relying on Andrew to fill up the church with guests."

"Who is your father?" Clara asked politely, relieved to see the soup was a light one served in small bowls. She was remembering why she rarely drank alcohol.

"Daddy owns the new rubber factory, well, he did other stuff before. But he has been in rubber since 1918. He makes tyres, that's how I got to know Andrew. Daddy shows off his tyres at Brooklands."

"And your mother?" Clara risked a small sip of soup.

"Ran off with a travelling salesman when I was a child, or so daddy says. She never writes."

The bluntness of the comment caused Clara a moment of hesitation. Laura seemed completely unperturbed by the effect of her honesty. She didn't even seem to realise how unusual it was to speak so openly.

"Daddy spoils me rotten because she left. He is really going to miss me when I leave with Andrew. I've promised him we will visit often, or I just don't think he would cope."

Through this announcement Andrew had been mute, working steadily through his soup. Now he glanced up.

"He'll be perfectly all right Laura, he has the factory to keep him busy."

"But we will visit?"

"Occasionally. Christmas and such."

Laura seemed to deflate slightly. For a while she toyed with her soup and conversation evaporated so Clara could over-hear what was going on down the far end of the table.

"Penelope, dearest, you will wear a dress on Saturday and a pretty hat." Glorianna was saying.

"Bloody nonsense! What's a wedding got to do with me wearing a dress? I'm not the bride!"

"Watch your language, young lady." That was Hogarth rumbling up from his soup, "You'll do as your mother says."

"Please do not refer to Glory as my mother." Peg sounded exasperated rather than angry.

"She is as good as. Besides, Saturday is about your brother, not you."

The angry conversation died down just as Laura seemed to revive herself.

"Peg said you are a female detective Clara, is that true?"

"I am, yes." Clara put down her spoon, her soup virtually untouched.

"Investigating crimes? Like in the American novels?"

"Sometimes. Also I trace missing cats, long-lost relatives and unravel all manner of other mundane problems. Last week a lady hired me to trace a knitting pattern she wanted."

"Sounds rather dull." Andrew butted in and Clara sensed a sneer in his tone.

"Only bits of it. I like helping people and some of us don't have rich fathers." As she said it Clara could have kicked herself. She bit her tongue in remorse. Her temper so often was her undoing, especially when people insulted her work.

"I'm sure it really is interesting." Laura moved in as peace-maker, "Have you ever had to find a murderer?"

"Yes. Twice."

"See? Now that is exciting!"

There was a sudden hammering at the door. All the guests looked up. The sound had apparently come from the entrance hall and within a moment they could hear the front door being opened and someone entering.

"Is that..." Glorianna went pale, "I thought he agreed not to come until after dinner."

"You know what Eustace is like with timings. Anyway, he had to turn up eventually." Hogarth placated.

Clara cast a curious eye about the table, hoping someone would offer to explain the sudden tension that had fallen over them all. Her eyes briefly met Peg's, but if there had been any thought of speaking it was crushed when the dining room doors burst open and a giant of a man stalked in.

Uncle Eustace was close to seven foot in height and favoured Hogarth's dimensions, though not on the same scale. He was also hot-tempered and prone to drinking too much. That was the best Clara could remember from rare comments she had picked up at home. He eyed the room with the look of an enraged madman.

"Started without me?"

"Eustace! What a surprise!" Glorianna rose from her seat and fluttered a hand at Hogarth to grab another chair, "I wasn't expecting you until 9 o'clock."

"I know you weren't. That's why I came early. I knew you would eat without me. What is it Glorianna? Ashamed of me? Don't want me sitting in at your nice dinner and perhaps saying something embarrassing."

Glorianna was flushing vivid red, she fanned herself awkwardly with one hand and gave a tight smile to the collected guests.

"Nonsense Eustace, I was thinking of the train timetables, that's all."

"You never could lie Glorianna." Eustace lumbered into the room, as he passed Clara she caught the distinct whiff of beer, "I don't really care, you know. I'm used to it. Father was always embarrassed by me too."

"Perhaps if you didn't turn up smelling like a brewery." Hogarth grumbled, herding his brother to a chair he had hastily placed between himself and his wife.

"I had a quick drink before catching the train." Eustace fell into the chair with an ominous creak of wood, "I hate waiting around, so a beer or two passes the time."

"Or five." Andrew grimaced at his uncle.

"Andrew! Hogarth!" Glorianna cast a stern glance at her menfolk, "Eustace is a guest and we will have none of that talk."

"Good old Glory, always trying to keep things peaceable. They should have sent you over to France in the war, saved us some lads if you could have calmed down the damn huns." Eustace gave a belly-laugh that failed to be taken up by the table.

"Soup, Eustace?" Glorianna was motioning to servants for extra cutlery.

"If you don't mind I'll skip to the real food." Eustace gave the guests a theatrical wink, before his eye fell on Peg, "Who's that fellow? Never seen him before."

"That is Penelope." Hogarth said with barely concealed exasperation.

"Thought Penelope was a girl's name?"

"It is."

Clara caught Tommy's eye. He was semi-amused by the performance of uncle Eustace, but it was apparent the family were not.

"Now where's the bride-to-be?" Eustace's eye roved up the table, briefly pausing on Clara, until Laura announced herself.

"I'm the bride!" She giggled, offering out a hand which Eustace struggled to reach over the table, "Nice to meet you uncle Eustace. I'm Laura."

"Well, you are a pip, aren't you?" Eustace's eyes had grown round, "How on earth did you catch her Andrew?"

Glorianna was trying to distract everyone with the arrival of the main course, but Eustace had honed in on Laura.

"Quite remarkable. What do you want to go marrying old grizzle-guts for? You should have someone lively and fun."

"Oh, but Andrew is fun!"

Eustace burst into another of his giant-size laughs.

"Well how do you like that?"

"Eustace, refrain yourself from insulting my children!" Hogarth snapped.

"But look at her, man! She's one of them flappers, all laughter and knees. She isn't the type for Andrew!"

"I think I can determine my 'type' for myself, thank you." Andrew responded haughtily, making himself appear every bit the stern bore his uncle was accusing him of being.

"If you say so Andrew. I'm not here to cause a stir." Eustace accepted a plate of duck and orange sauce, and for a moment peace descended on the troubled table.

Clara picked at her duck. The effects of the cocktail were wearing off with the addition of food, but her mind was too distracted to have sufficient time to restore her appetite. Eustace nothing like his brother Hogarth; he was boorish, blunt, and rude. His brother played the amiable, considerate host, while Eustace seemed determined to upset everyone around him. Clara had no knowledge if he had always been this way or whether family tensions had made him into this man of insults. Knowing what large families were like, there was usually always something brewing just beneath the surface. Was Eustace the black sheep because he couldn't hold his tongue, or had resentment made him that way?

She snuck a look down the table. Eustace was absorbed in sopping up sauce with potatoes. Glorianna looked disgusted by the performance and was merely toying with her food. Hogarth was making a determined effort to ignore his brother.

Clara returned to her duck and Laura caught her attention.

"Is he always like this?"

Clara gave a shrug. Andrew had overheard.

"Always." He sneered, "That's why, even though Eustace is the oldest, father inherited the estate from grandfather. Eustace fritters his money away in London."

Laura's eyes widened and she looked on Eustace with a new understanding, but it was not necessarily a look of revulsion. Clara thought she seemed rather fascinated with him. It occurred to Clara that she too wondered what Laura could see in her future husband, though she would never voice such thoughts aloud like Eustace.

Dinner ended with a selection of ices and coffee. Almost as soon as he could Andrew deserted the gathering, claiming he was going to smoke on the terrace. Laura watched him leave with a strangely fretful look. Glorianna suggested the ladies retire to the drawing room. Peg started to protest but a look from her stepmother silenced her. Tonight was not the time for petty quarrels. Clara retreated with Laura, managing to catch Tommy's disgruntled look as he was left virtually alone with the over-weight and now heavily sweating Eustace.

"What's up with you then?" She heard Eustace bellowing at Tommy as the ladies hastened to the drawing room.

Once inside Glorianna took a cigarette from a box on the mantel and lit it with impatience.

"Make us cocktails Peg, something strong." She pleaded.

"Not for me." Clara quickly added, "I can only take my cocktails in small doses."

"By the Dickens, that was awful." Glorianna paced before the fireplace, puffing on the cigarette with unconscious obsession, "What possessed him to come early?"

"He wanted to cause trouble." Peg walked over with a tray of drinks, "You know what he is like."

"I can't stand him!" Glorianna took a glass and almost poured the contents down her throat, "How can that man be related to Hogarth?"

"Quite easily." Peg said, taking her own cocktail, "Don't take him to heart Glory."

"Was he always like this? Or is it me? Does he resent me?"

"Uncle Eustace was always queer. I don't remember exactly when he stopped being so welcome at the house, but it was when I was still a girl."

"He didn't upset you Laura, did he?" Susan reached out a hand to grip her friend's wrist.

"Don't be silly!" Laura grinned at them all, "I found it all rather interesting. Dinner parties can be so dull. Oh, except yours Glorianna."

Glorianna waved off the unintentional insult.

"So…" Clara decided it was her turn for questions, "What is Eustace's story?"

"He's a drunken wastrel." Glorianna said bluntly.

"He doesn't get on with father, never has from what I understand." Peg added, "The pair of them are virtually enemies, from what I make out. Eustace keeps his distance, which is just as well. We see him maybe at Christmas, or at gatherings like this, but otherwise he keeps at his Club in the city."

"Does he resent that? You know, being exiled from his family home?"

"If he does he can hardly complain, it's his own fault." Peg shrugged her shoulders, "I think there was a huge rift between him and grandfather. The only reason he wasn't disinherited is because father stood up for him. Eustace should be grateful."

"People don't always think that way." Clara observed.

"Well he drives me to distraction." Glorianna stubbed out her cigarette, "I'll just be glad to get rid of him after the wedding. I shan't be asking him to stay on any longer. I try to be nice and you see how he throws it back at poor Hogarth."

"Andrew is certainly blistering about it." Laura said, with almost a hint of mischief.

"Oh Andrew understands his uncle." Peg reassured them all, "He'll get over it."

"I don't know if I ever will." Glorianna raided the mantel box for another cigarette, "I'll kill him if he ruins Andrew and Laura's wedding."

Clara wished people wouldn't say such things in her presence; they had a nasty way of etching themselves onto her brain.

Chapter Four

Clara accepted the invitation more out of curiosity than anything else. Why, after all, was Laura Pettibone asking her to call round the day before her wedding? She decided not to mention the invite to any of the Campbell family and headed across the family estate, aiming for the rough direction of the village where Laura lived. It was a fine day and spring was reassuringly in the air, soon it would be summer and the welcome warmth would revive everyone after the damp and cold of winter. Clara ambled down the path enjoying the freedom of a quiet stroll away from the tensions of the house. What to make of it all? Would Eustace really upset the wedding? No, he didn't seem to be that insensitive. Just inclined to make his presence known by being as rude and aggressive as possible. Hogarth would surely keep him in check.

"Good morning."

Clara woke from her thoughts to see the local vicar tipping his hat to her. She smiled back. Their paths crossed as he headed passed her towards the church on top of the hill. She supposed she would be seeing more of him tomorrow.

The lane wound into the village taking Clara past a small sweet shop and a pharmacy with big, elongated glass jars of blue liquid in the window. The post office loomed and she nipped inside for directions to Laura's house. Within moments she was back on her way, taking a right turn passed the pub and finding herself suddenly approaching a grand, grey building. It was not on the lavish scale of the Campbell residence, but nor was it humble. The front door was set beneath a pillared portico and a string of windows gazed out onto the front drive. A deliveryman was just leaving as Clara entered the gate and the house had a bustling feel to it, as though it was alive and busy in its own right. She took two steps to the front door and rang the bell.

A maid showed her to Laura's sitting room upstairs. The bride-to-be was reclining on a white sofa in a silk dressing gown, her hair heaped in bouncy curls about her shoulders. She cast aside a movie magazine as Clara entered and stretched out her arms.

"Is it eleven o'clock already?" She asked languidly.

"A little after."

Laura swept off the sofa gracefully and enfolded Clara in her arms. For Clara, always rather reserved with affection, the sudden embrace of a virtual stranger caught her off-guard.

"I'm so glad you could come. Would you like to see my wedding dress?" Laura grabbed her guest's arm and hauled her into the bedroom next door.

The bedroom was decorated in an assortment of cream and white colours, the effect almost blinding. In another home it would have seemed barren, or even bleak, but it was off-set by the piles of gowns in rainbow colours cast everywhere. Shoes were haphazardly discarded on the carpet and scarves and wraps hung off the bedstead in a row. Clara found the room strangely claustrophobic despite its brightness and wondered how anyone could sleep in it.

"This is it." Laura pulled out a white dress that, in contrast to the rest of the clothes in the room, was neatly contained on a hanger. It was just the sort of dress Clara had imagined Laura in. Straight-cut, low-waisted with a plain sash cutting across the hips and the skirt in straight pleats. It would hang just above the ankle, exposing a pair of white calf-skin shoes with a thick heel and a ribbon to tie them rather than laces.

"This is the veil." Laura pulled a tight hat onto her head, almost masking her short bob and pulled the long and vast veil about her.

Clara came forward and helped her arrange it.

"It is very pretty."

"Do you think so?"

"Certainly, and it will suit you down to a 'T'."

"I think it the bees' knees." Laura removed the veil and put away the dress.

Clara wondered if this was all she had been summoned for. To examine a dress and pass comment, or whether there was more motive behind her urgent invite. After all, if Laura wanted a mother-substitute Glorianna Campbell was by far the better choice.

"I noticed your dress yesterday." Laura had sat at her dressing table and was combing out her hair, "I thought it suited you well."

Clara hoped that was a compliment; her dress had been made up by Annie her maid following a pattern in a women's magazine. She couldn't pretend it had the grandeur of a designer dress but she did think it had a certain flair to it.

"Do you wear lipstick?" Laura asked.

"Sometimes." Clara produced a round case from her bag and showed its crimson contents.

"But not mascara? You should, it would bring out your eyes. Here, I'll show you."

Clara was sat on another chair at the table and Laura produced a box of black mascara and a fine brush.

"If you think it too expensive to buy, have your cook make it from Vaseline and coal dust. It works just as well, I have used that in emergencies."

Clara consented to having her eyes 'made up'. She was

still certain there was an ulterior motive to her invitation and perhaps being co-operative would draw it out. Besides, having her eyes done enabled her to be silent while Laura chatted away.

"I've worn mascara since last year. Daddy thought it ghastly at first, but he has gotten used to it. Andrew never said anything, I'm not sure he noticed."

There was a hesitation that Clara felt certain was meaningful, even if she was currently looking up at the ceiling to enable Laura to paint under her eyes.

"Do you have a boyfriend Clara?"

"Not really."

"It isn't easy these days, I know a lot of my friends complain that there are so few young men about. I suppose it was that awful war. I'm sure several of my friends will never have the chance to get married, and they know it too. Just look at Peg. She has clearly given up. Still, I don't blame her for wanting to dress like a man, they still have it best don't they?"

"But you were able to find a man to marry?"

"Oh yes! I mean, when Andrew asked me I just, well, jumped at it. I might not get another chance and I don't want to end up an old maid."

Clara wondered if this was the key to her sudden summons.

"How long had you been going with Andrew before he proposed?"

"I hadn't." Laura paused, "I had hardly noticed him to be honest, but then he asked me to marry him, just like that. It was 1919 and he was looking all dashing in his uniform and I thought, why not? Up till then everything had seemed so hopeless."

"Didn't it worry you that you barely knew him?"

Laura put down the mascara.

"Suppose it did? Just suppose?"

"Well?"

Laura wiped the mascara brush on a tissue.

"What do you think?" She said, referring to the make-up.

Clara examined her reflection. To her surprise she liked the way the make-up had made her eyes seem bigger and wider.

"Not bad."

"Add some lipstick and it will be perfect." Laura was rearranging the table, "Would you marry a man you hardly knew because you were desperate not to be alone?"

"No." Clara was blunt, but she knew Laura was craving her honesty.

"Not at all?"

"Loneliness does not frighten me as much as the idea of spending my life with a stranger. Are you having second thoughts Laura?"

"Oh no!" Laura rapidly stood up and walked across the room, "At least, not big doubts."

"I think everyone worries about getting married." Clara said, "Now you have got to know Andrew, do you like him?"

"Oh Clara I love him!" The out-burst was so impassioned Clara was in no doubt it was the truth.

"But?"

"What do you make of Andrew?"

"I don't really know him."

"But you are a detective, Glorianna told me and I was so excited. To think my husband's cousin is a female detective! Even Peg was impressed."

"That doesn't mean I can judge a person on sight. You are the person best set to know Andrew through and through."

"That's the problem, I don't really know him, not like that. I think he masks so much of himself from me." Laura sank onto the bed, "Sometimes I don't understand him at all. I'm not scared of him, or anything like that. I just can't quite get my head around who he is. I think he has secrets."

"Most people do."

"I want to know everything about him, yet he won't

let me in and some people..." Laura quirked her lips and stared into the distance, "What was your first impression of him, honestly?"

"Honestly?"

"Absolutely."

Clara decided this was dangerous territory and tread carefully. Honesty had a low tolerance threshold.

"I think Andrew is clever, commanding, very much built in a military mould. A little reserved perhaps, shy of his emotions. I doubt he tolerates fools graciously, but I saw no reason to consider him cruel about it. I suspect, like many men who served in the war, he aches inside a lot for a host of reasons neither of us can truly understand."

"Yes. Yes, that is Andrew. See? I knew you were clever enough to understand him all at once!"

Laura clapped her hands together excitedly.

"And do you think he will make a good husband?"

That really was dangerous territory.

"Most men do, with a little time. Has someone said otherwise?"

Laura seemed to sag.

"Susan... Susan seems to think I am rushing in."

"Andrew's sister?"

"Yes. She says I have hardly had a chance to know him and to know if I want to be a wife. She says I am setting myself up for disappointment. But Susan isn't me. Susan wants to have a life, a career. She is good at things like typing and learning facts. I'm not good at anything, except, well, getting dressed up." Laura wafted a hand at a heap of clothes, "I'm sure Susan says it out of my best interests, but it rankles so."

"I can imagine. Look, this is very much your decision, only you can say for certain how you feel about Andrew and marriage. If you want to marry him and are happy to accept all that married life entails, then no one should try and dissuade you. Susan has her own view on life, but that doesn't mean she knows what is right for you."

Laura perked up.

"You really are a wise bean! Have you considered marriage Clara?"

Clara had, but she kept those ideas tucked in a dark corner of her mind, since marriage seemed a far off hope.

"A little. But you know not everyone can get married, sometimes there isn't the right person out there for them."

"Oh, I know, which is why I feel so lucky finding Andrew. I sometimes wonder if Susan is jealous. She's never had a young man of her own and Peg lost hers during the war."

"Really?"

"Didn't you know? They were engaged and everything. It was 1918 I think. That's when she began dressing like a man."

"I'm sorry to hear that. So many people lost loved ones that way."

"Well, I was very lucky that Andrew came back in one piece." Laura picked up a turquoise bangle and lazily spun it round in her hand, "Was Tommy in the war?"

"Yes, that's how he lost the use of his legs."

"That's a shame. I didn't get a chance to speak to him, but he seems nice. Does he like cars?" Laura was suddenly off her bed and rummaging through a drawer, "Here, I've been dying to find the right person for these. Brooklands has a race meet on Sunday, an informal thing but there will be lots of drivers racing. Andrew is in it, we are postponing the honeymoon so he can race! Just think! I consider that very understanding of me." Laura expected approval and Clara quickly agreed.

"Oh yes, very understanding."

"Well, Andrew got these tickets and, golly, if I know who to ask! But if Tommy would like to go, and you of course, two tickets are yours."

"I think Tommy would like that, but we weren't planning on staying beyond the wedding, it might inconvenience Glorianna."

"That's simply solved! You can move in here after the wedding, we have tons of room and it will be lovely to have you stay on a while. The honeymoon isn't until a week after the wedding, what a bore! And Andrew will be so busy with this race he'll hardly notice me, so won't you keep me company, please?"

Clara supposed a few more days in the country could not hurt, it was nice to get away from Brighton and the demands of business. She accepted the tickets.

"Tell Tommy he must absolutely insist on a ride in Andrew's Napier. She is smashing."

Clara's mind was taken back to another young man who had loved fast cars. The dashing Captain O'Harris had never been content on standing still, or for that matter standing on the ground. His last flight in the Buzzard still haunted her dreams.

"Gosh Laura, look at the time. I'm expected for lunch. Will you excuse me?"

Clara hastened away from the over-powering sense of romance and hope that pervaded Laura's rooms. Suddenly it had become too much. Those few days in the company of Captain O'Harris had awakened a strange dream inside her, one she had carefully locked away. Now he was gone and the pain was still raw. She had not loved him, Clara insisted that to herself. She had been infatuated maybe, attracted yes, but love takes time. Even so, this wedding was starting to feel as though it might be a painful exercise for her.

Chapter Five

Peg sat opposite Eustace in a leather armchair, smoking a cigar.

"Come on man, spill the beans, why did you and father fall out?"

Clara was sat at a table by the window writing a postcard she had almost forgotten to send for a friend's birthday, as Peg began her interrogation. Eustace gave a rumbling gruff and swilled his whisky in its glass.

"What does it matter to you?"

"It doesn't matter one jot, except I am curious." Peg sucked contentedly on her cigar, "Bet Clara is too."

Clara kept her head down and pretended not to overhear.

"My fraternal differences are too complicated for light conversation."

Peg made a noise expressing her disbelief.

"Seriously uncle Eustace, what a bore, here I am prepared to listen to your side of events and you won't speak up. Exactly how is that a defence?"

"A defence? A defence to what?"

"To everything! To the tension at dinner last night, to the clear disharmony between you and father. As it is I am inclined to make up my own views on the cause, and they are unlikely to be complementary to you."

Eustace made his rumbling noise again, which seemed to be a sign of irritation.

"Was it drink that did it?"

"A man's entitled to drink." Eustace drained his whisky glass to prove it.

"Then women. Or maybe money?"

"Make up your mind as to my failings, won't you?"

"Then again, it could be all three." Peg tapped the ash from her cigar into an onyx ashtray and waited for a response. It came from an unexpected quarter.

"I believe you will find the rift that occurred between Hogarth and Eustace was fuelled by little more than the unhappy knowledge that Eustace could not be the son his father wanted and Hogarth could, except Hogarth was younger and that meant he should not inherit the lion's share of his father's empire."

Peg and Eustace both looked up at Clara who had tired of the baiting antics behind her.

"Eustace didn't care for business, Hogarth did. But it is traditional to pass these things on to the eldest son, so Eustace was forced into a mould that did not fit him and naturally he failed, or perhaps you would rather I say 'rebelled'. The end result was alienation, long spells away from home, resentment towards Hogarth for being the 'favoured' son and an overriding sense of having shamed himself and his family."

"By Jove." Eustace's hand trembled as he put down the glass, "How did you know?"

Peg was just as astonished.

"Honestly Clara, are you psychic or something?"

"No, but I am afraid Eustace your story is nothing new. For the eldest son to have been ostracised in such a way it had to be pretty much the case." Clara shrugged, "Rather fairground stuff after that, like fortune-tellers, all vague but pointing in one direction. Sorry."

"Sorry? You are bloody insightful!" Peg roared with laughter, "Did anyone tell you she was a private detective

Eustace."

"No. Is that what you are Clara?"

"Yes, but it really is not as exciting as it sounds. Lots of lost dogs and absconding husbands most of the time."

Eustace sank back in his chair.

"You were spot on. It quite shook me, but spot on. I never was the son my father had wanted. Could I have another whisky?" Eustace held his glass out to Peg who obediently poured, "Hogarth was a different story. He was business minded, could do his sums, never caused a bother. I was always the odd one out."

"That doesn't mean you are less important than him." Clara said soothingly.

"No, but it knocks a man down." Eustace took a reassuring sip of alcohol, "Now I'm just a rich fool, too old and fat to be much use anywhere."

"That's a sad thing to say." Clara walked over and joined them, "And I doubt it too. I think deep down you have plenty of skills to be proud of, you just mask them a great deal because you lack confidence."

"You are too kind Clara."

Clara gave a shrug. At that moment Glorianna burst into the drawing room.

"Have you seen Susan?" She demanded.

Peg was startled by her stepmother's ruffled appearance and fraught look.

"No." She said, "Why?"

"Look, don't worry, but I went to her room because she was supposed to be trying on her bridesmaid gown and she wasn't there. We had arranged to check her outfit for tomorrow."

"She's no doubt around somewhere." Peg emphasised 'around' by circling her cigar in the air. She had relaxed considerably now she knew the crisis was merely one of fashion.

"That's the thing, I've looked in all the likely places."

"She'll turn up in a moment." Peg persisted, "Susan is such a butterfly-brain, you know."

Disgruntled, Glorianna swept out of the room. Clara watched her with a feeling of anxiety building inside.

"Susan doesn't always see eye-to-eye with Glory." Peg whispered to them conspiratorially, "You must have noticed the way Glory tries to dress like a girl of twenty? She is always trying to rival Susan in gowns. That's why I like to wear trousers, no competition from the step-mum."

"Does Susan normally vanish when Gloriana wants to discuss clothes?" Clara asked.

"Well, not vanish. Just kick her heels, waste time, you know. So Glory gets fed up and goes off to do her own ensemble."

Clara still felt it was a strange moment to choose to be defiant; the eve of your brother's wedding.

"Does Susan mind being a bridesmaid?"

"Mind? I should think she is quite used to it, this will be her third go. You know what they say about the girl who is always the bridesmaid, never the bride?"

"That's the tagline for that tooth powder advert." Eustace joined in, "Reminding girls that bad breath keeps the boys at bay. I have to say I have never met a girl with bad breath."

Clara's sense of unease was rising. She glanced at the door, wondering what to do.

"Susan is always the third pin at a party, crying shame because she is such a spark. I suppose she isn't so pretty and a little bit dumpy, but she has a charming singing voice." Peg reflected.

"Trouble is there are ten girls for every young lad and they are getting fussy. In my day we were happy if they were single and knew their right foot from their left." Eustace grinned at fond memories, "Of course, we weren't half as forward as they are now."

Clara suddenly couldn't bear her own anxiety.

"I think I'll go see if they've found her." She stood, taking the pair by surprise and hurried out.

Glorianna was in the study with Hogarth, wringing

her hands and talking about search parties. Clara entered without knocking.

"So you haven't found her?"

"Oh Clara, where can she have gone?" Glorianna gave a little gasp.

"I'll round up the servants and send them out looking. Susan wouldn't wander off." Hogarth cast a glance at the clock which was just coming to quarter to nine, "Perhaps she just went for some air."

"It's dark Hogarth! And I checked the terrace."

"I'll start looking while you organise the others." Clara went back into the hall and grabbed her coat, her mind was whirring with possibilities and none of them were appealing.

She didn't head out the front door but instead went downstairs to the servants' quarters. As she expected the male servants were gathered in the kitchen with cups of tea. She spotted the driver who had brought her to the house, yet again his name escaped her and she opted for her best guess.

"Jimmy?"

"Yes miss." He responded, looking worried.

"Susan is missing, you will all be called shortly to help search, but Jimmy I would like you to come with me."

Jimmy hastened from his seat, everyone else was looking confused and one or two were reaching for coats. In the corridor leading to the back entrance Clara started asking questions.

"Are there lakes, ponds or rivers on the estate or nearby?"

"A river runs through the far end of the estate. It has a bridge over it. What are you thinking miss?"

"Oh, some dreadful things Jimmy, but I sincerely hope I am wrong."

"Very well miss. By the way miss, its Timmy." The driver ducked his head sheepishly for correcting her.

Clara gave him a smile, it was all she could manage at that moment.

"All right, Timmy, we have a girl to find."

Timmy led the way down the back steps and passed the garages. He paused briefly to collect two large torches and handed one to Clara. Then they made their way into the dark reaches of the estate. The night was cloudy. There was no moonlight to guide them. Timmy seemed fairly assured of the route to take, while Clara kept her torch low and tried to avoid tripping over. Her new shoes, bought specifically for the Campbell visit, were not the best for hiking across damp ground. Her heels kept insisting on sinking into the soil.

The estate was rambling and soon Clara was lost. Timmy guided them, but with more hesitancy now. His torch beam caught on bushes and trees, the odd forlorn statue and forgotten benches. In the distance Clara could hear voices and knew they were not alone in their hunt. People were calling for Susan, but they were so far back, circling the house, expecting her to not have gone far. Clara was thinking other things.

Always the bridesmaid, never the bride... Susan had seemed so bubbly, so kind and friendly, yet she had tried to persuade Laura to reconsider getting married. Was it genuine concern or something more akin to jealousy? When Laura married, Susan lost a brother and a girl she had come to consider a good friend. Did that upset her? Scare her? Clara hoped to God she was allowing her imagination to run wild and nothing more.

"That's the river." Timmy pointed his torch at a fast moving stretch of water.

"For how long does it cross the estate?"

"Mile or two." Timmy shrugged, "At a guess."

Clara wished she had shared her ideas with more searchers, with just Timmy the river would be difficult to scour.

"Where's the bridge?"

"Miss, do you think she jumped in?"

"I'm not sure what to think, but I want to take a look."

Timmy escorted her to the bridge; it was made of

stone in a classical three arched design. At another time Clara would have admired it, now she was just thinking of all the parapets a person could jump from. She shone her torch underneath the first arch, scanning the rippling water, looking for any sign. Timmy was doing the same on the far side.

"She would be swept away miss, if she jumped."

Clara grimaced.

"I know, but where would she end up?"

Timmy gave it some thought.

"Where the river ends the wall reaches over it with a shallow arch and a ledge. She would have to stop there."

Neither of them mentioned that this was contingent on her still being alive. Clara swept the waters with her torch beam again.

"All right, show me."

They followed the river to the left, the water flowing upstream fast. Along the way Clara's eyes were drawn to the dark water. She kept expecting to see a glimpse of skirt or to hear a voice call for help. Behind her there were still the sounds of the search party calling for Susan. If only they could find her, discover her asleep in the gazebo or walking through the trees. But Susan wasn't answering their cries.

Clara's shoes were certainly ruined by the time the estate wall came into sight. She wasn't thinking of them, instead her eyes were fixed on the narrow arch that was just becoming visible. The river ran under this arch at the base of the wall, allowing fish in and out, but preventing the intrusions of poachers. Clara aimed her torch at it, but the beam wasn't strong enough and all she could hear was the rushing of the water. She started to hurry, Timmy picked up pace too. Tortuously slow, the torch light travelled up the water and picked out the archway and something… something else.

Timmy gave a cry and ran forward. Clara slipped on the grass she followed. Both torch beams alighted on the figure clinging to the ledge that ran over the arch.

Susan looked like a drowned rat barely able to prevent herself from being dragged away by the current. She looked into the torchlight, but could see nobody.

"Susan! We'll help you!" Clara called out.

Timmy was already slipping off his jacket and shoes. He handed his torch to Clara and plunged into the water. Clara held her breath as he swam to Susan. As he grasped her about the middle she easily relinquished her hold on the ledge and almost seemed to faint. He hauled her back to the bank, a dead weight, fighting the fast current all the time. On the bank Clara hurried to reach down and grab Susan. Between her and Timmy they pulled Susan up the grass.

"Oh Susan!" Clara felt herself sob looking at the bedraggled woman.

Susan was crying softly. Her dark hair was stuck to her face and her clothes were ruined. She was dressed in the outfit she had had on for dinner.

"Why Susan? Why?" Clara rested a hand on her back, "Well never mind that, we better get you back to the house. Everyone is so worried."

Susan was unresisting as Timmy and Clara lifted her to her feet. Timmy went to pick up and carry her but Clara stopped him.

"Better if she walks. She is freezing cold and the movement will warm her a little."

Susan was still weeping to herself. Timmy put her right arm around his shoulder and Clara took the left. Together they half-walked, half-dragged Susan in the direction of the house.

"It was an accident." Susan suddenly blurted out as the lights of the house came into view.

"Really?" Clara raised an eyebrow, "If you want to tell Glorianna that so be it."

"I didn't really mean it." Susan insisted, "I mean, I slipped."

"Let's not think about it for the moment. You need warm clothes and a hot drink."

"But Clara, if you hadn't found me…"

"I did find you and that is all that matters." Clara gave the girl a smile.

They were on the back lawn, light was pouring out of a set of open terrace doors and people were milling about.

"She's here! We found her!" Clara called out.

Hogarth pushed past a pair of servants, hastily followed by Glorianna. He ran to his daughter and embraced her to him.

"What in the world?" He exclaimed as he realised she was soaking wet.

"I had an accident." Susan said quickly, "I went for a walk near the river and I missed my footing."

If Hogarth disbelieved this answer he gave no sign.

"Let's get you inside and drinking a hot totty. Martha! Fetch some towels and get the water bottle heated!" Hogarth waved at servants and the crowd slowly dispersed back to their usual duties

Susan was herded inside, shielded in the arms of her father with Glorianna clucking about her and brushing at her wet hair and clothes. Clara was left alone with Timmy.

"Thanks for the help." She said to him, "I think your uniform is ruined."

Timmy pulled at a shirt sleeve and gave it a sniff.

"Nothing a bit of carbolic won't solve." He shrugged, "Goodnight miss."

"Goodnight."

Clara headed indoors wondering just what on earth the drama of that evening had been all about.

Chapter Six

Weddings were meant to be happy events Clara reflected, but the atmosphere in the Campbell house that morning was rather sombre. Susan was tucked up in bed, suffering from a chill and officially relieved of bridesmaid duty. There was no indication of who would replace her. The events of the night before had cast a pall over proceedings. Susan might protest it had all been an unfortunate accident, but Clara was not alone in thinking otherwise. The atmosphere around the breakfast table that morning had been particularly tense. Somehow uncle Eustace had managed to have the sense to not put in an appearance.

As Clara arranged her dress and brushed her hair she agitated herself by thinking Susan's swim was a rather bad omen. To begin blissful nuptials with such a near tragedy in peoples' minds seemed hardly fortuitous. It made Clara uncomfortable, almost nervous.

"I think too much." Clara scolded herself, putting down her brush and glancing at herself in the mirror. She wondered if Susan had any mascara? It was as good an excuse as any to check on her.

"I'm too curious as well." Clara nagged herself as she left the room, but it didn't stop her heading upstairs to

Susan's bedroom.

Susan called out when she knocked. She was propped up in bed among mountains of pillows and eating quite heartily from a plate of kedgeree. Rather than someone with the appearance of a chill, she seemed rosy-cheeked and merry.

"Morning Clara."

"Morning. Sorry to disturb you, do you happen to have any mascara?"

Susan pointed to a dressing table piled with bottles and small containers.

"How are you feeling?" Clara asked as she ransacked the pile, if she was honest she wasn't entirely certain what she was looking for.

"Heaps better. I don't know what came over me last night."

"I'm relieved to hear that."

"Sorry to scare you all like that. I'm not usually the morbid kind, just things got on top of me." Susan forked up some rice, "I wasn't thinking straight and I wasn't really thinking about, you know, ending it all."

"I understand." Clara found a small pot of black cream, "Is this it?"

"Oh no, that's awful stuff. Look in the blue box. Anyway, turns out missing this jolly wedding has improved my mood no end."

"Why's that? I mean, most people look forward to weddings."

"I know, just for me this one was different." Susan adjusted her pillows, "I can't say why and it was only this morning I really understood that it was the thought of the wedding that had made me so miserable. Knowing I couldn't go was such a relief, isn't that strange?"

Clara found a small, round blue box and held it up for Susan.

"That's it, there's a brush about somewhere too."

"I suppose losing a brother and a friend at the same time would make anyone sad." Clara replied as she fumbled through jars, earrings and the odd scrap of paper, "After all, Laura will have a new life, as will Andrew. As happy as that is, it can also feel upsetting."

"Yes, I had thought about that." Susan sighed, "I've seen three friends get married in the last year. I'm the only one left single. Talk about feeling left-out."

Susan gave an unconvincing laugh.

"But you have other things. Laura told me you want a career?" Clara found a brush and went to Susan, "Would you mind?" She held out the jar.

"No, no of course. Bend down." Susan carefully began to paint in Clara's eyes, "You see Clara, I would like a career, well I would like something. Something I could show to people and be proud of. The only problem is I don't know what."

"There are a lot more opportunities these days for women."

"I can't deny that, though there are still too many things we are excluded from. Tell me Clara, how did you decide to be a detective?"

"I'm afraid it just sort of happened. Saying I decided to become a detective would imply that I gave it more thought than I actually did. It just happened to be something I was good at and liked doing."

"There you are, you did decide. You picked something you could be good at and which you liked. So why can't I find something similar?"

"What do you like doing?"

"That's the problem, I quite like doing nothing." Susan finished Clara's eyes and set the box down on a side table, "I'm not exactly a modern woman keen to rush into business and push the limitations of society. Rather I like being at home and spending daddy's money. Doesn't that sound appalling?"

Clara smiled at her as she stood.

"I won't condemn you for it. But I don't really think that is enough for you, else you would not have had this upset over the wedding."

38

"True." Susan nodded, "Perhaps I would like a family?"

"I think you have plenty of time to make up your mind." Clara examined her eyes in the mirror and then headed for the door, "Thanks for the mascara, I'll bring you back some cake."

"Oh don't bother, there will be loads left over. We'll be eating it for weeks." Susan frowned as she sank back into the pillows, "Don't tell Laura about this."

"My lips are sealed." Clara promised as she headed back to her room.

The church was crammed with various branches of the Campbell family, they had spread themselves out so liberally that they had overflowed onto the bride's side of the church, but since the Pettibone guests were rather limited in number this didn't really matter. Clara was escorted with Tommy to the far side of a pew by an attendant, who apologised briefly for the positioning.

"I should think so!" Clara grumbled to her brother, "Shoved up a corner, five rows back, not even in line with the other cousins. It should be pointed out that we are fairly close blood relations, at least we should have been in the third row. Considering we are actually staying with the bridegroom's family!"

"It's this thing." Tommy tapped the side of his wheelchair, "They didn't know where to put me so I wouldn't block an aisle."

Clara's frown deepened.

"That is unfair Tommy, did you not lose the use of your legs fighting for most of these souls here? I'm sure we could have squeezed you into a pew briefly. I shall talk to someone!"

"Clara!" Tommy hissed, his tone suddenly sharp, "Don't make a scene, I do not want to be manhandled out of this chair and into a pew in front of everyone."

Clara sank into her pew.

"I know. I know that." She said softly, "I just… I feel hurt that they didn't consider you better when they organised this. Glorianna has spent enough of Hogarth's money after all. She could have arranged something, instead of shunning us, sticking us up a corner, like we were outcasts."

"It doesn't upset me." Tommy said soothingly.

"What would mother say? She would be so upset."

"But I'm not." Tommy persisted, "It's just a wedding, and quite frankly I would rather be here than be sitting next to weeping aunts and uncles."

"Yes. Yes, you are right. At least they didn't put us behind a pillar."

"Talking of uncles, watch out here comes Eustace."

Eustace squeezed his girth into the narrow space between the rows of pews and edged down towards Clara. He collapsed onto the hard wood with a groan.

"Mind if I sit here? They don't want me at the front, I know that without asking. Look at Glory's face." Eustace raised a hand and gave a silly wave to Glorianna who had momentarily turned in her seat. She glared back and turned away quickly.

"How did you offend Glorianna in the first place? She has only been married to Hogarth these last, what, five years?"

"Eight. Married him shortly after Maud Campbell popped her clogs. I thought Hogarth couldn't get a worse wife than old Maud, oh she was a battleaxe! Ruled her husband and her children with an iron will. Andrew is like her ever so much. She was barely cold in her grave when Hogarth announced he was marrying again, for the sake of the girls, of course."

"Glorianna isn't such a bad thing, she has been very pleasant to us." Clara replied.

"Hah! You don't know her yet, just you ask Susan. That little drama last night? If you ask me Glory had a fair hand in it."

"She was very worried about Susan, you saw that."

"And so she should be, if it were her sharp tongue that sent Susan out into the cold to do herself in."

Clara stiffened a little.

"It was an accident."

"You and I both know she jumped." Eustace grimaced and rubbed at his breastbone, "Damn indigestion, won't leave me be."

"Are you suggesting Glorianna and Susan do not get along?"

"How many teenage daughters get along with a stepmother their father married within weeks of their real mother's death? Typical bitterness and angst. Susan is a dear thing, but rather sensitive. She takes things to heart and Glory has a cruel tongue when she wants. Of course, she is all sweetness and light to her special guests."

There was an unpleasant emphasis in Eustace's words that made Clara uncomfortable. She knew she shouldn't ask, but if she didn't she would wonder what he had meant.

"Special?"

"Glory likes her charity cases, anyone she can fuss over and feel better than. Sorry to say you are it Clara. The poor relations. That's why you are staying at the house and no one else is. You're Glory's project that she can usher around and show to her friends to prove how generous and nice she is. The reason she doesn't like me is that I wouldn't play her game." Eustace snorted, "She wants her friends to remember how she looked after her husband's poor cousins, how kind she was, how nice. That Tommy is a cripple just makes it an extra bonus, 'oh look how Glory takes care of the war wounded!' Didn't you even wonder why she suddenly got in touch after all this time?"

"Ignore him." Tommy said promptly, refusing to look at Eustace, "This is his way of getting attention."

Clara did ignore him, she had more sense than to take Eustace's 'honesty' at face value. But a little seed of doubt had been sown, perhaps not even sown, perhaps just watered. Something deep down had always wondered if there had been more to the sudden invite than the wedding. After all, they had been asked to stay at the house, how often were distant cousins given such privilege?

"Eustace, would you mind moving over to Laura's side of the church, we are uneven." Glory had appeared like a Valkyrie ready to clash shield and spear with a recalcitrant foe.

Eustace scowled at her.

"Yes, I mind. I don't know anyone over there!"

"You know great aunt Bess and her companion Irlene."

"Bess Campbell! You want me to sit next to that deaf old post?"

"Yes we need to make up the numbers on that side, else it all looks rather awkward. Now come, come Eustace, you weren't going to sit with us anyway, so why make a fuss about moving?"

"Typical! Typical!" Eustace pried himself from his seat and started to edge away, "You have it in for me Glory!"

"Nonsense! I've already asked cousins Bert and Freda to move and they were very gracious about the matter."

Eustace launched himself into the aisle of the church, already panting hard from the exertion. Glorianna carefully motioned him to an opposite aisle, made the introductions to great aunt Bess and left him in her mercy. She quickly returned to Clara and Tommy.

"I'm so sorry about that Clara."

"No harm done." Clara assured her.

"He really drives me to distraction. You never know what he will do next. And I'm sorry about you being so far back, this is really most trying. I was assured by the vicar he would arrange somehow to accommodate Tommy's chair in the third row, but as you can see he completely forgot." Glorianna fanned herself with a hand, "I really wonder sometimes, I really wonder..."

She was distracted by the whispered announcement the bride had arrived and rushed back to her place.

"Let the show commence." Tommy said to his sister with a slightly morose grin.

Laura looked stunning as she appeared at the church

doors. The private viewing of the dress she had given to Clara at her house had not done justice to the outfit designer. The slimming lines and low waist, coupled with a hemline that revealed ankle and white shoes, turned the dress into something a starlet might wear. It helped that Laura had the dainty figure to accommodate its unforgiving cut. Her veil draped down behind her and spilled out on the floor like a grand spider's web. Minus one bridesmaid, the remaining girl fought to keep the veil lifted and snag-free.

Clara watched Laura walk up the aisle with a strange flutter in her stomach. To be getting married to a man one loved so dearly in that moment seemed the greatest of things. Clara found herself tight-throated as Laura took her place by Andrew and looked up into his eyes with blissful happiness. Would that ever be Clara? She tossed away the thought; it made her angry getting so emotional and silly. She had her place in this world as did everyone, so far it had been a rather lonely journey and with her twenty-fifth birthday approaching hopes of it being otherwise were looking dim. But she had other things and she was pleased with the life she had created for herself. Still, there were so many missing; her mother, her father, those who had gone to war and never come back. A tear rolled unnoticed down her cheek.

Tommy reached out and took her hand, squeezing it hard. She glanced at him, gave him a smile to assure him she was all right and then held tight to his hand.

The reverend was working his way slowly through the marriage service. Andrew stood bolt upright, wearing his military officer's uniform, his medals proudly displayed on his chest. He did not reveal a flicker of emotion, but surely deep down he was moved by the momentous occasion? Laura was breathless and giddy, she was trying to grasp the words being spoken but was too excited and elated to really catch them. It was all like a strange dream come true and her mind was on the moment they could leave the church man and wife.

Reverend Draper was just getting into his stride as he reached the part where he turned to the congregation and asked, in his most dramatic manner for he had once performed in youth theatre, if anyone among the audience knew of any reason the couple should not be wed?

There was a steady silence, a moment when everyone glanced at everyone else. A silly anxiety infiltrated Clara and made her wish that the long pause could be over. She tensed, but no one spoke. Reverend Draper moved back into action.

"That being the case…"

"Oi! I have a bloody good reason!"

As one the congregation turned to the open church doors. They looked at the women in red in the doorway as though she were a stray dog who had accidentally wandered in. But she was no stray and she knew exactly where she was. She walked forward on black heels, pulling at a mink fur stole over her shoulders.

"Fine turn out, old Andrew, my boy. Did you miss my invite?"

Clara was almost alone in taking her eyes off the woman and looking for Andrew's reaction. He was stony silent. Impassive. Nothing seemed to break his façade of calm.

"Excuse me, who are you?" Glorianna, the avenging Valkyrie, was astride her horse again and galloping into the fray.

Clara had a nasty feeling she wasn't going to succeed this time.

"I'm his wife! That's who I am!" The woman snarled at her.

"Whose wife?" Glorianna demanded.

"Andrew Campbell's! That's why he can't get married to this peewit of a thing. He's already married to me!"

Chapter Seven

Clara suspected there had been very little in Glorianna's life that had ever defeated her, but the presence of the strange woman in red changed that happy circumstance sharply. Glorianna's mouth worked, but no words came out. What was there to say?

"In case you doubt me," The woman continued, snapping open a purse, "Here is the marriage certificate."

She handed it to Glorianna who studied it in a daze.

"No funny business now, they keep copies of those." The woman looked delighted with herself.

Laura was half collapsed in her father's arms, her face as white as her dress. Hogarth emerged from his pew and carefully took the certificate from his wife. He studied it for several moments before turning to his son agog.

"Andrew?"

Andrew was implacable. He moved toward the woman without a hint of anger, remorse, or grief even. He just took her by the arm and muttered in her ear.

"All right, I'll go." The woman said, snatching back the marriage certificate, "But I had to show myself, didn't I? Wouldn't be right letting this carry on."

She stuffed the certificate in her purse as Andrew, still holding her arm escorted her to the church door.

"Will you come and see me?" Clara heard her say as she left, what Andrew replied she never heard.

"Ahem, perhaps the bride and groom and the, erm, parents should come with me into the vestry for a moment and discuss this matter." Reverend Draper looked terribly shaken, his face had lost all its colour and his voice trembled.

"Poor sod's never had this happen before." Tommy whispered to his sister.

"Who has?" Clara returned, shocked herself at the turn around.

Laura, Andrew and their respective parents retired with the vicar while everyone else looked around and wondered what had just occurred.

"Is it true?" Tommy found himself saying.

"She had the certificate and she definitely knew him." Clara fixed her eyes on the vestry door, as if she could bore her way in and find out what was happening. She was worried about Laura, she had looked so… destroyed, when they had walked away.

"I mean it happens." Tommy continued, "During the war there were a lot of lads who married girlfriends quickly in case they never had the chance again."

"How many abandoned them to find another wife?"

Tommy gave a shrug.

"All I am saying is this is feasible. Andrew marries the girl before he goes to the front, a little bit of foolishness and then he comes back and forgets all about her. Goes on with his life, thinks no one will ever know."

"That isn't terribly honourable." Clara said.

"War warps your sense of honour. Maybe she was a girl he wanted in a…" Tommy screwed up his eyes.

"You can be honest with me, Tommy, I am very difficult to offend these days."

"Well, say a fellow wants a good time with his girl, but she refuses without him making her an honest lass. So they pop to a registry office and deal with the necessities and everyone is happy."

46

"She didn't look like the sort who would care about such things." Clara answered darkly, "She looked a tart and by my reckoning several years older than Andrew."

Tommy pulled a face.

"That's not very nice."

"Perhaps not, but I stand by my statement. Besides, whether she is a good-time gal or a lady of strong moral-fibre, Andrew abandoned her, forsook his vows and embroiled Laura into a marriage that would have been wholly illegal. Whatever he might have thought, it would have come out eventually."

"So better now than later. Just as well the woman came."

Clara harrumphed.

"I'll tell you this now Tommy, that woman has been here several days and has been biding her time to reveal her secret at the worst possible moment for Andrew. She could have quietly gone to the Campbells and explained the matter before today. Instead she storms in and humiliates poor Laura who has done nothing to her and is innocent in this matter. That in itself lowers her in my opinion."

"How can you be so sure she did not just arrive?"

"Where were her bags? If she had just come off the train and walked here – it's a good two miles you know – then why were her shoes spotless? Did she look like a woman who had just come off a train? Did she look worn out by her travels? No, she was fresh as a daisy, her hair and make-up faultless. She has been planning this little scene for a while."

"I guess she would have seen the marriage announcement in the papers. Hogarth made sure it featured in most of the nationals."

"The real question is why now? Why not sooner? She must have known how to find him, his name would have been reasonably easy to trace, especially if she had his service number."

"Not everyone is you Clara." Tommy smiled at her,

"Some people don't think like that."

"So say they don't, what does she want? Money? Andrew to return to her? She must realise the latter is impossible!"

"Maybe she teases herself with the hope he just might."

"She looked a little too experienced to dabble much with hope." Clara remarked grimly.

Reverend Draper reappeared. Hogarth was a step behind him. He walked up to the altar and looked uncomfortably at his guests.

"As you may appreciate there has been a small complication in the arrangements for the wedding. We are therefore postponing it until matters are resolved. If you would please head into the village, the Bon-Bon is hosting the reception and we would not see good food go to waste. So please, do go and enjoy yourselves. My wife and I will join you shortly." Hogarth glanced at his attentive audience, "I'm sure everything will be sorted out soon. There seems to have been some confusion. I need not add, please do not spread any rumours about this business abroad, as it really is a very mundane matter."

"Mundane!" Clara half-laughed, "I would hate to see what his definition of a real crisis is."

Guests began to stand and leave.

"Do you want to go to the reception?" Tommy asked her.

"I would rather go back to the house."

"You are too curious, Clara."

"Nothing of the sort! I have merely lost my appetite after this debacle."

Tommy gave her a disbelieving look, just as Glorianna emerged from the vestry. She was clearly flustered as she found Hogarth.

"Laura and her father have gone out a back door. She could not face walking through these people." Glorianna swept hair from her forehead, "Good God, is this really happening."

She hurried down the aisle, half-chaperoning, half-chasing the guests to the reception. Soon there was no one inside the church except Clara and Tommy. Hogarth had wandered away, though it was not apparent where to. Andrew had vanished like his bride. Reverend Draper started putting away his Bible. His hands were still shaking.

"Dreadful thing." Clara said to him as she negotiated Tommy into the aisle, "I hope it didn't affect you too badly?"

The reverend glanced up, he looked almost gaunt with shock.

"Strangest thing. I never expected that. To see her walk in like that!" The reverend shook his head, "Strangest thing."

"There's a man heading for a nervous breakdown." Tommy said quietly as they left the church, "He really got himself worked up over the matter."

"It no doubt shook him deeply. It must be awful to think of someone breaking vows you, yourself hold sacred, so easily."

"Most of the vicars I knew at the front were made of sterner stuff."

"Well yes! They had to be, to be there."

They rumbled down the hill towards the Campbell residence, ignoring the lonely wedding car still parked in the lane.

"I hope Laura's all right." Clara repeated.

"People bounce back quite well." Tommy reassured her, "And she is still young."

That didn't seem entirely comforting to Clara, what did youth have to do with the way one experienced devastating news?

It was just over a mile from the church to the Campbell house and they spoke little on the way. Tommy kept insisting on wheeling himself and making Clara let go of the handles of his chair. The hill gave him extra speed and Clara had to run to keep up, clutching onto her hat and grabbing at the wheelchair when it threatened to run into a wall. By the time they were approaching the drive of the house both were out of breath from their antics.

"I feel quite guilty being so jolly after what has gone on." Clara said as she fought with Tommy's chair to get him up the drive.

"Don't be wet. If everyone was sad when everyone else was sad, because they thought they should be, no one would ever be happy!"

Clara took a moment to drag the logic from that fuzzy statement.

"Probably you are right."

"I am always right, it is a gift."

"Pish! You keep fooling yourself into believing that!"

They were in high spirits as they reached the front door, but that soon changed as they spotted Peg.

"Is Glory with you? No, no, of course not, she is attending that damn reception. Damn! Damn!" Peg had lit a cigarette and was puffing away feverishly, "It's all so ridiculous. Andrew has vanished, just vanished. Probably tinkering with that car of his. I don't know what Laura is thinking right now, did you see her as you left the church?"

Clara answered in the negative.

"Damn again!" Peg finished her cigarette and started a new one, "What a state she must be in? And I get home and Susan is not in her room, talk about having a fit, I had kittens and puppies. I raced downstairs thinking the worst when she saunters in the French windows with a bunch of flowers in her hand. Had been out to get some fresh air. After I near enough squealed at her in righteous fury, I had to reveal why I was home so soon and the disaster of the wedding. She wanted to go to Laura at once, but I insisted she go back to bed. Honestly, this family is a wreck! What do you make of it all Clara? Tell me?"

"Quite frankly I'm as baffled and stunned as you. I

hardly expected what occurred in the church." Clara picked up Peg's discarded fag end which was beginning to singe a hole in the hall rug; they didn't need a fire to complicate matters further.

"So what now? I ask myself." Peg blew out a cloud of smoke and sank back against the wall, "Is it true? I mean, could Andrew really have married that woman?"

"Bit of a pain he isn't here to ask." Tommy remarked.

"If you could get any answer out of him." Peg grunted, "Andrew, you may have noticed, is hardly the forthcoming type. He was bad enough before the war, you could never get anything out of him, it would make you scream."

"I'm sure this will all be resolved. The woman may be a fraud, just trying to stir trouble and get some money." Clara suggested lamely.

"She had the certificate, I saw Glory and father look at it. It seemed genuine enough to them. Glory might have been fooled, but my father is a wily man and he knows what a legal document should look like."

"Peg, try to calm down. We have to take this matter step-by-step, and if it is true, well there are ways and means of solving that as well. It will be Andrew's decision, depending, of course, on whether Laura still wants to marry him."

"Gads, I wouldn't want to." Peg reached the end of another cigarette, "After such nonsense, I mean the shame of it! Poor girl. Poor, poor girl."

"Well, you can't do much until Andrew decides to reappear, so I suggest trying to put it out of your mind for the moment." Clara collected the second cigarette butt as it tumbled to the floor.

"I suppose I could make father some tea." Peg wandered off abruptly, looking half-dazed, "And I could get out of this damn dress."

Clara let out a small sigh of relief as Peg disappeared.

"Right mess, isn't it?"

Tommy and Clara both looked left to see uncle

Eustace hovering in the drawing room doorway.

"It's flared up my indigestion no end." He rubbed at his chest again, pulled a face and then exited to the drinks cabinet.

"Right, how fast can we be packed and off home?" Tommy asked his sister hopefully.

Clara wasn't listening. Her mind was caught up with all the small dramas around her that had culminated in one huge disaster. She was wondering if they should track down Andrew, or even visit Laura. But in the end she knew they would do neither. They would keep their heads down and watch things develop until either Clara was asked to help or asked to leave. In the meantime she thought it advisable to keep out of the way of the family.

"Why do I have the feeling this is going to get worse before it gets better?" She murmured.

"That's because you are a pessimist." Tommy said, "I, on the other hand, am an optimist. For instance I am optimistic we can pack and be on the next train home to Brighton in a few hours."

He watched his sister.

"Except we're not going home, are we?" He added miserably.

"Not yet, it would be like abandoning a sinking ship. We'll hang on until tomorrow, that's all. Anyway, you have those race tickets."

"Think Andrew will be brazen enough to still take part?"

"Oh, who knows? He is mad enough on his cars to postpone his honeymoon! Anything is possible."

"That's what worries me." Tommy shook his head, "Well, don't come running to me when you wish you had gone home on the first train."

"I won't." Clara assured him, "Besides, we are family!"

Chapter Eight

Clara went to bed early that night. Dinner had been an unpleasant event, with mournful faces and downcast eyes. Everyone fudging over a cold montage of dishes left over from the reception. It seemed a lot of wedding guests had felt it indiscreet to eat a reception feast without an actual wedding taking place, so they had made their excuses and returned to their hotels or homes. Far too much food had been left over, so Glorianna had swept it up and had it transported home for dinner. She was trying to put a brave face on the matter, but was clearly drained and miserable.

Peg had smoked herself sick and was toying with a plate of cold meat and potatoes. Hogarth was the opposite, downing his food in record time and demanding more, clearly comfort eating to assuage his misery and confusion. Susan had fluttered down from her room, but was morose, aware that her own performance the night before had not aided domestic harmony. Only Eustace ate with what seemed a normal appetite, his indigestion fast forgotten. Andrew was still missing.

Clara picked her way through some cold chicken, guiltily casting an eye to an assortment of exquisite looking desserts stocked on the sideboard. At home dessert tended to be occasional and consisted of rice pudding or a fruit crumble. The extraordinary dishes that had been prepared for the wedding were a far cry from her usual sweet delight, and her eyes were unerringly drawn to a sherry trifle, with thick cream and gold flakes on the top. The wedding cake had not returned home, at least, not to the dining room. It had been dismantled, its many layers parcelled out between the staff at the hotel and the Campbell servants. At least for them the day had ended with a pleasant surprise.

Dinner finished abruptly. There was dessert for those who wished it, but Glorianna, Susan and Peg retreated solemnly. Clara decided it prudent to discreetly pile a bowl with dessert and disappear to consume it in her room. Tommy followed her example and they quietly made their excuses leaving the two Campbell brothers alone.

"I hope they don't fight." Clara briefly thought to herself as she locked herself in her bedroom.

It was oddly relaxing to suddenly be free of the Campbell drama and safely shut away. Clara dumped her bowl of trifle, lemon torte and chocolate mousse on a writing desk and began spooning her way through while composing a letter to her maid, Annie, informing her she was likely to be delayed in coming home.

Dessert dealt with and the house strangely quiet, Clara found herself at a loose end. She opened her window a touch as the night was stuffy and sat thinking of nothing much for a while. She listened to an owl calling and noted how silent it was in the countryside. At any given time at her house in Brighton there was bound to be some noise coming from outside.

Just before midnight she gave up trying to think of something to do and went to bed. Naturally this was not conducive to instant slumber and she lay awake for a while, her mind working over-time.

The woman in the church had to be genuine. No one would try such a scam otherwise, it would be so easy to dismiss. And Andrew had not said a word, not denied her, not laughed, not even shown a trace of anger. He was so mute over it all. That chilled Clara. Laura had acted as expected; complete shock, outrage and horror. She had drooped back in her father's arms, clearly overcome. Then there was Mr Pettibone, yes, that was curious. Surely any normal father would have ranted and raved over his only daughter being so humiliated? But Mr Pettibone had gone along with things so quietly and meekly. No furious outpourings. No blustering denials. Was this really the wealthy businessman Clara had been told about? She supposed everyone had their own ways of acting; perhaps Mr Pettibone was not the demonstrative type. Glorianna, at least, had acted true to form.

So, if the crisis were true, as it very much seemed to be, where did that leave things? And what did it say about Andrew? Well, in the second case it meant he had lied and kept secrets not only from his wife-to-be, but his family too. Tommy was probably right in that it was a wartime fling, a moment of madness that Andrew had endeavoured to forget. But secrets like that tend to catch up on people. Had he really thought he could get away with having two wives? Surely he realised once it was in the papers there was a high chance his first wife would see it? Or had he made arrangements with her, expecting her to keep her distance and she had reneged? That was always possible. In any case the matter had to be resolved and that left two options; return to his first wife or petition for a divorce. Option one was liable to be difficult. Andrew had left his wife and Clara was of the opinion that if a man abandoned his spouse, press-ganging him into coming back was not going to result in marital bliss. Perhaps, Clara told herself, that was blatant cynicism. But she knew of few cases of people being forced into doing something they didn't want to, where they ended up liking the situation. It went against human nature. Force a person and they had a natural instinct to revolt.

That didn't mean she was softening to Andrew's

plight. He had been a cad. Whatever her thoughts on the woman in red, Andrew had married her, taken sacred vows and then run off. Supposing, just supposing, there had been a real reason. Perhaps the woman had gone first, or he had thought her dead, then that might just excuse his actions. Yet even so he should have checked before his second marriage and assured himself he could legally wed Laura. Imagine if they had had children and then it had all come out! Any offspring would be illegitimate and Laura would have been doubly disgraced! It was all so horrid a thought.

Well, if Laura could forgive him, and as Peg had said that would take some doing, that left only one option – a divorce. Which was messy, public and controversial. They would not be able to wed in a church for a start, and there was a dreadful stigma attached to divorcees, more so women than men, but still...

Laura would need to be prepared for scandal. It would be a real test of her love for Andrew, if not her endurance, and that was assuming her father was prepared to have his daughter marry a divorced man. Very complicated.

Clara rolled over on her side and watched the hands of her wristwatch ticking round slowly in a shaft of moonlight. Pity Andrew wasn't a widower, that would have made things so much simpler. Widowers were allowed leeway, they were pitied not derided. They were victims, not sinners. Perhaps Andrew had convinced himself the woman was dead and that it was fine to marry Laura. If he had he had been extremely foolish. What a mess this all was!

Clara yawned and snuggled down in her pillow. Sleep came smoothly on despite her over-indulgence on sugar.

She was woken at quarter to one by the cold draught coming in the window. She roused from her bed, freezing, and went to shut it. A car roared throatily somewhere in the distance as she dropped the sash and it made her wonder if Andrew was home yet. Had he really gone to look over his car, or had he paid a call on his wife?

Clara dropped back on the bed and drew up the blankets, aware she was suddenly wide awake again. She had been dreaming of the wedding vividly, the woman in red had been as clear as a photograph down to her hat and shoes. The more Clara thought of her, the more she sensed the wrongness of it all.

The woman had been wearing a dress in the latest style, dyed scarlet but there had been a hint of faded charm about the outfit. It was possibly homemade from a pattern book. There had been something about it that implied it was trying to mask an otherwise impoverished lifestyle. Her shoes! Yes her shoes had been old, but recently polished. When she walked they were badly scuffed on the soles and she had not worn stockings. That had not registered at the time, but now it struck Clara for stockings were such an essential of life, yet they could also be expensive.

She had had no jewels, except a half-hidden string of pearls, only they could easily have been costume jewellery from Woolworths, at a distance it was hard to tell. The hat was nondescript, a little knocked out of shape. It had had sequins, but Clara was certain some had been missing. However the woman's make-up had been perfect, if heavy. She was masking her age, but nothing could hide the crows' feet at her eyes and the thin lines along her lips from smoking. She was older than Andrew and it had shown.

But the fur stole! Oh that had caught Clara's eye at once because it was thick mink, fawny brown with a soft cream lining. The sort of thing you wore in the depths of winter for warmth and there she was swaddled in it on a balmy spring day! It was so out of place, except it wasn't. Not if the woman was intending to prove that at one time she had been loved by someone who could afford such things for her. Not if the mink had been given to her by Andrew. Oh yes, she would wear it then. Her one prize from her wedding. She would wear it and march up the steps of the church and rub it in Laura's face. Look what

57

he gave me, just look!

Clara collected her thoughts, what did this tell her about the woman? Well, she was used to poverty and it was real poverty, the kind where even the essentials of stockings were unaffordable. The dress was homemade, maybe even borrowed, the shoes were likely her only pair polished up for the occasion. The hat had been battered around, handled a lot, maybe even been in and out of the pawn shop. But she had once known such wealth it had spun her head. The mink was worth a fortune, she could have sold it at any time to feed herself or buy dozens of stockings. But she kept it because it meant more to her than money, it represented a lost love, a moment of hope when she had thought she could rise above her poverty and be something else.

Who was she? Clara didn't like to think it, but she had the hallmarks of a woman of the night. They were far from infrequent in Brighton and they were made by poverty. There had once been a reform home for them in the town, but more often than not the girls came to the seaside resort because of the money that could be made from the tourists and the soldiers stationed nearby. Clara had seen prostitutes haunting the town. It wasn't precisely hard during the season. Her mother had told her not to look at them, but it was difficult not to when they were dressed to dazzle and falling off the arms of some toff with too much money and not enough discretion. For all their flaunted 'good-times' and cheeriness, there were grim lines on their faces which they tried to mask with heavy powder. It made her think so much of the woman in red's face. Those same lines, that same hardness. In their world it was girl against girl, anyone younger than you was a threat and treated with disregard and no sympathy. Why should Laura be viewed any differently?

Clara shuddered off that line of thought. It had all grown so muddled and dark, now she was comparing marriage to prostitution. Yet it made sense. During the war London was a regular stopover for men on leave, some preferred to stay there and indulge rather than go home. Indulging meant drinking, sometimes drugs, and very often women – the bought kind. The truth was prostitution had become quite a business in those strange days and the police were barely able to keep on top of the brothels and call-girls. So Andrew wanders into a den of vice and he meets a woman, and he likes her, he thinks himself in love even. Then tomorrow he is headed to war, perhaps he shall die on the front and he is swept up in a tide of passion and fear, and he thinks he shall marry this woman, the woman he loves. He shall go to the front with a sweetheart's name on his lips.

Clara paused. Had Tommy ever done something like that? If he had, would he even tell her? She was not naïve, or stupid. The men who refrained from consorting intimately with girls, whether prostitutes or not, were remarkably few. She would not blame Tommy if he had, she didn't blame any of them. Not when the future they faced was so bleak.

Clara shut her eyes and concerned herself with falling back asleep. Her clock ticked reassuringly and the silence seemed peaceful, even if it hid a wealth of torn emotions. Slumber found her again.

When she woke for the third time she wasn't sure the cause. Her wristwatch said five minutes past four and there was a faint glow outside that hinted at dawn not being far off. Clara rolled onto her back and heard the sobbing. It was a woman weeping, softly but heavily. Perhaps she would never have heard it, never have woken from her sleep, had it not been so near. Clara drew a mental picture of the house in her mind and tried to think whose room was closest to hers. Susan's bedroom was surely just above her. It could easily be Susan who was weeping so solemnly. Clara listened a while, she was not tempted to go up and check on her. People who pick the middle of the night to start crying usually do so because that is the time when they are least likely to be disturbed by a well-wisher. They don't want someone to creep in and start sympathising.

If it was Susan, Clara fully understood her anguish. She could be weeping for the sake of her friend's broken marriage, but weeping in young women is usually self-centred, unless they are mothers. Weeping comes from the heart and it tends to break when we are weakest and when we are thinking the hardest of ourselves. Clara knew what that was like. She only ever cried in private and when she did it was because something had penetrated her usual shell of self-confident calm. She wouldn't be surprised if Susan was weeping over her own misfortunes in life. Her bubbliness masked a deep-centred unhappiness. Susan was lost, she didn't know what she wanted from life, yet at the same time she wanted something. She had no husband, which might have been off-set if she had a career of some description, even a hobby, but she had none and, truth be told, life as a housewife was still the only career most women could expect. So she was jealous and that made her feel guilty, and guilt made her angry at herself and so she wept.

Oh yes, Clara knew all about that. How often had she sat and wondered where her future lay? Yes, she had her work and it was good work, but she was still lonely. For a brief period a few weeks ago that loneliness had been assuaged by a dashing ex-RFC captain. O'Harris had been everything that normally drove Clara away; brash, over-confident, boastful, driven. Instead he had drawn her in and within a short time Clara had begun to think of him a lot more than was usual. His disappearance had hurt. She denied loving him, because Clara Fitzgerald did not fall that easily, but he had shown her an insight into another world, a world where love, maybe even marriage was possible. And then he had gone and blown it.

Clara tossed onto her side gruffly. He had ruined her last hopes. She had opened a small, yet firmly sealed door inside herself, for him, and when he left it was murder closing it again. Perhaps it hadn't really closed. A faint smile played on Clara's lips because a thought had struck her. That silly man Oliver Bankes was still around. She wasn't sure if he irritated her or appealed to her. He definitely drove her insane. He was so disorganised and scatter-brained. Sweet, but hopeless. He was the sort of man who would need a full-time wife just to ensure he got dressed and had breakfast in the mornings, not a woman who had her own life to lead. Still, he was nice company and he had taken her out for afternoon tea every day after the loss of O'Harris was known, just so she didn't get down in the dumps. Silly man! But, bless him, he was so amiably reliable. Clara rested back. Her last thoughts were of Oliver Bankes and his endless photographs of Brighton.

Chapter Nine

"We're heading to the race track, come on."

"Tommy Fitzgerald don't pester me! I barely slept." Clara splashed cold water on her face.

"You know Andrew didn't come home last night? Peg wants to see if he is there. He will be of course. I'm sure of it."

"Perhaps we should have checked the river again." Clara said grabbing up her purse.

"Don't be cruel." Tommy frowned at her, "Come on! Come on! We have some cars to inspect!"

Clara rolled her eyes at her brother.

Brooklands race track fitted neatly into the rolling Surrey landscape, strangely at peace with its country surroundings. Built in 1907 by Mr Locke King, a wealthy car enthusiast, the circular track lolled up and down the rough ground and man-made hills. It was rather alien to Clara's eyes, these huge swathes of tarmacadam and concrete, coursing at angles and tight turns to give the cars and drivers a good run for their money. Though the landscape had grown up around it and removed some of its 'newness' it still stood out against a backdrop of trees and fields.

"The track is 1,000 feet wide and 2 miles, 1,350 yards

in circumference." Tommy read off a small leaflet a man at the gates had given them, it seemed it was too early in the morning to be worrying about tickets and the man had waved Tommy, Clara and Peg through without asking to see them, "The total length is 3 and a quarter miles. Now, over there were the land rises, that's the Byfleet, made from two huge bankings that are so tall they tower over the roofs of nearby houses."

"I'm sure that delights the householders." Clara said.

"When the land you live on is owned by Mr Locke King you don't exactly have an option." Peg added, catching Clara's tone.

"It says here at one point the track crosses the Wey itself and at another it runs in the lee of a railway line. Oh and Clara, Alcock and Brown's Vickers Vimy aircraft they used in the World Record crossing to America was made here."

"They make a lot of planes in the sheds near the track." Peg pointed into the distance, "The long straight is an ideal landing strip. Ask Andrew and he will tell you the mess the Royal Flying Corps made of the racetrack during the war."

They were approaching a series of white garages. Cars were sitting idle in front with men in overalls tinkering with them.

"Last minute touches." Peg nodded, "If Andrew is anywhere it will be here. He usually has garage 10."

"Peg, what do you make of Andrew staying out all night? I mean, is that usual for him?" Clara asked as they threaded through scattered tools and spare tyres.

"He can be like that." Peg answered carefully, "Prone to brooding. Trouble is, I can't say for sure if he is upset because the woman was a nasty fraud or because she was real."

Clara had been thinking the same. The line of garages was well-lit in the sunlight and it was not hard for Peg to suddenly give a cry and point out Andrew's Napier. It was painted a dark green and sitting on the very edge of the garage area, between two pillars. A pair of legs stuck out from underneath, moving slightly as their owner stretched to reach into the belly of the beast.

"Andrew!"

The legs twitched and went still for a moment. Then their owner cautiously pulled himself out from under the car. Andrew's face was smattered with oil and he looked as tired as Clara felt. When he stood, wiping his hands with a cloth he only briefly looked at his sister then refused to meet her eye.

"I was so worried!" Peg hopped forward and flung her arms about his neck, "Silly boy!"

"Don't make a fuss Peg." Andrew brushed her away, "What are you all doing here?"

"Well firstly we have tickets for the race." Clara motioned to two slips of paper in Tommy's hand, "But secondly, and I dare say most importantly, we came to ensure you were here and all right."

Andrew gave a sullen shrug.

"Why did you run off like that?" Peg demanded, "We were beside ourselves! Where were you last night?"

"I slept in the garage." Andrew vaguely waved in the direction of the building behind them, "I didn't much want to face everyone last night. I knew you would only ask questions."

"What do you expect after yesterday's drama?" Clara asked a little hotly, feeling irritated she had ever been worried at all about the surly man before her.

Andrew made no reply, just flicked at a strand of loose cotton on his steering wheel.

"Bonzo, Herr Campbell!" A man in driver's cap waved at them as he walked passed, "I am trying my Opel. See if she remembers the track!"

Andrew lifted a hand in response, but he was still distracted. Clara looked enquiringly at Peg.

"Mr Francke, Austrian." Peg answered, "So he is racing today?"

"Yes, just to top off my bad luck. I thought his Opel

would be in crates and hay for at least another year." Andrew finished off with the loose thread and sat back on his car, "Look, if you are here to natter on about yesterday I don't want to know."

"Come off it Andrew! You have to discuss it!" Peg looked at him aghast.

"It's between Laura and I. I'll find a way to put things right, but I don't need you barging your noses in. Especially you." Andrew's last words were adamantly directed at Clara, "I don't need a busybody interfering in this."

"Mind your tongue!" Tommy snapped before Clara had the chance, "That's my sister and she isn't a busybody, she is a very clever detective and you might be grateful for her help one day."

"Might I?" Andrew scoffed, "When I next lose my gloves I'll let you know then."

"You are insufferable Andrew." Peg snapped at her brother, "I hope you damn well lose this race, you don't deserve to win."

Andrew gave her an unpleasant smile as she walked away with Clara and Tommy.

"He isn't usually this bad." Peg apologised, "Isn't this business hateful?"

Clara put a friendly hand on Peg's arm.

"Try not to fret."

"It's just such a mess Clara. Who is this woman? Does she have a claim on my brother?" Peg fumbled in her trouser pocket for a cigarette, "I'm desperate for a gasper. I can't stand this."

"There goes Herr Francke's Opel." Tommy leaned forward in his chair as a silver car streaked past on the racetrack, "She's a nimble thing."

"Oh yes, Andrew absolutely hates Francke and his car." Peg muttered lighting her cigarette, "He hasn't really got much chance against him."

The thrum of an engine reverberated into the distance. The Surrey countryside seemed unmoved by the

65

commotion, even a flock of rooks in a nearby tree ignored the noise.

"I really can't see how Andrew can even think of racing." Peg dragged hard on her cigarette, "He doesn't seem to give a damn about Laura."

Suddenly there was a screech of brakes and a horn blared. Everyone froze. The workmen glanced up from the cars, other drivers stopped in the middle of checks and donning goggles. A silence descended. Had the Opel crashed on an open stretch of road pre-race? No one seemed to want to move and find out. Then, just as suddenly, an engine roared again and the Opel was heading back towards them, coming the wrong way on the track.

"What's the blighter doing?" Tommy was trying to see Francke's face, what could have turned him about?

In moments the Opel was drawing up before a building Clara understood to be the racing steward's office and Francke was jumping out.

"Perhaps a problem with the track?" Peg shook her head, "And after all that effort they put into repairing it."

Clara was edging forward. Her eyes had been caught by the look of shock on Francke's face in the brief moment before he left his car. He didn't look like someone who had found a pothole, so what did it mean?

Several officials ran out of the hut at undignified speed, heading up the track in the direction Francke had originally gone. Francke went to follow but he was driven back by gestures from the officials. He stomped instead towards the garages.

"Herr Francke, what is it?" A mechanic stood up and asked.

Francke gave him a grisly look, grimacing with his lips curled back on his teeth.

"A body." He said, "A woman on the track."

"Oh Lord!" Peg gasped and dropped her cigarette, "What if it's Laura? What if she…"

"Don't jump to conclusions, it could be anyone." Clara

said quickly, "Maybe an accident?"

"Damn fool woman, right in the track. I nearly hit her." Francke scowled, "If she weren't already dead, she would have been."

"Mr Francke, what did she look like?" Peg was gnawing at her lip, "Not a young blonde girl?"

"Nein, she was older with dark hair and a red dress."

Clara felt a shiver go down her spine.

"A red dress?"

"Someone has rung for the police." Francke continued.

As he spoke there was a distant ringing of bells that indicated the peelers were on the march.

"We need to go look." Clara said quietly in Peg's ear, "If it is the woman in red…"

Peg's eyes went wide.

"What an awful thing Clara, but I suddenly thought wouldn't that solve a lot?"

"Perhaps. But we need to look first."

"What about Andrew?"

Clara glanced backwards and could see Andrew walking down with the other men, curious as to what was happening.

"Tommy, keep him here a moment will you? I don't trust him not to scarper again if he finds out who I think is lying on the racetrack."

Tommy turned his head, not relishing his task.

"I'll do what I can."

"Good. Come on Peg, let's see what all this business is about."

They walked up the track, Clara's arm through Peg's, mainly because the latter was looking reluctant to come. Three stewards were standing at a point in the track where it turned and ran between two man-made banks – the Byfleet as Tommy had called it. Clara did not anticipate they would welcome her arrival and she was far from surprised when the nearest marched forward.

"I'll have to ask you ladies to turn back." He said brusquely.

67

"I'm sorry for the bother, but we have an awful feeling we know the lady." Clara couldn't quite see past him to confirm her suspicions, "We thought we better come up and make a formal identification."

"I don't know about that, that's police business." The steward said firmly, "And I don't care for showing ladies around corpses."

"Then we will just wait here until the police arrive." Clara responded, "I think they will want to see us."

"You do that." The steward snorted, then he walked back a bit and took up a position that blocked the view of the body from the two ladies.

"Clara, it can't really be her, can it?"

"Now you are sounding hopeful."

"I know, I know, that is so awful. But just think if it is, then all this business is over and Andrew can get on with the wedding. If Laura wants him of course, I'm not sure I would."

"If she is dead," Clara picked her words cautiously, "If she is, then I think matters are liable to become a lot more complicated before the day is out."

"Surely not? She must have fallen down one of those banks, or come over unwell. Perhaps she was trying to find Andrew like us and got lost in the dark. I dare say it would be rather unpleasant falling down that steep bank and onto concrete. It could break your neck!"

Clara was reserving judgement until she had more details, there was no point running off at a tangent until they knew it was really the woman in red, and, of course, what had killed her. The loud bells of the police cars were growing nearer, gates were being flung open and a black car slid onto the track and rumbled up to within a foot or so of Clara. The passenger door opened and a man in a suit and hat climbed out. He was a little rumpled around the edges and his suit had seen better days. Clara had no doubt he was a police inspector. Clara let go of Peg and hurried towards him.

"Inspector, I'm sorry to butt in, but my cousin and I

believe we may know the woman up ahead."

The inspector gave Clara an amused look.

"Do you now?"

"You may sneer inspector, but we have good reason to believe the woman is someone we met only yesterday and, if that is the case, we may be able to help you with this matter."

The inspector was close to laughing now, looking at the young lady before him who was acting in all seriousness as though she was a police officer.

"When we need public opinions I will let you know." He smirked.

"Inspector," Clara's tone darkened, she was not about to be ignored or talked to so impertinently, "Though I am certain you are a man of the world who knows his job from top to bottom, on this occasion I fear you have made a misjudgement. I am not a fanciful creature who has come for a spot of sight-seeing. My name is Clara Fitzgerald, I am cousin to the Campbells. You may recognise Penelope Campbell behind me."

The inspector observed Peg and his expression changed, some of his cockiness evaporated.

"I am sure you are aware of the influential nature of that family in this area. Now, I have reason to believe that this woman is connected with the Campbells and, if I am right, this could prove to be very serious. I need not add that the family will do all in their power to avoid publicity of this."

"And where does that leave you Miss Fitzgerald?"

"My position is equally complicated. If this case unfolds as I imagine, or should I say dread, then at some point I likely will be called upon to aid the family. You see, in my home town of Brighton I operate as a private detective. And before you smirk again inspector, I shall have you know I have already solved two murder cases this year. If you doubt me you may contact Inspector Park-Coombs of the Brighton constabulary, who will inform you of my credentials." Clara dug a business card out of her purse and wrote on the back in pencil the number for Inspector Park-Coombs, "I'm sure he will be completely honest with you and will not hold back from outlining my faults, but so be it. As I say, no doubt at some point my job shall be remembered by the Campbells and I will be called upon to assist. I would, therefore, appreciate it if we could get off on the right foot."

The inspector studied the card at length.

"A female private detective?"

"Is it so surprising inspector? There have been female police officers since 1914."

"That there have." The inspector nodded, "But you are jumping the gun, you don't know yet if this woman is connected to the Campbells."

"Call it a dreadful hunch." Clara replied, "That and I have a very cynical view of the way the world works. Meaning if the worst can happen, it shall."

The inspector gave a little smile and slipped the card into his coat pocket.

"Perhaps you best come this way Miss Fitzgerald."

The body was sprawled on the tarmac. The woman was staring up at the sky, like she was looking doggedly for something or someone. She was very pale and very dead.

"So, is your hunch confirmed?" The inspector asked.

Clara looked at the worn shoes, the red dress, crumpled up over her stocking-less knees, the forlorn black hat, twisted forever out of shape and the hard-lined face.

"Yes." She said sadly, "My Lord, I was so hoping I was wrong."

The inspector crouched by the body and studied it a while.

"Is the doctor here yet?"

"Coming!" Shouted a voice, and a fat balding man ambled up the racetrack.

He dumped a black medical bag by the side of the woman and wiped at his flushed face with a handkerchief.

"I fear we are in for a hot summer inspector." He muttered.

"Could you confine yourself to the body for a moment."

The balding doctor knelt down and felt for a pulse, rather superfluous since the body was stone cold. He gave a cursory look at the clothing, and then carefully lifted the woman's head. There was a very small patch of blood and a smeared stain in her hair.

"She landed on her head." The doctor mused, "But she was already dead. No bleeding, you see."

His hands strayed to her face, then down to her neck. He pulled at the collar of the dress and then gave a satisfied huff.

"Strangled. Clear as day."

The inspector leaned forward, Clara found herself doing the same.

"So she was strangled then dumped here?"

"Looks like it."

The inspector turned his attention on Clara.

"Who is she then?"

"I don't know her by name, only by sight."

The inspector's expression was not nice.

"You persuaded me to let you through here for a woman you had only ever glanced at?"

"It is not so simple." Clara said quickly, aware the inspector's patience would not last long, "Yesterday was the occasion of Andrew Campbell's wedding to Laura Pettibone, and yesterday this woman marched into the church and declared herself Andrew Campbell's wife. The ceremony was ruined, the bride-to-be humiliated. And now the culprit of the drama is lying dead. Do you see why I was so concerned?"

"Where is Andrew Campbell now?"

Clara gave a small sigh.

"Garage 10, working on his Napier. Inspector, the obvious assumption is to think Andrew did this."

"Is it now?"

71

"I know where this will all lead, the family are in a state as it is. Andrew bolted after the wedding, we only just found him a few minutes before the discovery of the body and he is refusing to talk to us."

"Then maybe he will talk to me. Sergeant, go fetch Mr Campbell."

The sergeant hurried away.

"I'm very worried inspector." Clara said, "There seems an awful lot wrong with the Campbell household, not least this poor woman's presence."

"Good job I'm here then." The inspector grinned.

Clara refused to rise to the bait.

"Miss Fitzgerald, that rings a bell? Weren't you involved in a case with that pilot who was trying for a flying world record?"

"Captain O'Harris." Clara felt the usual sadness as she spoke his name, "I discovered what had happened to his late uncle."

"That's right, it was in all the papers. The dead uncle whose corpse vanished." The inspector paused a moment, "I showed that to some of the new lads, had them work on it as a sort of theoretical case. So tell me, did the solution come to you as another hunch?"

Clara gave him a long look.

"Sadly inspector that was indeed the case, though as it happens I had a number of clues to assist me, including some threatening messages which implied I was on the right track."

"Really? Some people take you quite seriously then?"

Clara was about to rebuke the policeman when she spotted the wry grin on his face.

"Inspector, are you trying to tease me?"

"Miss Fitzgerald I would never even think of doing such a thing." The inspector's smile belied his statement.

Clara suspected they would get along just fine.

"Well, I don't intend to get involved in this case if I can help it. I would much rather go home to Brighton."

"That would be a shame." The inspector said, "Since I

have a feeling the Campbells are going to need all the help they can get in this matter."

"I know." Clara answered, "Oh, I know."

"The name's Jennings, by the way." The inspector held out a hand. Clara shook it.

At that moment the sergeant came into sight escorting a truculent Andrew Campbell. He had a stormy look on his face and chaffed at being ushered by the sergeant along the track.

"He has an unpleasant manner and a gruff temper, but that does not make him a killer." Clara said quickly.

"Miss Fitzgerald, just as I must not imply you are any less suited for detective work since you are a woman, please do me the same honour and not regard me as lacking in common sense or intelligence because I happen to work for the police."

"I do apologise." Clara replied, "You do just so look a typical policeman."

It was her turn to give a smile and mock the inspector. He went to speak and then noted her look.

"Yes, we will get along just fine." She said aloud, trying to avoid laughing.

Andrew Campbell appeared in front of them. His first look was a harsh one at Clara.

"What is she doing here?"

"Never mind that." The inspector's tone hardened, "I need you to come this way and see if you recognise this woman."

"I don't want my business being known by everyone." Andrew baulked.

"Then perhaps you should have considered divorcing your first wife before attempting to marry your second?" Clara told him sweetly.

The jibe hit home. Andrew bit his tongue and followed the inspector. It was not long before the body was fully in view. Clara waited for the natural emotion that must now arise from Andrew. He hesitated. For a second he disbelieved his eyes. Then he starting to sway ever so faintly and his face flushed.

"You know her?" The inspector asked.

"Yes."

"May I ask how?"

Andrew pulled a face, he was warring between relief and rage at the sight before him.

"She is my wife."

Clara gave an unconscious sigh. She had known it, but she hadn't been certain. A part of her had hoped that the woman was a fraud. Clearly not.

"Can you tell me her name?" The inspector continued.

"Shirley Cox." Andrew spoke quietly, "If you need to know more than that I can't help you. We have been estranged some time."

"Here, Sir." The sergeant had been examining the body again and had found Shirley's handbag half tucked under her, "It's empty except for this."

The wedding certificate emerged once more from the handbag, a little more crumpled and rubbed around the edges, but still declaring its accusation.

"You married in 1915?" The inspector read the paper, "What of the witnesses?"

"One was the subaltern in my unit, he died six months later. The other was a friend of Shirley's." Andrew was solemn, "What happened to her? Did Francke hit her?"

"No." The inspector folded up the certificate and placed it in his pocket with Clara's card, "She was strangled."

The shock Clara had been expecting finally came over Andrew. It was like he had been jolted by a spark of electricity. His face, as far as emotions ever registered upon it, seemed to indicate he was genuinely surprised.

"Strangled? By who?"

"That is what I shall be investigating." The inspector said coolly, "I will ask you to keep close to home for the next few days so I can contact you easily."

Andrew's temper kicked.

"I didn't do it!"

"Andrew," Clara came alongside him and gently took his arm, "The police will have to ask questions of you, that is what they do. Perhaps we should go home."

"Will you get off me?" Andrew snatched away his arm and stormed off, back in the direction of the garages.

"Delightful man." The inspector huffed.

"I would try to defend him because he is in shock, but I really don't like him enough." Clara was thinking she should get back to Brighton sooner rather than later, and yet knowing full well she was stuck here, "Good day inspector, do give Park-Coombs a call. I suspect I shall see you again."

"Good day Miss Fitzgerald."

Clara collected Peg as she left behind the murder scene. Peg was upset and trembling, she wouldn't say a word as they went back to fetch Tommy. Clara wondered how long it would be before the Campbells realised how bad this situation could get.

Chapter Ten

Clara would have preferred avoiding a cocktail session with the Campbell family that evening, but it had been made clear to her that refusing the invitation was out of the question. The family had gathered in the drawing room, a very unhappy arrangement. No one was talking, despite them all being summoned under the pretence that they must 'discuss' things. Glorianna was heading the conference, but she was as quiet as the rest. Peg had found some old magazines to read and Eustace was working his way through a bottle of whisky. Tommy gave his sister a sombre look, wishing there was some way he could extract them both from the situation.

"Is Andrew joining us?" Eustace asked knowing precisely that he wasn't.

"He refuses to speak to anyone." Glorianna rubbed over one eye as a headache crept on.

"He's a silly lad. What is all this wife business about anyway?"

"Eustace, it's not your business." Hogarth told his brother gruffly.

"Then why are we all here?" Eustace poured himself another dram, "Unless this is a little charade until you can work up the courage to ask Clara to investigate this nonsense?"

Clara closed her eyes, her stomach sinking. She had the same suspicion. Glorianna coughed politely.

"Now Eustace has mentioned it, have you given the matter any thought Clara?"

Clara opened her eyes. She didn't drink much but right now she could do with a large sherry.

"Only as the rest of you have. It is not my place to interfere."

"Oh but Clara, you must. We insist! This whole scandal is too much to bear. If it gets out Andrew will be ruined and what about poor Peg and Susan, what reputation will they have left? What prospect for marriage?"

"I can't change the fact Andrew was married to this woman." Clara answered.

"No, I don't say you can. But you must find who murdered her. I know it was none of us, but until the real culprit is caught people will look at us askance. I don't trust the police, I never have."

"The inspector seemed competent." Clara was trying to think of a way to turn the topic in a different direction.

"I do not care for the police. No, I think it best if Clara investigates this matter on our behalf, don't you agree Hogarth?"

Hogarth suddenly came alert, his sharp brown eyes caught Clara's and she felt the plea behind them as he said,

"Yes, you must Clara, you really must."

Clara tried to think of an excuse, but there was really none.

"I shall look into this, but if I find something detrimental to Andrew or anyone else I shall hand it over to the police, unless I consider it of no importance to them."

"We fully understand." Glorianna pressed her hands together and smiled, "I'm sure you will do a superb job. Now, cook said she had made some biscuits? I think we all deserve one before dinner."

Glorianna was on her feet and ringing the bell pull.

"Bet you are wishing you stayed in Brighton." Eustace winked at Clara.

"How is the indigestion?" She replied, looking askance at the nearly empty whisky bottle.

"It comes and goes. Bane of my life, honest it is. But better that, then a strumpet wife who can't help getting herself killed."

"Oh Eustace you are coarse!" Peg groaned.

"I didn't marry her. I have managed to have the sense all my life to avoid such a problem. Girl was clearly a tart anyway, why didn't he just throw her a few shillings and be done with it?"

"Eustace!" Hogarth rumbled.

"Come on brother, we have all thought it. Isn't that why you want Clara to investigate? So she can dig up the dirt before the police? What do you expect her to find? That this Shirley Cox was a secret princess fallen on hard times?"

"I don't know why Andrew married her, but I give my son some credit for being morally upstanding." Hogarth bristled at his brother, "Aren't you due back in London soon Eustace?"

"Not until Friday night. Have an appointment with a card table." Eustace gave a wicked grin as his brother snorted in disgust, "I'll give Andrew's regards to the local ladies."

"Eustace!" Hogarth jumped to his feet, "If you weren't my brother..."

"Yes?"

Hogarth rumbled something under his breath, then he spun on his heel and left the room.

"Satisfied Eustace?" Peg said coolly.

"I only say what others think." Eustace shrugged.

One of the maid servants made a fortuitous arrival at that moment with fresh-baked shortbread biscuits. Clara took one, relieved that for the moment everyone was distracted. Eustace took three, naturally.

Susan was sitting to the far right of her uncle. She was looking pale and morose. She had only joined the group downstairs because Glorianna had insisted. It seemed her stepmother was aiming for a united front, better for withstanding the slings and arrows destined to come in their direction. When Susan took a biscuit it was out of politeness rather than real desire. Clara was more worried about her than any of them.

"Are you feeling a little better Susan?" She asked.

"A little." Susan forced a smile.

"You must be so bored up in your room alone."

"It does get a little tedious, but I hardly mind."

"I shall come and read to you, or just talk." Clara offered.

"That is kind. You needn't worry."

But Clara did worry. She wasn't as convinced as the rest of the family that Susan's suicide attempt was completely forgotten. That sort of emotion did not evaporate so fast. She wanted to talk with Susan alone. Until she did she would find it hard to convince herself the girl was not at risk of trying anything again. Of all the Campbells it was Susan who Clara was really anxious for. Andrew could hold his own, so could Peg, and Hogarth and Glorianna were old enough to weather any storm, but Susan seemed suddenly so fragile.

Eustace started to splutter on a biscuit. He banged a fist on his chest.

"You eat too fast, that is why you always have indigestion." Peg told him.

"Nonsense! I only get my indigestion badly when I eat here. I put it down to the miserable atmosphere in this house, tension over the dinner table does no one any favours."

Clara had had enough and now it seemed Peg was about to resume battle with Eustace she was inclined to escape. She gave a wink to Tommy and then excused herself.

"I must really write another note to my maid if I am to stay on, I shall want her here."

No one paid her much notice except Susan who had suddenly realised she was to be left behind in the room with Eustace and Peg. Clara gave her a wink too.

"Susan, would you mind finding me some more stationary, I am very short of envelopes."

Susan almost leapt from her place, she excused herself with Clara, and Tommy made his exit shortly after.

"Thank heavens!" Susan breathed as they left.

"Is Eustace always this way?"

"Always, thank you for getting me out of there. I think I shall go lie down again." Susan gave a tight cough and released herself from Clara before heading upstairs.

As she went away Clara still had that overriding feeling that something was just not right with her.

Chapter Eleven

Clara's decision to visit Laura Pettibone had not been taken without a considerable amount of argument with herself. Would the girl think her intrusive? Would she prefer to be left alone? Yet at the same time none of the Campbells had paid her a visit and surely she would appreciate some company? Whichever way Clara looked at it she could not decide the best course, but someone had to visit Laura and explain the new circumstances. She was sure Laura would rather it was a friend who broke the news that her husband-to-be was now embroiled in a murder case, than the police.

There was no sign of the elusive Mr Pettibone when Clara arrived around midday. She had refrained from coming earlier knowing the well-heeled often did not arise before the sun was high in the sky. As it turned out she was still a little early for Laura Pettibone was reclining on her sofa draped in a silken dressing wrap, with a night mask pushed haphazardly up onto her forehead. She brightened when she saw Clara, in fact she shot to her feet and embraced her in a bear hug.

"Wonderful Clara, you have come at last! I knew you would not let me down! Has the maid shown you the room I had prepared for you?"

Clara felt her heart sink. She had not intentionally forgotten the invitation to stay at the Pettibone household, but she had assumed with the calamity of Saturday she would be an unwelcome intrusion. Clara's policy in these situations was to be honest but gentle.

"Dear Laura, I have to discuss that with you, for something rather serious has come up."

Laura drew back.

"More serious than my disaster of a marriage ceremony?" The girl looked petulant.

"I'm afraid so. You see the woman who claimed to be Andrew's wife, well she is dead, and the Campbells want me to investigate what happened. Andrew is implicated in the matter and they want me to prove his innocence. So you see it is prudent for me at the moment to remain at the Campbell house where I am at the heart of things."

Laura was dazed by this rush of news. She shook her head as if to dislodge the confusion.

"That woman is dead?"

"Yes."

"And Andrew is implicated, why?"

"For one thing she interrupted his wedding to you, and then her body was found on the Brooklands racetrack, where Andrew was all yesterday. And finally because, unfortunately, she was genuinely his wife."

Laura sat down heavily on her sofa. Her face had turned ashen. One hand plucked unconsciously at the hem of her sleeve.

"She really was his wife?"

"Yes."

Clara had expected tears, but Laura took the news with great calm. If anything she looked resigned to the matter.

"I feared as much. I mean, a woman doesn't march into a church like that with no reason."

"No, I suppose not. I'm very sorry though." Clara perched herself on a stool, "How has your father taken it?"

"Daddy goes quiet when he is upset. He must be very upset because he has not spoken a word since Saturday. I wish he would say something, just anything, so I could know what to do."

"Do you still want to marry Andrew?"

Laura's face sagged.

"I don't know. He lied to me and he was committing a crime by marrying me."

"Bigamy. Yes."

"And he hasn't been to see me at all. Not to explain or ask forgiveness." Laura scrunched up her face with anger, "He should have come. Instead he ran away. How can I marry him after that?"

"I imagine it depends if you love him." Clara sighed, "But right now we have to think of other matters. As I say the woman is dead and the police are looking for her murderer."

Laura gave a little start.

"She was murdered? They are certain?"

"She was strangled." Clara wished there was an easier way to break this to Laura, "There main suspect is naturally Andrew. Though no doubt they will look at the rest of the family as well. They may even consider you or your father Laura."

"Oh daddy would never kill anyone!" Laura gasped, "Nor would I for that matter!"

"Even when your honour and reputation have been so brutally harmed?"

Laura blanched again, it was clear she had not considered the full implications of Saturday's fiasco.

"Daddy still wouldn't!"

"Well at least you now know what to expect if the police call. Where did you go after Saturday, anyway?"

"Straight back here." Laura gave a small sniff as if tears really were now threatening, "Where else was there to go? And I have been here since. This is an awful mess, isn't it?"

"I'm afraid so."

"Oh why did I agree to marry him at all? My friends said he was not right for me, too serious and stiff, even Susan said not to. But when he asked me at the dance all I could think of was how nice it would be to be married to an officer, and how Andrew was so much more of a man than the boys who haunted around me usually. Look where such thinking got me?"

"You are not to blame for this." Clara patted Laura's hand, "You did nothing wrong by following your heart, and I for one would not blame you if you still wanted to marry Andrew after all this."

"You are nice Clara, but I really need to think hard on this. Would you mind leaving me alone?"

"Of course not." Clara stood and got her handbag, "If you want me I shall be at the Campbells and I shall come at once."

"Thank you Clara, you have been such a friend! You know Susan has never come to see me?"

"She is still rather ill." Clara said defensively.

"Really? I could have sworn I saw her in the field next to the church when I came out with daddy. No matter, who am I to determine how poorly someone is?"

Yet the bitter edge to Laura's words suggested she was sorely hurt by her friend's apparent betrayal.

~~~*~~~

In the meantime, while Clara was facing Laura, Tommy had took it upon himself to deal with the obnoxious uncle Eustace. He had come to the conclusion that while it was highly unlikely Eustace had murdered Shirley Cox, he might know something about the whereabouts of the other Campbell family members. And he was not limited by loyalty as to what he would or would not say. In fact Eustace would quite happily implicate most of his relatives in the crime, should it suit him.

Tommy found him once more in the drawing room, making a vain attempt to read The Pickwick Papers, while a brandy and soda was cupped in his right hand.

"Is lunch served?" Eustace asked without looking up.

"Not yet."

"Blast them, I'm famished." Eustace flung down the book, "I can't stick Dickens, I don't know why I try."

Eustace gave a loud belch. Tommy grimaced.

"The stomach is all in knots again, I swear it's the cooking here." Eustace swallowed hard, "I lie in bed at night with my gullet on fire and my belly bubbling. I always have a decanter of tonic water at the bedside, but these days no matter how much I drink it fails to improve my bilious attacks. I blame it on a childhood of bland food, you know."

Tommy would rather have blamed it on Eustace's girth and fondness for alcohol.

"I came to see who was around." Tommy wheeled himself to the drinks cabinet and poured out a gin and tonic, "The house is bally quiet all of a sudden."

"Oh they are all wretched, hiding themselves away from the truth."

"How do you mean?"

Eustace waggled his glass at Tommy.

"I see it this way. My nephew gets swept away by this Shirley Cox in the war and marries her without telling a soul, but a few weeks back in the trenches and he sobers up, thinks to himself what has he done? A few more weeks and he is ignoring her letters, pretending she doesn't exist, thinking she will go away if he ignores her. She doesn't know his real address after all, she writes to him at the front. So he avoids London, keeps his head down and weeks turn into years and Shirley Cox all but vanishes from his mind. Maybe she's dead? Maybe she found someone else? Whatever, he doesn't care as long as she doesn't bother him. Then he meets this pretty slip of a thing called Laura, none too bright either, but with a fair amount of money and the only child to inherit a fancy estate. What could be better? Andrew proposes and everything goes as planned.

"So the wedding comes round and maybe once or twice in his darkest dreams Andrew thinks of Shirley Cox and wonders where she is, hopes she is dead or living another life. But he brushes it all off, because what does it matter? He never imagines she will turn up at the church! What a commotion! What bad luck that she happened to read the wedding announcements in the paper the very day his was listed! And now she appears to reclaim her husband. Well, Andrew is embarrassed and upset. He has been made a fool of and everyone now knows his secret. He seeks out Shirley, she wants him back, but he has no intention of returning to her. There is no love there, instead there is bitterness, hate even. She has trapped him and what can he do? I doubt he meant to kill her, but they argued and it grew out of hand. Suddenly he has her by the throat and she is dead. Voila!"

"An interesting hypothesis." Tommy said, without mentioning that it was also the obvious one that everyone had considered, not just Eustace who deemed himself so clever, "But why put the body on the Brooklands racetrack?"

"I see it this way. She found him at the racetrack, that was where the argument took place. He leaves her body on the track hoping one of the other racers will go round the corner and run over the body. Isn't that what that foreigner Francke almost did?"

"Yes, but the police aren't stupid. They would see she was strangled."

"But he isn't thinking straight!" Eustace sneered as though Tommy was being impossibly stupid, "He acts spontaneously!"

"Andrew isn't the sort who strikes me as being prone to spontaneous actions."

"All right Mr Clever-Clogs, who do you think did it then?"

Tommy sipped quietly at his drink, noting how the pause irritated Eustace further.

"I don't have a 'suspect' in mind. Too early to say."

"Pish! It's obvious one of this lot did it!"

"Some would say it rather odd that you are so keen to accuse your own family of murder." Tommy said with a morbid smile.

"You don't know them all that well, that's your problem. I told you that!"

"So? What can be so bad about them that it makes you believe them murderers?"

Eustace gave a harrumph.

"You don't understand at all, I mean the girls, Peg and Susan, I dare say they are harmless enough, though both a bit loopy. Look how Peg dresses! And Susan runs off in the night to drown herself, you can't tell me those are the actions of a person living in a perfectly normal, happy family."

"I admit that was troubling me." Tommy agreed, "But people can act oddly for no real reason."

"Have you not seen how Glory treats that girl? Typical wicked stepmother. Let me tell you it's Hogarth and that witch I blame for all this. She has a negative influence on everyone around her, see how Andrew has become a walking tree stump, never uttering a word? It's because he doesn't dare. She'll jump on the slightest thing. I've heard her say some spiteful things to Susan, she treats her like a rival, always trying to dress to outdo her. Oh you didn't see the Christmas when she forced Susan into this ghastly frock that made her look a frump and then Glory turns up in the exact same dress which she can carry off like a dream because she has the figure of a gnat. If she had been my wife I would have had some words for that performance."

"There are often problems between stepdaughters and stepmothers." Tommy frowned, "But I didn't realise it was that bad. Didn't Hogarth marry her quite soon after his wife died? I didn't attend that wedding, but I think my parents did."

"The first Mrs Campbell wasn't cold in her grave." Eustace snorted triumphantly, "It was scandalous, people talked. Eugenie Campbell was dead a week when the banns were read. I suppose you might argue she had been ailing for some time, but whichever way you look at it Hogarth had to have known Glory and fallen for her before his wife departed this earth."

"Was she a family friend?"

"Hogarth's secretary. Now another clue, note how she won't allow him to have another secretary in the house? It can hardly be because of financial considerations, so what?"

"Perhaps she fears another woman in the house will distract him, like she did?" Tommy finished Eustace's train of thought.

"Precisely! Glory isn't going to risk that. Oh no, she has her claws in Eustace and it wouldn't surprise me if she has seen to it that all of his estate, when he passes, goes straight to her. Then where will poor Peg and Susan be? I dare say it will be a Hell for them. Quite frankly I went and revised my own will to ensure they had a portion each. But don't tell a soul, as they think I am leaving it all to the League of Dumb Friends."

Tommy found that an interesting aside into uncle Eustace's character. Perhaps he was not such the bad humoured and mean soul he made himself out to be.

"You've told me how Glorianna is perhaps an adulteress and not necessarily nice to her stepchildren, but hardly why she could be a murderess."

"She could be though." Eustace grinned, and it was a decidedly nasty look, "She could kill. I've often wondered if she would have had the guts to hasten Eugenie Campbell off this mortal coil. Eugenie had tuberculosis, but her death came faster than most had expected. You have to wonder, don't you, what with the quick wedding. I mean there was no real inquiry because Eugenie was known to be dying. Who knows?"

Tommy was reluctant to admit to himself that it did all sound very odd, at the very least it was improper.

"It must have been hard on Andrew and his sisters."

"Andrew was already away fighting for his country and the girls were at boarding schools. What say did they have? Mind you, I do wonder how the dates of Hogarth's marriage tie up with those of Andrew's. That could be interesting, say he did it out of retaliation?"

It was a possibility no doubt.

"Would Glorianna have motive to kill Shirley Cox, though?"

"Glory hates scandal. She would kill for that."

Tommy fell silent, not for the first time it amazed him how a sudden death could start bringing out the worst in people. He had taken Glory at face value, but now she was revealed as a woman who could lie and plot against another. That was disturbing.

"Then there is Hogarth." Eustace had a twinkle in his eye as he continued his assassination of the family character, "My brother was always the tough one. He could withstand anything. Boarding school knocked the stuffing out of me but Hogarth thrived, you know why? Because he never took any trouble from anyone. If a boy tried to punch him he would punch back first, and not stop until the boy was knocked senseless. Even the masters kept a cool eye on Hogarth. He was good at his lessons too, never a fault, never a wrong sum, never a piece of muddled Latin grammar. Unlike old Eustace, who had more than his fair share of beatings for getting the wrong answer. It was a brutal world and only the brutal thrived."

Tommy nodded in understanding.

"Hogarth was never afraid to get his hands dirty. If he had been young enough for the war I could imagine him as one of those tough-as-old-boots sergeants who sends a man to his death without even blinking and sleeps peacefully the same night. The sort that could run a Hun through and not give it a thought."

"On that I have to correct you Eustace, many of us in the trenches became that way. We were inured to the cruelty, it was the only way to carry on."

"Yes, but Hogarth would have started that way. All I am saying is that Hogarth would think no more of murdering a woman who had ruined his son than he would of wringing the neck of a pheasant his dog had brought back to him."

"By that logic, you should have been dead years ago." Tommy suggested much to Eustace's humour.

"But I'm family!" Eustace rumbled with laughter, "Blood family! That means a lot to the Campbells."

"And what about you Eustace? Are you a killer?"

Eustace's good humour evaporated.

"What sort of a question is that?"

"An honest one. I know I am a killer, I have killed. It just wasn't called murder because there was a war on."

Eustace clamped his lips together so hard they formed a stiff line.

"I could never kill." He said firmly, "Never."

Tommy stared at him for a long time.

"No, perhaps not."

Tommy quietly rolled himself out of the room, uncertain what to make of Eustace's revelations.

Chapter Twelve

Clara was hardly in the door of the Campbell house when a footman ran up and offered her a letter that had just been hand-delivered for her. Clara was curious enough to open it without removing her hat or gloves. The paper had the words Surrey Police Constabulary heavily printed in black ink at the top, this in itself was enough to make Clara excited.

Dear Miss Clara Fitzgerald,

Subsequent to our conversation I contacted Inspector Park-Coombs of the Brighton Constabulary. He has assured me you are an honest and reliable person who has been of great use on occasion to the Brighton police and has advised me to take you into my confidence. I hope we may be able to work together on this matter, as you are clearly placed in a better position than I am to know the Campbell household. Therefore would you please call at your earliest convenience to the local police station?

Yours sincerely, Inspector Jennings

Clara wedged the letter in her handbag and was out

the door again before the footman knew what was happening. Inspector Jennings wanted to speak to her! It was more than Clara had hoped for. She knew she would have had to eventually go to the police and ask for assistance during her enquiries, there was simply no alternative, but to have it offered was another matter. Thank God for the kindness of Inspector Park-Coombs! They might have started out on the wrong foot, but by the time Clara had concluded her first investigation the inspector had come to respect her intellect and intuition. It was just such a pity women couldn't be promoted to inspectors, he had said on one occasion. Not that Clara wished to work for the police, she preferred being a free agent, but she was never one to turn down their help.

She hurried into the village and had to ask directions of a passing postman. The police station was set in a former house and was far from expansive. In this corner of Surrey crime was hardly high and on most days only a constable and a sergeant could be found at the station. It had been slightly fortuitous that Jennings had been down doing an inspection when the body at Brooklands had been discovered, else he would have had to come from the main station.

Clara hastened inside and informed the desk sergeant of her urgent summons. He was mildly surprised to see someone so keen to be called to the police station. He sent an idle constable up to tell Jennings she was here.

"You were on the racetrack yesterday." He nodded, and Clara realised she was staring at the same sergeant who had had the unpleasant task of dragging Andrew Campbell before the inspector, "Nasty business. You knew her then?"

"Sort of." Clara didn't like to reveal too much.

"We don't get many murders here and when we do it's usually strangers that get themselves knocked off. Shame though, when it's a woman."

Clara wasn't sure how to reply, all sudden death to her seemed a shame no matter the gender or age of the victim. She was saved from further conversation by the constable returning and asking her to accompany him to the inspector.

~~~*~~~

Jennings was sitting uncomfortably behind someone else's desk. He wasn't sure who the 'someone else' was, as the constable did not have an office and the sergeant had a small room at the back of the house where he could catch up on paperwork. He had to assume, therefore, that this office space was intended for casual use, hence why it was so poorly appointed. The desk was old and Victorian and too high for the chair that had been supplied, which was uncomfortable enough without banging your elbows on the edge of the desk every time you reached for a paper clip. There were a series of filing cabinets to his right which provided the sum total of the station's archives, and a window that looked out on an apple tree and next door's compost heap to his left. Jennings had learnt quick enough that opening the window to let in some air also tended to let in the smell of decomposing vegetation. It was behind this inadequate and slightly embarrassing work station that he met with Clara once more.

The inspector had thought Clara something unique when he first glimpsed her. Not the usual girl he was used to dealing with, she was quite cool upon sighting the body and very practical about the situation. She was also pretty and slender, with a fashionable bob and just a hint of red lipstick. He really wasn't sure what to make of her and after his conversation with Inspector Park-Coombs he was even more baffled, but there was one thing the Brighton inspector had said that had stuck in his mind.

"Let her in on this Jennings, or she'll find her own way in and that can only mean trouble."

Jennings had thought Park-Coombs was teasing him, but after the phone call he had not felt so sure. He had a worrying suspicion that Clara Fitzgerald was more than just an interfering busybody, she might actually be a good detective.

Clara reached his desk with a quick glance at the room. The constable was behind her and quickly dragged over a chair for Clara to sit in. Clara settled down and took her own first good look at the inspector. Inspector Jennings was in his late thirties with bright, dark eyes and hair that had a distinctive curl to it. His suit, though clearly worn, was clean and neat and ornamented by a rather bright tie that limply hung over his shirt. He looked hot and Clara wondered why he didn't open the window on such a fine day.

"Thank you for coming Miss Fitzgerald."

"Thank you for asking me, I appreciate the invitation."

"Well Inspector Park-Coombs implied it was better to work with you than against you." Jennings gave a crooked smile as Clara raised an eyebrow, "He also reminded me how useful it would be to have someone on the inside, so to speak."

"Spying on the Campbells you mean?"

"I would rather think of it as looking for clues. You are a detective after all. Anyway, isn't that why you are staying with the Campbells?"

Clara had already admitted as such to Laura Pettibone, but she had no intention of doing the same to the inspector.

"They insisted I stay there."

"Of course, but it is useful. Anyway," The inspector pulled a cardboard folder towards him, "I thought you might be interested in the coroner's findings on Shirley Cox."

He removed a sheet of paper and handed it to Clara.

"It includes an inventory of the things we found on her. Not a lot as you can see."

Clara scanned the paper.

"So strangulation was the cause of death." Clara read the paragraph further, "With a fine cloth, possible silk, but no rope or cord."

"No, it did not leave a pattern so the coroner infers it was a smooth fabric with a very fine weave. I've seen people throttled with silk handkerchiefs before now. They don't leave much of an impression."

"He estimates she was dead between 12 and 18 hours."

"Yes, the warm day might have speeded things up a little."

"That could put her murder time worryingly close to the wedding." Clara did a quick calculation in her head, "None of them have alibis for that time, except Glorianna who was attending the reception dinner."

"They held the reception?"

"It seemed foolish to waste the food."

"I suppose, but you see this opens the field when it comes to suspects. Not only does the time mean several of them could have done it, but the method could implicate a woman as much as a man."

"The coroner found no other signs of violence."

"No, and her clothes were not damaged in any way. He did the obvious checks for…" The inspector almost blushed.

"She was not violated then, I take it?" Clara finished for him.

"No, but you will note that the coroner saw signs to indicate she had been with child at least once in her life, but at the same time it did not appear she had ever delivered a baby."

Clara read through the coroner's careful notes.

"He says there was scar tissue and damage within the womb to suggest some sort of invasive treatment. He suggests a crude abortion. He was very thorough."

"I asked him to be, it seemed appropriate considering the strange circumstances and I had a hunch." The inspector caught himself using a term he had accused Clara of, "I did a little work on Shirley Cox's background, not that it was challenging, the Metropolitan police were very aware of her. Shirley Cox was a call girl, one of the better sort since she didn't loiter around alleys, but still a woman of the night. She liked hanging out at the dance halls and around the cinemas and theatres looking for trade. Now I asked myself if that is the sort of girl a young man like Andrew Campbell marries for no real reason?"

"He would not be the first man to fall for a prostitute. Love makes fools of us."

"Andrew Campbell does not strike me as the impulsive type." Countered the inspector, "I rather fancied there was more to it than just a passing infatuation. I wondered if the girl was pregnant and told him it was his and a sense of duty swept over him; that seems more like a Campbell thing to do. But then this Shirley Cox isn't one for motherhood and once she has him snared she quickly gets an abortion. But she miscalculates and when Andrew discovers there is no child he feels duped and abandons her. There go all Shirley's plan for a comfortable future. She is back on the streets, living day by day until she happens to see that wedding announcement."

"I see where you are leading." Clara nodded, "Andrew Campbell might be sour-faced but he has a sense of duty akin to his father and he would not abandon his wife without a reason."

"He more than abandoned her, he treated her as though she were dead. The actions of a very angry, bitter man who has had his love turned to hate."

"Then again," Clara laid down the report, "Shirley Cox may have been pregnant years before she met Andrew, the abortion could just be coincidence. Call girls do get pregnant."

"Yes, and a back-street butcher is the usual solution." Jennings sighed, "I know it's a long-shot, I suppose I was curious more than anything."

"It is a good theory though." Clara threw him a line, "I agree this whole mess does not strike me as something Andrew would do, not that I know him exceptionally well, but he is not the sort to fall head-over-heels for a girl on the spur of the moment. His engagement to Laura

Pettibone, for instance, almost seems calculated. And it also bothers me that he would abandon a wife in that way. Andrew, I don't think, is the sort to avoid his commitments once he has made them unless there is a good reason. What else do you know about Shirley Cox?"

"She was aged somewhere around 38 and 42, police couldn't say for sure her exact date of birth. She was an independent, didn't have a pimp. The police were aware that on occasion she was living in relative luxury as a mistress to certain well-known names. Shirley knew her worth and she didn't go for anything less than a man with a decent bank account. There was a brief period in the books when she vanished from sight, between 1915 and 1917 she was invisible. No trouble, no incidents. She was always known for her temper and if she wasn't in trouble for soliciting, she was under arrest for disturbing the peace by starting a cat fight. But for two years she was off the scene. The police wondered if she was dead."

"Instead she was married."

"Yes, and then the Christmas of 1917 they find her tight in the gutter. They haul her in and let her sleep it off in a cell. From then on it seems Shirley was back to business. But she was older now and she had been off the scene for two years. Her patch was taken by younger women and she struggled to make her way. Her clients became cheaper; she hung out with the soldier boys more and more. The last record they have on her was three weeks ago when she was picked up with a number of other girls hawking their trade at a nightclub. Police say she was in a sorry state and looked like she needed a decent meal. Shirley Cox had truly fallen from the heights."

Clara listened, her mind conjuring the image of the woman in the church. Her malicious grin, her laugh, her missing stockings and the mink stole. A stole that she could have pawned and lived off the proceeds for weeks. Yet she kept it, a treasured memento of a failed marriage...

Clara picked up the report again quickly and scanned through the list of things found on Shirley's body.

"Where is the stole?"

"The stole?" Said the inspector dumbly.

"When Shirley Cox came to the church she was wearing an expensive mink stole, but it was not with the body and you clearly did not find it on the racetrack."

Jennings mulled over the suggestion.

"She could have left it wherever she was staying before she encountered her killer."

"Maybe, but bear in mind she specifically wore that stole to the church. I think she wanted to remind Andrew of the things he had given her, of what she had once meant to him. Now, if she went to meet Andrew again after the ceremony she would have gone in the stole. It was important."

"I see what you are saying, the stole could lead us to the killer. Unfortunately I have not tracked down where Shirley was staying yet so I cannot say if her stole was with her belongings or is truly missing."

"Leave that to me inspector." Clara rose from her chair, "I appreciate you sharing this with me and I will make my own discreet enquiries and let you know of anything I turn up."

"Thank you Miss Fitzgerald, but if you do find where she was staying before us, please call the police immediately without removing anything." Jennings gave her a stern look which Clara deemed unnecessary, she was not an idiot.

"Of course inspector, we are working together after all." Clara swept up her handbag and headed off, the fire of curiosity burning brightly inside her now.

Chapter Thirteen

Clara worked on the assumption that asking enough questions eventually produced a result, unless of course you were interviewing a suspect, in which case being circumspect was better. But when tracking something, such as an address, a polite question here or there usually worked wonders. For instance, while there was a hotel in the village Clara was convinced Shirley would have stayed in one of the small guest houses dotted around. And as the summer season was yet to be in full flow, more attention was paid to the few guests that were around. So it was with a few choice questions in the post office and grocers, that Clara discovered a woman answering Shirley's description had been staying at a tiny boarding house down Oak Street, run by a Scottish landlady and her husband. The postmistress had in fact been present when Shirley sent off a postcard to London and had briefly caught sight of her name.

The boarding house was well-presented, with early pansies in a window box and a mown lawn, but it was clearly very small. Clara knocked loudly, wondering if it was getting a bit late in the day. Her watch was telling her it was close to four. Perhaps the landlady was serving tea? But when a broad Scottish woman, with her grey hair in a bun, answered the door with a smile Clara felt she could proceed as planned.

"I do apologise for disturbing you at teatime, but I've come to see Shirley Cox."

"Disturbing me? Nonsense! This is the time all my guests arrive, not that I'm expecting any. Do come in, won't you? I'm afraid Shirley's out but I expect she will be back soon."

The Scottish landlady ushered Clara through to a surprisingly large kitchen, where a teapot stood on the stove and a homemade cake adorned the table.

"Sit yourself down. I only have Mr Robins at home today so you might as well share in the cake. As you can tell I like my little teatime treats." The landlady rubbed at her rotund belly, "I'm Mrs Macphinn, by the way."

"Clara Fitzgerald." Clara introduced herself, "I've been trying to find Shirley all day, I'm so glad I tracked her here."

"She is a friend." Mrs Macphinn presented the teapot on the table topped with a stripy knitted tea cosy.

"Actually she is a relation by marriage."

"Och, I didn't know she were married?"

"I'm afraid it wasn't the happiest of situations. A wartime marriage, you know."

Mrs Macphinn nodded her head earnestly.

"You hear it all the time. A rash marriage made in the heat of the moment and it doesn't last as long as the wedding cake. So why have you come to find her?"

"I thought maybe I could be helpful, though I'm not really sure how. But it's awful being in a mess all alone, isn't it?"

"Poor thing, yes now you say it she did seem rather tense. I said to myself there is a lass who has known a lifetime of worry. What was she doing here?"

"Trying to find the errant husband."

"Oh, shush, what a thing…" Mrs Macphinn cut at the cake, jam oozed out thickly from the middle and Clara wondered where the Scottish lady managed to get all her sugar from, "Cake?"

"Thank you." Clara accepted a large slice and watched as Mrs Macphinn devoured hers with mammoth sized bites, "When did she arrive here?"

"She came on the Thursday. Said she wouldn't be staying long. I gave her the nice room at the back of the landing, right next to the bathroom."

"Do you think she will be back shortly, only I can't stay long?"

"Surely, surely. She is always home for dinner. You see I cook breakfast and dinner for the guests, what with there not being many places to eat late in the village. Then I can also provide sandwiches for lunchtime if it's arrange beforehand. Shirley has been so kind-hearted, she comes in to help with the dinner, doesn't have to but insists. And she eats with such relish, I swear the girl looks half-starved. She says my cooking reminds her of her mother's."

"You run a fine house Mrs Macphinn, I wish I had found this place before I stopped over elsewhere."

"Ah, you can move here"

"I paid in advance for three days." Clara said regretfully.

"Well now, I never but ask for the first night and expect my guests to settle the bill at the end of their stay and they always do!"

That, decided Clara, explained how Shirley Cox was able to afford to stay in the house.

"You are clearly a very considerate woman Mrs Macphinn." Clara said with a smile, "I'm glad Shirley pitched up here, she hasn't had an easy time of it."

"No, I could see that." Mrs Macphinn nodded sagely and cut herself a second slice of cake, "I wouldn't call her a happy person. Looked very sad to me. First night here she hardly spoke, but then I brought her out of her herself. Between her and Mr Robins we have fine talks over dinner."

"What sort of things do you talk about? The landlady

at my establishment is rather strict about what can be discussed at dinner."

"Aye, I reckon I know who it is you are staying with." Mrs Macphinn tapped the side of her nose conspiratorially, Clara felt a tad guilty for whoever she had just slandered, "I don't mind what the guests talk of as long as it's not sordid. I mean you do have to watch out. We have families stay here and respectable old people. They don't want to be eating their liver and tatties listening to someone prattling on about nasty things. I did have to remind Shirley once to watch her tongue. It was when I mentioned about the church and she was rather rude about vicars, called them hypocrites. I said 'Now Shirley, it's all fine and good having opinions, but I won't have the House of God criticised in this house.' She was very good about it."

Distantly a clock chimed the half hour.

"She is rather late today." Mrs Macphinn glanced out the kitchen window and then observed how much cake she consumed and felt mildly abashed.

"Did she say where she was going when you saw her this morning?" Clara fished for extra information.

"Actually I didn't see her this morning. She was gone early. I did check on her room and found the bed all made neat and her trunk still sitting there. I confess for a moment I thought she might have run out on me."

"Oh not Shirley!" Clara lied swiftly.

"I can't say where she went." Mrs Macphinn started to fidget, thinking about the potatoes and carrots she had to get on with and peel.

Clara took a look at her watch, as if she had not just heard the chimes.

"I'm afraid I must be getting on. I'm sorry to have bothered you and to have missed Shirley."

"Wasn't a bother at all, do you want to leave a message?"

Clara hesitated. It was difficult to think of leaving a message for someone you knew was dead.

"Could you mention I dropped in and say I will call again?"

"I can do that." Mrs Macphinn started clearing up their plates, "I reckon she has just got delayed somewhere."

Clara said her goodbyes and headed out the door. She walked a few paces then called over a boy who was playing with a pebble in the street.

"Can you take this message to the police station?"

The boy gave a nod and she pressed a shilling and a swiftly written note into his hand so he skipped off in haste. As she had promised Inspector Jennings, she had found the place Shirley had been staying, now he could collect her trunk and break the news to Mrs Macphinn about what had happened to her latest guest. It didn't stop Clara feeling guilty, however, for leading the poor woman astray. She sometimes wondered at how skilled she had become in lying since she had been a detective.

Chapter Fourteen

Clara sat down next to Tommy in his bedroom. They had both retreated once more from an unhappy dinner and were settled down to dessert in Tommy's quarters. Clara was wondering if all this fine dining would soon have her letting out the waist of her dress. That didn't stop her delving into a hearty portion of gooseberry jelly, strawberries and cream.

"So Eustace pins it on Andrew." Tommy summed up his conversation earlier with the Campbell uncle, "Though he doesn't dismiss any of the others from being possible candidates."

"Useful." Clara said with a groan, "The problem is they all have a strong motive, but hardly any of them have alibis."

"Do you ever think that concentrating our efforts on Andrew, as he seems the most likely murderer, gives the real killer an unfair advantage to slip the net?"

"I suppose it depends if Andrew did it or not." Clara licked cream off her spoon, "What is your opinion of Andrew as a killer?"

"He could have done it, but I just don't see him being so rash."

"I saw him when he reached the body and his shock

looked genuine. Unfortunately trying to talk to him is like drawing blood from a stone. Perhaps you could try, he might open up better to a man."

"Andrew is very much a closed book, but I'll give it a go." Tommy put his bowl on the bedside table and leaned back on his bed.

"You'll be pleased to know Annie should arrive tomorrow." Clara added.

Tommy's eyes twinkled.

"So you'll be sending her down into the servants' quarters to get the inside scoop?"

On past cases Annie, the Fitzgeralds' unconventional maid, had proved an asset when it came to learning the truth from servant circles. People all too readily forgot how much servants overheard and saw.

"Annie can help us pin down exactly when everyone was about. The servants are our best bet for their exact comings and goings. Servants see all."

"Well I've missed Annie. She is far better company than that stuffy lot in there." Tommy gave a derisive snort, "I can't get my head around them all. I thought Eustace was the mad one, but I'm beginning to think he is the sanest one of the lot."

"Yes, they do have that effect on you. I wonder when the police will call and take statements?"

"They're letting them stew." Tommy stretched his arms over his head, "The inspector is building up his background knowledge so he can come in here and strike hard."

"Still, I would have thought they would have called by now…"

As Clara spoke the front doorbell rang and echoed about the house.

"You've talked them up again sister."

"Surely not!" Clara hopped to the door and peeped outside, she could not see the front hall from here, but she could hear voices and she recognised Inspector Jennings instructing the butler to summon the family, "It is them, you know!"

Tommy gave a laugh. Clara left the bedroom and hurried to the hall where she spotted the inspector standing with a constable.

"Evening Miss Fitzgerald." Jennings would have tipped his hat to her had he not already removed it.

"I wondered when you would come!" Clara came forward, "Are you taking statements?"

"Yes we are. I presume you want to be present?"

Clara studied his face, wondering if he was mocking her. She relaxed when he seemed genuine.

"Yes, I would appreciate that. I could sit in a corner and take notes."

Glorianna emerged a step ahead of the butler who had fetched her, still dressed in her dinner gown. Her face bore an expression of perfect horror at the sight of policemen in her house.

"What on earth is all this?" She demanded.

"I have come to take statements from the family." Jennings answered politely.

"Could it not have waited until the morning?"

"No, it could not." Jennings said firmly.

Clara sensed what he was up to, putting the family on the wrong foot, catching them at a moment when they would be least prepared for attack. They had had a day to relax, even to come to think the police were not going to question them at all. Now here was the wily inspector.

"I... I suppose you should take over the drawing room." Glorianna pushed open the door to the room and stood there anxiously, "You want to speak to all of us?"

"Yes, but one at a time. We can start with you if you like."

Glorianna's eyes went wide, then she composed herself.

"Well, yes, let's get it over with."

She headed into the drawing room in a daze. Her whole evening had just been turned upside down. She couldn't quite fathom why the police would want to talk to her. After all, she was not even Andrew's real mother. She had just been there, and yes she had been cross about the ruined wedding, it had taken a good deal of effort and money to arrange. But it was not the end of the world, Hogarth's reputation would survive it. Andrew might have to be sent away. She had been considering that on and off the whole day, but otherwise they would survive.

She perched herself awkwardly on a sofa and motioned for the inspector to sit where he pleased. Clara quietly took a place at the far side of the room, behind Glorianna and out of sight. She removed a notebook and pencil from a pocket in her skirt and quietly prepared to take notes.

"What could you possibly want to know from me?" Glorianna asked, trying to laugh off the matter and failing.

"Could you tell me where you were during the course of Saturday afternoon, from the time of the wedding?" The inspector began.

Glorianna looked at him as if he were being incredibly foolish.

"At the reception, of course!"

"You had the reception?"

Glorianna grew a little angry.

"The food was all prepared and paid for, I hate waste inspector. Perhaps the aristocratic thing to do would have been to have it all thrown away. But I grew up in a poor family and I know the value of food. Besides, many of the guests had travelled some distance to be there and I could not send them home with empty stomachs. It was the only decent thing to do."

"Who among the immediate family attended the reception?"

"Only myself." Glorianna stiffened, "Naturally Eustace was there, anywhere there is food and drink Eustace is bound to be. Everyone else went home, I assume."

"You were there the entire time?"

"Yes, where else would I be?"

"Until what time?"

Glorianna frowned.

"We sat down at one, there were no speeches so the meal proceeded through all the courses without a pause. I suppose it was about four when we had all finished. But then some of the guests had to wait for trains, so I hung around until the last of them was gone. I suppose I was home just after five. My arrival came with quite a procession because I ordered the remainder of the meal packaged up and brought with me."

"Did you see anyone on your arrival home?"

For the first time Glorianna had to give a long pause before she could answer.

"I'm sorry, I'm not sure who I saw first. Obviously the butler, he took my coat. I was avoiding Eustace, Hogarth was in his study. I think I saw Peg a few minutes after I came in the door. She was in here, reading. We didn't speak so I went upstairs to get changed."

"And you were home all the rest of the night?"

"Yes!"

"Can anyone confirm that?"

"I did not kill that awful woman." Glorianna rubbed at her forehead with a thumb and forefinger in a pinching movement, "I saw everyone at dinner. Afterwards I was in here with Peg and Eustace. Hogarth went back to his study. It was around eleven when I went to bed. I saw no one after that until the morning."

"And what did you make of Shirley Cox?"

"Who?"

"Your stepson's late wife."

Glorianna opened her mouth but words failed her.

"Is that for certain?" She finally managed.

"Yes."

"Well, I... I didn't like her. She was so common and vulgar. Walking into that church in red and making such a spectacle. I thought her an awful creature. But that doesn't mean I killed her."

"I appreciate that Mrs Campbell. Perhaps you would be kind enough to fetch another member of the family for me to chat to?"

Glorianna looked affronted at the sudden dismissal, but she stood without a word and headed out the door. Within moments, suggesting she had been waiting in the hall outside, Peg appeared.

"What ho inspector!" She threw herself down on the sofa Glorianna had just departed, as usual dressed in shirt and trousers with her hair slicked back.

Inspector Jennings was not easily surprised, still it took a moment for him to adjust to the appearance of Peg. He had only glimpsed her on the racetrack and the full manner of her outfit had escaped him. He also had to reluctantly admit to himself that at Brooklands he had made the error of thinking her a young man.

"You must be…?"

"Penelope Campbell. Call me Peg." Peg offered a hand to be shook. The inspector declined.

"Could you tell me where you were on Saturday after the wedding?"

"Easy, I was here. I came straight home to get out of that awful dress Glory insisted I wear. I was here all day after that."

"Did anyone see you?"

"Well Clara did," Peg pointed over her shoulder, "She came in a moment after me."

The inspector glanced at Clara for confirmation.

"She is correct inspector, I walked in with Tommy and Peg was in the hall."

"That's right," Continued Peg, "I had got home to find Susan out of bed and nowhere around and I was having a bit of the collywobbles about it. Then Susan comes swanning in the French windows with a bunch of wild flowers. Next moment Clara is home. Then I went and got changed and was rather aimless for the rest of the afternoon. I just sat in here and read a magazine."

"And in the evening?" Asked the inspector.

"I had dinner and went to bed. There isn't much else to do in this house."

"And what did you make of the late Shirley Cox, your brother's wife?"

Peg's jolly façade cracked a little.

"I don't know what you mean."

"She must have made an impression on you, bursting into the church like that."

Peg still struggled.

"She was just... a woman. She was a bit tarty and I thought her shoes rather worn, but I can't say much else crossed my mind."

"It did not upset you she had ruined your brother's wedding?"

"That was Andrew's fault! Running off from a wife, disgraceful. Perhaps if she had been a fraud I would have been angry, but she was the genuine thing. I was sad for Laura, but gosh, there have been plenty of women over the last few years who never got the wedding they were expecting. Look at me, I was engaged and the silly sod goes off and gets killed in Belgium. I imagine that rather hardened me. Anyway, Andrew is still alive if Laura wants him."

"Thank you Miss Campbell, if you could send in someone else?"

The next person in was Hogarth Campbell, who looked dyspeptic and cross at the intrusion. A brief thought flittered across Clara's mind concerning what Eustace had said about his brother. Could he be violent if he needed to be? The way he appeared as he entered the drawing room, he certainly looked like someone who had a temper. It was not the calm, quiet Hogarth who was usually presented to them.

"Will this take long?" He asked gruffly.

"I doubt it, if you could tell us your whereabouts after the wedding on Saturday?" The inspector was unfazed by his new suspect's grumpiness.

"I came straight home, what else could I do? I puttered for a bit, I wanted to give a piece of my mind to Andrew but he had vanished. Finally I settled down to work on a history of my family I've been busy with."

"Anyone see you?"

"The maid who brought in my coffee and sandwiches at 3 o'clock, and I saw everyone at dinner, but otherwise no one." Hogarth was glaring at the inspector defiantly.

"What were your feelings about your son's first wife?"

"Plainly? She was a nuisance. I couldn't understand why he hadn't spoken to me about it and we could have sorted something. A quiet divorce to be rid of her. Instead he bottles it all up. He's been like that since the war, he never says a thing about what he is thinking or feeling. It can drive you to madness all that introspection!"

"Are you suggesting your son could have had something to do with his first wife's death?"

"Of course not!" Hogarth bellowed so loudly the room seemed to echo, "Weren't you listening? I just said I couldn't understand why he didn't mention it, that's all. Andrew would no more harm that woman than I."

Clara felt that was a statement rather open to interpretation.

"I was going to pay her off, if you need to know. Pay her off, hush it up, sort out a divorce and then have a quiet marriage between Andrew and Laura. I was thinking I would pay for them to have an extended honeymoon and then they could settle in France or even South America. Get away from all the gossip-mongers here. It would have come right in the end. The girl winding up dead is just an added nuisance."

"What if she had refused to be divorced?"

"Her type don't refuse, not if you wave enough cash at them. I would have set her up nicely, a little cottage somewhere. She would never have had to worry again. It's not as though she loved him, for crying out loud! She was a gold-digger, simple as that."

"You never had any hint your son had married?"

"Didn't I just say that?"

"It is a difficult thing to keep hidden from family."

"Well he did, and I've had enough of this." Hogarth

thrust himself up from the sofa, "I take it you will want someone else? I shan't bother Eustace as he is having one of his bilious attacks and has gone to bed. Besides, he had no reason to do anything."

The inspector refrained from snapping, though the temptation was great.

"Yes, if you could fetch someone else."

Susan appeared after a long pause of some ten minutes. She was nervous as she peered around the door. Hastily dressed in a light day gown, her hair barely brushed, she shuffled into the room looking so washed out her skin seemed almost translucent.

"Miss Susan Campbell?" The inspector asked gently.

"Yes." Susan replied in a timid voice.

"You didn't attend your brother's wedding?"

"No, I was unwell."

"But you weren't home when your sister Penelope returned?"

Susan swallowed anxiously. Her eyes flicked over the constable behind Jennings.

"I fancied some fresh air and I thought if I walked to the boundary of our garden and into the next field I could just glimpse the church. I wanted to see Andrew and Laura come out."

Susan swallowed again.

"You didn't see them, of course."

"No, I waited a while, but the bells never rang, and then the guests were coming out. I knew something wasn't right and I was feeling rather grim again so I headed home."

"Did you see a woman in red enter the church?"

Susan considered the question.

"I think so. She was going in as I reached the hedge."

"Did you know who she was?"

"No."

"But you know now?"

Susan licked her lips, which were suddenly so dry.

"Yes. She was Andrew's wife. Before you ask I never

knew he was married. I only found out when Peg came home and told me."

"Have you been out of the house since?"

"No."

"Not even to collect more flowers?"

"No." Susan shook her head vigorously, "Honestly inspector I have nothing to do with this, I have enough worries of my own…" Susan gulped as the words spilled out. She clamped her lips shut on further admissions.

"Thank you Miss Campbell, perhaps you could fetch for us your brother Andrew." The inspector decided to throw her a line, but instead Susan's eyes seemed to bulge.

"I…" She glanced over her shoulder helplessly at Clara, "I don't know where he is."

The inspector looked as though he had been jolted.

"I instructed Andrew Campbell to stay at home, where has he gone?"

Susan shook her head.

"Well, when did he leave?"

Again Susan shook her head helplessly.

"Inspector," Clara interrupted, "I have an idea where he is likely to have gone, why don't we allow Susan to rest and try and track down Andrew ourselves?"

Susan's relief at Clara's intervention was palpable to everyone. The inspector, however, was still annoyed.

"He was told to remain here, does he not listen to anyone?"

"Not often." Susan gave a little smile. Clara had moved behind her and was quietly helping her to make her escape.

"Go fetch your hat inspector and have a car ready for us. I know where we need to head."

The inspector stood, muttering to himself, and disappeared to organise their departure. Susan relaxed as he left their presence.

"Another escape thanks to you Clara."

"Don't mention it." Clara squeezed her shoulder.

"I'll go back to bed now, I still feel rotten." Susan moved off, Clara hesitated to say more until she was almost at the staircase.

"You know, if you ever want to talk to me... I'm a very good listener and nothing shocks me, not these days. So if you want to talk..."

Susan gave her a very sad smile.

"We all have our burdens to carry, don't we Clara? I'll be all right, you just sort out Andrew."

She made her way up the stairs slowly. Clara felt more anxious than ever about her.

Chapter Fifteen

"When I find that swine I'll wring his neck for all this trouble." Inspector Jennings fidgeted in the back of the police car. His plan to catch the Campbell family unawares had been a good one, it had worked before. He caught his suspects when they were vulnerable and least prepared, but that Andrew Campbell might slip the net had not been foreseen. Jennings had not expected him to ignore his orders.

Clara decided it was safer to remain silent than to engage Jennings in conversation as they wound their way to Brooklands.

"I've had men out sweeping that blooming racetrack for the missing stole all day!" Jennings grumbled, "Surely they would have seen him if he had gone there."

"He will be tucked away in the garages, inspector. Very safe from police eyes." Clara noticed the gates of the racetrack looming, the place was pitch dark, except for a few odd lights down near the garages, "See?"

They headed swiftly in the direction of the lights. Jennings had the constable head out onto the track, determined not to lose his suspect again.

"I don't think he will bolt inspector."

"I'm not taking any chances."

Just before garage number 10 a man walked out in front of them cursing to himself and carrying a bag of tools. It was Francke. He pulled up short when he saw them.

"What you doing here?" He asked curiously.

"Is Andrew Campbell around?" The inspector asked hastily.

Francke gave a nod towards garage 10.

"It about that woman I nearly hit. I didn't hit her!"

"We know that Francke." Jennings said reassuringly, darting past the German as he spoke.

Clara followed in his wake. Francke watched them disappear into garage 10, then dropped his tools and went to see what was happening.

Andrew was stretched out on an old sofa at the back of the garage, almost asleep in his oil-stained overalls. He observed Jennings approach him through bleary eyes.

"So you found me." Andrew yawned and pulled himself upright, then his attention fell on Clara, "What is she doing here?"

Clara was a little stunned by the expression of hatred on Andrew's face, she couldn't understand how she had offended him so.

"Miss Fitzgerald is helping with the investigation." Jennings said smartly.

"Interfering more like! I've never seen someone so nosy, she's probably glad there's been a murder so she has something to gossip about."

"Andrew Campbell, I have been asked to assist you in any way I can by helping solve this murder. But I refuse to be insulted. I would much rather be back in Brighton than having to sort out the sordid mess you have gotten yourself into." Clara snapped, finally fed up with her cousin.

"Sordid? Who are you to say that of me? The poor relation, that's who you are! Staying at the house because you don't have the money for a hotel! I didn't want you at the wedding, I didn't want any of you. If father had kept it

116

low-key as I had wanted than none of this would have happened!"

"And you would have committed bigamy." Clara said coolly, "Which is also a crime. You're a scoundrel Andrew Campbell, whichever way you look at it."

Francke gave a round of applause behind Clara, grinning from ear to ear.

"That's enough all of you!" Jennings interrupted, "Clara is present because I have asked her to be present and if you insult her, then you are effectively insulting me for inviting her. Do you understand Mr Campbell?"

Andrew scowled at them. For the first time Clara saw a spark of violence that made her re-evaluate her view of him. Perhaps, in the right situation, he could be driven to dangerous actions.

"I want to ask you about your movements after the wedding on Saturday." Jennings began in a calmer voice.

"I was here, all the time. You can ask Francke." Andrew pointed at the Austrian.

Francke gave a broad shrug of his shoulders.

"I saw him once or twice, maybe, for a few moments." He said noncommittally.

"Liar!" Andrew shouted, "You came in here and drank tea with me! Your mechanics were outside all afternoon next to my car and you were sitting in that stupid deckchair of yours flicking through a newspaper. I was a few feet away from you all afternoon!"

"I can only answer honestly." Francke was nonplussed, "I actually saw you only briefly."

"Bloody swine! So you'd see me hang to ensure your own winning place at the next track meet? We all know my Napier will do over your Opel unless I can't drive it."

"As you please." Francke didn't react to the accusation, "I merely state what I know."

"But your mechanics would have seen him?" Jennings once more interrupted.

"Maybe." Francke gave his calm shrug again.

"He'll tell them to say different, they all need the work

he gives them." Andrew deflated somewhat, he sank down on the sofa and pressed his head into his hands, "I'm not a fool inspector, I know you are looking to me to have done this. But I didn't kill Shirley."

"Perhaps you can help me to believe that." The inspector folded over a new page in his notebook, "Tell me about your marriage to Shirley."

Andrew sighed into his hands.

"You want all the gruesome details?"

"Yes."

"And she has to hear it?"

Clara stiffened.

"I will never spread a word of what you tell me, whatever you think of me I am not a gossip." She said.

"She might be the only one able to save you from the noose too." Jennings added with emphasis, "Remember that."

Andrew was silent for several moments, except for the sounds of him taking deep breaths through his fingers.

"I met her on leave in London." He stated softly, "She was a dancer. She danced very well. We were at the Empire dance hall, a gang of us from the unit and she was looking for a partner. She picked me and we hit it off. She told me her name was Shirley and she wanted to know what I had been doing at the front, whether I was one of the brave lads in the trenches. That sort of thing. We talked, we danced. Eventually I took her for a meal."

"Did you know she was a prostitute?" Jennings asked bluntly.

They all waited for Andrew to explode again, but he didn't. It seemed his fight was gone. Instead, very quietly he said.

"Yes. I knew."

"What happened then?"

"I had a month's leave because I had taken a bit of gas and needed to recover. I saw her everyday rather than go home. There was nothing at home for me except father and Glory. I would rather be in London with Shirley.

Soon we were walking out. I stayed at Shirley's place at night. I'm not sure what I was thinking, only there was this nag inside of me that I might not be around long the way the war was going, so why not enjoy that last month home? I treated her well, I bought her gifts. We were always eating out and going to dances. Sometimes one of her old... friends, would come around and I would have to see them off, make them understand she wasn't into that business anymore."

"Were you planning on marrying her?"

"I don't know, maybe, eventually. I was only thinking of the moment. What was the point of thinking a week or month ahead when I might be dead? You can't plan for anything when you have that looming over you." Andrew raised his head, he looked exhausted by it all, "Then she fell pregnant. She said it was mine. The other lads laughed, said I was being led a merry dance, but I didn't believe them. I thought to myself, if I'm killed what will happen to the child? At least if we were married Shirley could claim some money from the Army and my family. So the day before I went back to Flanders we were married in the registry office. I bought Shirley a mink stole for the occasion, it was a cold day. That was the last I ever saw of her until Saturday."

There was a glint in the inspector's eyes as he looked over at Clara. So his theory had been right.

"Why?" He asked, not letting on his own suspicions.

Andrew fell back on the sofa, his face ashen, the lines around his mouth and eyes suddenly so deep. He seemed to have aged many years. He couldn't look at them as he spoke, he just kept staring at his Napier off to his right.

"There was no baby. There never had been. We wrote letters for a while, I was still eager, but nine months came and went with no mention of a child and I started to wonder. All those taunts the other lads had mocked me with came back to my mind and ate away at me. Day after day I sat in those trenches, clinging to one vain hope that there was a part of me that would survive the slaughter.

119

A child that would bear my name. I lived for that, but she lied to me, there never was a child. I had been used, but worse she had given me this false hope that suddenly crumbled to dust. It felt as though I had nothing left." Andrew cringed as the memories returned, "I suppose I have to be honest with you, but from that moment I hated her. I wrote to her once and asked her about the baby. She made some strange excuse about losing it, but she couldn't explain why she had not told me. I felt such a fool. I cut myself off from her. Stopped sending money to her, that was the worst I could do to her, I knew that, she was so mercenary stopping the money would hurt. I never wrote again and I never saw her again. As far as I was concerned I didn't have a wife."

"Yet legally speaking you did." Jennings pointed out politely, "When you proposed to Laura Pettibone didn't that worry you?"

"You don't know how I had eradicated her from my memory. I convinced myself the marriage was not real, like everything else. It had been done in such haste I didn't think it could be legally binding. I suppose I was just happy to stumble on blindly pretending it had never occurred."

"What about when Shirley turned up at the church?"

"I was stunned. It was like a nightmare, there she was dressed exactly like the day we got married, even with the mink stole. I didn't know what to think, I just felt numb as if it couldn't be her, not really."

"You whispered something to her as she left the church, what was it?" Clara risked a question.

Andrew looked at her with resentment, but he answered.

"She wanted me to meet her so we could talk, I promised I would call on her."

"Did you?"

Andrew shook his head.

"I never saw her again."

The inspector folded over the leather cover of his

notebook.

"I think that will do for the moment Mr Campbell, but I would prefer it if you keep close to home as I reminded you before."

Andrew made no reply. The inspector nodded to Clara and they turned to leave the garage. Francke was at their side, his face contorted in thought.

"How did she get here, I ask myself?" Francke remarked as they strode out into the night, "She did not walk here, I think. No, I think someone brought her here."

"Yes, we had already come to that conclusion. It's the 'who' that is more important now." Jennings said, irritated at the continued presence of the Austrian.

"Let me think, something comes to me..." Francke tapped at his forehead, "It was here, about midnight. I was in the workshop. I couldn't sleep so I got up and came outside for a cigarette, and I see some lights. Car lights. I think nothing of it, because people travel at all times, but I'm certain it stopped above the Byfleet for a few moments. Not long, but for a short time the lights were stationary and then it moved off again."

Clara glanced at Jennings, he was listening riveted.

"You are sure?" He asked.

"Of that? Yes." Francke gave them both a smile, "I don't like Andrew much, but I tell you this, he was not in that car. He was fast asleep on the sofa. I saw him."

The inspector thanked Francke and he moved away with Clara as the Austrian returned to his abandoned tools.

"Well, it looks like Andrew is in the clear." Clara said, "He couldn't have dumped the body."

"No, that is true."

Clara stared at Jennings.

"But something is worrying you?"

"Yes, and it might mean Andrew as not as innocent as he protests."

Clara felt herself go cold.

121

"Are you going to tell me?" She asked.

"It's just a little thing, you see just now when we were talking to Andrew and he was professing his honesty he to us? Well, I know for a fact, without a doubt in my mind, that honest Andrew was lying."

Chapter Sixteen

The inspector showed Clara into his office at the station. She had declined going straight back to the Campbells, instead wanting to know what Jennings had meant by his cryptic comment. Jennings turned on the gas light, muttering something about electricity not having reached the police yet and motioned towards a battered trunk under the window.

"Go ahead, I'm sure you want to examine it."

Clara did want to look at Shirley Cox's trunk, but refused to show undignified haste, so removed her gloves and hat first before kneeling in front of the box. It was not overly large and had been in use for many years. The corners were bashed in, their paper covering ripped revealing the cardboard that comprised the trunk. Someone had mended one with parcel tape and attempted to use boot polish to hide the damage.

Clara lifted the lid gingerly. The box interior did not smell musty as she had anticipated, but was sweet with the scent of old roses and the light fragrance of face powder. Tucked under some straps in the lid were several small theatre programmes.

"Andrew did say she was a dancer." Jennings mentioned as Clara looked at the faded booklets.

One was orange and white with illustrations in black, another was pale green with bold lettering. A third had a drawing of a man and woman performing acrobatics on the front. Each had the name Shirley Cox printed on it and the description 'child dancer'. So this was how life had begun for Shirley. On the stage in London theatres and music halls, one of the many children who performed in pantomimes and variety acts for a few pence. It was a hard life; long hours, difficult work and often having to travel to and from the theatre alone at all hours. Then, of course, there was the moment the child grew too big to be deemed 'sweet' on stage and their novelty evaporated just as adulthood and the need for an income beckoned.

"The boys in London never knew her as a dancer." Jennings confirmed, watching Clara thumb thoughtfully through the programmes, "They first picked her up soliciting when she was eighteen or nineteen. A lot of child actors and dancers struggle to find work when they grow up, there are so many of them out there, and they no longer have youth in their favour."

"Remarkable that you can be 'too old' before you are even twenty." Clara put the programmes down, they were depressing her.

She went through the rest of the trunk, its catalogue of belongings rather limited. A make-up bag nestled next to a hair brush; two pairs of spare knickers were rolled up in a blouse and crammed beneath them was a pair of stockings with a hole in one larger than Clara's hand – no wonder Shirley had gone bare-legged; under those was a worn coat and two embroidered handkerchiefs; at the very base there was a small purse with a few pennies inside and a thick book tied up with string.

Clara removed the book and looked through its pages, to her surprise it contained scraps from newspapers, a torn page from Who's Who and another from a Surrey Directory, along with notes and jottings all concerning the Campbell family.

"She has been searching for Andrew a long time."

"Wouldn't you if all you had as an alternative was walking the streets." Jennings was matter-of-fact, "Look at the last completed page."

Clara thumbed through pages thick with cheap glue paste to almost the last sheet. There she found the final entry, a notice badly snipped from The Times concerning the forthcoming marriage of Andrew Campbell and Laura Pettibone. Clara put down the book, how sad it all was, how depressing. She understood Andrew had been angry, wouldn't anybody having felt that way after being so duped? But she also saw Shirley's perspective, a woman driven by this overruling desperation to survive. It was difficult to blame someone for clinging to one last hope of salvation.

"There were two more things in the box that I removed to look at further." Jennings opened a drawer at his desk, "These are all the letters, as far as I can tell, that Andrew Campbell sent his wife during the war, and this is her diary."

He positioned a bundle of letters and a thin black book on the desk.

"The letters weren't particularly helpful. They mainly concern Andrew's life at the front and are naturally censored. The diary was more interesting, especially the last entry."

Jennings handed the black book to Clara and she flicked through its contents briefly to get an idea of Shirley's style. She didn't write every day, rather she added entries when something interesting had happened. They were often brief. The very last one was no different.

"Saturday 15 May 1920." Clara read aloud, "Blew Andrew's wedding as planned. His face was priceless. Persuaded him to come see me. He came at 2pm. We argued. He threw a bundle of money at me, told me to leave. I said I couldn't do that. He was furious and marched out. Not sure what to do now. He doesn't seem to love me anymore."

Clara checked the date of the entry again, then looked

towards Jennings.

"That's how you knew Andrew was lying when he said he did not see Shirley after the wedding."

"Not just that, Mrs Macphinn, the landlady, was naturally upset when she heard about her guest's demise and wanted to be helpful. I asked her if Shirley had ever had any visitors while she was staying with her. Your name came up of course," Jennings grinned, "But she also mentioned that a young man came over on the Saturday afternoon. He was tall, stern-looking and never smiled. Sounds like our Andrew, doesn't it. Well he went up to see Shirley in her room, which Mrs Macphinn didn't approve of, but he insisted. So being a landlady with her respectability to think of dear Mrs Macphinn loitered on the stairs. She heard Shirley and the gentleman argue, then after ten minutes he stormed down the stairs and left."

"That does sound like Andrew." Clara sighed, "And just when I was beginning to think he might be in the clear. Still, he didn't murder her there and then, so he either asked her to meet him sometime later or our murderer is someone entirely different."

"I know, none of this makes things any plainer."

"I don't suppose you asked when Mrs Macphinn last saw her guest?"

"That would have been around 4.30pm on Saturday. Mrs Macphinn visits her sister on a Saturday and leaves dinner for the guests cooking in the oven. Mr Macphinn serves it up on her behalf. Shirley was still in the house when Mrs Macphinn left, but she has no idea if she was still around when she returned. She just assumed she was."

"And Mr Macphinn?"

"As observant a fellow as an ostrich with its head in the sand. He couldn't be sure, but after a great deal of thinking and complaining about his memory he came to the conclusion that Shirley was not there for dinner on Saturday."

"That narrows down when she could have been murdered. It had to be after 4.30pm, when most of the Campbells were home. Unfortunately they were so scattered about the house none have a solid alibi."

"For all we know Shirley came to the house and was bumped off there, in the gardens perhaps. Then moved."

"What do you make of the car Francke saw." Clara asked, "I recall hearing a car as well that night. It's not exactly a common sound."

"We can't say for certain it was dumping the body, but it seems likely. That narrows the field further since there aren't that many people with cars around these parts, except the Campbells of course."

"There must be others with cars?"

"The doctor, perhaps, the police naturally." Jennings shook his head, "No, that line of thought brings us right back to the Campbells again."

"It would be pretty foolish of Andrew to dump the body on the racetrack."

"Ah, unless he was trying to throw us off the scent! A double bluff, banking on his friend Francke to provide an alibi."

"I think it likely Andrew was at the track all day after he saw Shirley." Clara said firmly.

"That doesn't rule out him having an accomplice. His sister for instance? He murders Shirley and heads to the racetrack to provide himself with an alibi, knowing that so many people are coming and going it would be hard for anyone to know if he had been there all afternoon or not. In the meantime the accomplice collects the body and hides it in one of the Campbell cars. Only to dump it on the racetrack late at night, making it look like a clumsy attempt to implicate Andrew. Thus causing us to assume he is actually innocent and had been framed." Jennings had to pause for breath after his long speech.

Clara gave him a moment.

"I'm unconvinced." She said calmly.

"Then name me another suspect."

127

"As good as Andrew? No, I can't think of one, but I'm not certain it was Andrew. If anything I am verging towards finding him innocent, despite his obnoxious nature."

Jennings smiled at her.

"I'm close to having enough circumstantial evidence to convict him."

"A court would not accept it." Scoffed Clara.

"Really? We have a damn good motive. Andrew was last seen arguing with Shirley at 2pm when he lied and said he was at the racetrack. When she vanished after half four how can we be certain he was not lying again when he said he was nowhere near her? Then there is the motor car, I still need to work on that, but if it did transport the body I only have one suspect with a car. Finally we have the dumping of the body, which could be a clever double bluff. There are holes, I admit, but people have been hanged on a lot less."

"I would not want to hang anyone on what you just told me." Clara tossed Shirley's diary onto the desk, "Could someone take me home now, I have a lot to think over?"

"Of course, but don't waste too much time worrying about Andrew. He has made a fine bed for himself to sleep in."

"Why is it I always end up feeling sorry for my suspects?"

Jennings gave Clara a light pat on the shoulder.

"You'll have to toughen up."

"I would rather not, I seem to be doing all right as I am."

Jennings gave her another smile.

"Don't expect any gratitude from Andrew if you prove him innocent."

"Oh I won't! I'm not that sentimental!"

Chapter Seventeen

Clara couldn't sleep late into the morning, though she occasionally tried. But the bright light of day and the call of birds berated her for her dawdling and she felt it impossible to not get up. So she was busy getting first choice at the breakfast table when she heard the front door quietly open and close. The next moment a familiar head poked around the door.

"I might have known you would be up already unlike decent folk."

"Annie!"

Clara dropped her fork and rushed to embrace her maid and friend. A lifelong bond had been formed between the two women when they met in hospital during the war. Clara had been a nurse, Annie her patient. When the frail girl had wondered what would become of her after she recovered Clara offered her a job. Even so, Clara found it difficult to think of Annie as a maid and struggled to keep her behaviour strictly formal.

"Give over Clara! What will the butler think?" Annie laughed as she pushed away her friend, "So what pickle are we in now?"

Clara grimaced.

"Murder, as usual. I couldn't put it all in my telegram,

but Andrew was married once before and his first wife showed up at his wedding. Now she is dead."

"Clear-cut case to me." Annie pretended to brush her hands of the matter, "So why hasn't he been arrested?"

"Because it's far more complicated than it seems and I, for one, think he is innocent."

Annie rolled her eyes.

"Why doesn't that surprise me?"

"But I'm so glad you are here, this house is driving me demented and Tommy misses you dreadfully."

Annie suppressed a smile.

"Does he now?"

"You know we are simply hopeless without you."

"And?"

Clara hesitated as Annie looked at her enquiringly.

"Come on Clara, I know you. You want another pair of eyes and ears in his household."

"Am I that obvious?"

"Yes!" Annie chuckled, "Fortunately I was going mad mooching around that empty house in Brighton, so I was pleased to come out to the country. Besides that young man, Oliver Bankes, has been calling for you every day. He is like a little lost puppy."

"Oh dear." Clara nibbled at her thumb, wondering what to make of Oliver Bankes, if anything.

"Well, anyway, I told him…"

Annie was cut off by the scream coming from upstairs. Clara only had to look at Annie and the maid dropped her suitcase, before both women went flying to the source of the sound. They had to head down one corridor and then turn left before they spotted the screamer. It was one of the house maids, stood outside a bedroom door and almost turning blue with the noise she was making. Annie swooped on her, making soothing sounds and trying to calm her, while Clara ventured into the room.

It didn't take much to recognise the cause of the commotion.

"Oh Eustace."

Eustace was lying on his back in bed, his arms flung out either side, his eyes bulging and staring at the ceiling. Vomit covered the bed sheets to the right of his face. His skin had turned a strange shade of chalky grey, as if his blood had been drained from him. There was no doubt he was dead. Still, to be certain, Clara walked forward and felt for a pulse. When it was clear there was none she took a step back and stared disbelievingly at the corpse.

"What's going on?" Glorianna appeared in the room wrapped in her dressing gown.

"You need to call a doctor Glorianna, and find Hogarth." Clara put a hand out to try and stop Glorianna coming forward but the woman pushed past.

She gasped when she saw Eustace.

"Go fetch Hogarth and ring the doctor." Clara turned her around and half forced her from the room. Clara wasn't certain what was making her act so urgently, but some instinct inside her told her she had to act cautiously. Eustace's unexpected death was troubling.

"What's happened Clara?" Annie asked from the doorway, unable to see in the room.

"Uncle Eustace is dead. It's all a bit messy. Perhaps you should take the maid downstairs?"

Annie gave a little nod.

"Be careful Clara."

"Always." Clara answered with a reassuring smile.

Annie led the maid away, who was now almost collapsed with shock. Clara was alone with the body only for a few minutes before Hogarth appeared. He walked in the room slowly and viewed his brother from the foot of the bed.

"I told Glorianna to call the doctor." Clara said.

"Yes, is that necessary?"

"I think so, he died rather violently." Clara hardly needed to point out the way Eustace was splayed on the bed as though he had been writhing and the awful look in his eyes, "You said he felt ill last night?"

"One of his bilious attacks. He took unwell after

dinner, said he would go lie down and asked for some tonic water to be sent up. Do you think it was something he ate?"

Clara was carefully looking at the jug of water on the bedside table, almost completely empty.

"Did he always drink tonic water at night?"

"Only when his indigestion was playing up." Hogarth reached out for a chair and sat down hard, "I wasn't expecting this. I didn't think him that ill."

"I never heard of indigestion killing a man." Clara was studying the tonic water intently, "Eustace has been rather ill during his stay here."

"He always complains our food doesn't agree with him. I don't know why it shouldn't, I think he just likes to moan about it. There's nothing wrong with the food after all, we are all here quite healthy." Hogarth rubbed at his eyes, "I know it sounds awful, but my brother always seems to make things worse, even when he is dead."

Clara walked over to Hogarth and gently took his hand. He was trembling, she felt his fingers shaking in her palm.

"He was still my brother." Hogarth said softly, "Despite his ill-manners and trouble-making. I thought he would be around another decade at least."

"I'm sorry."

"Clara, this has been one of the worst weeks I can remember. Worse even then when Andrew was away. That was different, everything was happening at a distance. This is all so… close. That damn woman! And now Eustace! I just don't understand how this can be happening. What have we done wrong?"

"I don't think you've done anything wrong Hogarth. Life can be difficult sometimes."

"Do you think the police will want to know about Eustace?"

Clara didn't answer immediately, Hogarth looked distressed and she didn't want to add to that, but she couldn't lie either. Something felt very wrong with

132

Eustace's death.

"I'm not sure at the moment."

"Eustace didn't deserve to go this way. Not like this. He was obnoxious, I know, I know. But he had a good heart beating inside him. He couldn't help that he was not the son our father wanted."

"Was it bitter between them?" Clara asked.

"Sometimes." Hogarth drew a shaky breath, "Who am I kidding? All the time! Eustace was not cut out for business and father resented that. He sent him to the best schools and tried his hardest and Eustace tried hard too, in return. It was just never that simple. Figures and sums never made sense to Eustace, he struggled with anything more complicated than simple addition. He would stare at a ledger for hours, under our father's gaze and still not have a clue what it all meant. I, on the other hand, picked it up so easily. I know Eustace resented that, felt I had taken his place. But just as he couldn't help being who he was, so I couldn't help having a head for arithmetic."

"I think Eustace knew it was not your fault."

Hogarth rubbed miserably at his face.

"Really?"

"Eustace didn't want to be burdened by running a business, it was best you took it over. His problem was he never really recovered from being a disappointment to his father."

Hogarth nodded.

"I can see that."

"The doctor's here." Glorianna peeked around the door, averting her eyes from the bed where Eustace lay, "I haven't told the girls yet, Peg was roused by the noise but I told her a maid caught her hand in a door."

Glorianna vanished again as the doctor appeared. Doctor Hogg was lean and tall with a stoop from years of looking down on patients from a great height. He was white-haired and wore gold-rimmed glasses perched precariously on his nose. He shuffled in, looking no less than ninety years old, and quietly shook the hands of

Hogarth and Clara. Then he turned to the bed.

"Oh dear. Did you realise he was already dead?"

Hogarth gave Clara a look of exasperation; she decided to take over matters.

"We were aware doctor, but we thought it best you take a look. After all, there has to be a death certificate and so forth."

Clara followed the doctor to the bedside. She had hoped to find him a competent man with an eye for the suspicious, she had her own doubts but she wanted the doctor to confirm them before she acted. Instead he looked the sort who would glance at the body and sign the certificate without a thought.

Doctor Hogg went through the usual checks for pulse and heart function for the sake of them. Then began a detailed examination of Eustace's face, from his wide open eyes, to the unpleasant staining around his mouth.

"Was he ill last night?"

"Just a little bilious." Clara said.

"He was definitely a very robust individual. In my experience such people suffer greatly from digestive disorders."

Clara was desperate to add that sometimes such people had a little help, but Hogarth was watching and what was she really basing her suspicions on? A hunch? A gut feeling something wasn't right?

"My first thought is a heart attack, very common in a man of this age with so much fat." Doctor Hogg sank a finger into Eustace's portly side. It sunk deep into the flesh, "The vomit is odd though."

"I thought so too, and he looks so…" Clara struggled for the right word, "Distressed."

"That can happen, if the victim becomes aware of the attack. Mind you, I say heart but he could have choked on his own vomit." The doctor opened Eustace's mouth and stared down his throat, "No, I'm afraid it will have to be a cut-up job. I'll inform the coroner. I can have a couple of men come to collect him later this morning."

Doctor Hogg took another long, assessing look at his patient.

"Make that four men."

"What do you expect to find?" Clara said, feeling a little more hopeful.

"Probably still the heart." Doctor Hogg checked his watch, "I must get on, there is a very live lady down the road suffering from an attack of the gall bladder. I should say give it an hour for the men to arrive to collect the body."

Doctor Hogg was wandering out of the room before he had finished talking.

"Why did Glory call him?" Hogarth snarled when the doctor had vanished, "Hopeless idiot."

Clara was looking at the bed and thinking calmly. She wasn't so sure Doctor Hogg was such a fool, but she also wasn't convinced by her own doubts concerning Eustace's demise. She had to act for herself. First things first she rang the servants' bell. Then she took the jug of tonic water off the bedside table and covered it with a cloth. Hogarth watched her curiously.

"What are you doing Clara?"

"Being thorough." Clara gave him a smile, "And possibly being over-suspicious."

A maid appeared in the doorway with her eyes downcast, not prepared to witness the scene of a gruesome death.

"Could you bring me a clean glass jar?" Clara asked the girl, "And a spoon."

The girl disappeared.

"You are worrying me Clara." Hogarth rested his arms on the high foot rest at the base of his brother's bed, "Are you thinking we have another murder on our hands?"

"I make no assumptions until I have some evidence." Clara answered, "I'm just curious, that's all. Why does your food disagree so with Eustace when, as you say, it suits us perfectly well? I do not believe Eustace had a weak constitution. He spent most of his time at his Club

135

and from the little I know of cooking in such places it can hardly be termed plain living. Eustace is clearly a man who loves his food, and rich, fatty food at that. Why should he have such problems with his digestion when he comes here?"

Hogarth's worried look creased his forehead into a deep frown. The maid returned with the jar, unable to bring herself to enter the room so offering it at the door. Clara took it with a slight pang of pride that her own sensibilities did not extend to being terrified of a dead body. Then she set to work scooping vomit into the jar. When she was done she gave the spoon back to the maid and covered the jar with a similar cloth to the one she had found for the jug.

"Amuse me Hogarth." Clara winked at her cousin as she collected the two samples.

Hogarth just gave a shrug, completely perplexed.

Clara removed the jug and the jar to her own room and carefully locked them inside, then she found the phone in the hallway and asked to be put through to the police station. The line rang for a long time before someone, slightly out-of-breath, answered.

"Could I speak to inspector Jennings?" Clara asked.

The speaker on the other end gasped air as he spoke.

"He's rather busy."

"It's important, tell him Clara called."

The speaker asked her to hold and then there was silence. Clara stared at the wall in front of her where a still-life of poppies and sunflowers in a blue and white vase hung. She was looking at the picture, but her mind was far off. Had Eustace known something useful? He had been very open when he spoke to Tommy, had someone heard him? Or was there another reason someone would care to dispose of him? It was all supposition of course, he may not have actually been murdered, but Clara was certain she had seen grains of something sitting at the very bottom of his jug of tonic water. They could just be particles of dirt from the jug being improperly cleaned.

But then there was the vomit and his clear distress —
there had been real anguish in Eustace's eyes.

"Clara?"

She jerked back to reality.

"Inspector, I thought I should inform you there has
been another death." Clara cast a look around the hall to
make sure no one was listening, "Uncle Eustace has
passed away."

"I'm sorry to hear that." Jennings replied, clearly not
understanding her meaning.

"With all that has been going on I thought it wise to
save some samples of material for your lab. Would you
mind sending someone reliable over to collect them?"

"Clara, are you saying Eustace was murdered?"

"I'm not sure, not yet. But I don't like the look of this."

Jennings was quiet a moment.

"What sort of samples?"

"A jug of water and a jar of vomit. Both may or may
not contain poison."

Another silence.

"Clara, this is getting serious. If he has been murdered
it will have been at the hands of someone in that house."

"I know."

"Just be careful, that's all I'm saying."

"I always am inspector." Clara said her goodbyes and
put the phone down.

"Who was that?" Glorianna almost snapped at Clara.

She turned calmly to see her a few feet away. She had
not apparently overheard.

"Only the inspector. I was informing him of Eustace's
death."

"Why?"

"He was intending to come today and interview him, I
thought it prudent to make him aware of the situation so
he did not disturb you all at this delicate time."

"Oh." Glorianna looked mollified, "That was a good
idea Clara."

"You have enough on your plate right now Glorianna

without a policeman nosing about."

"Yes, yes."

"The doctor is sending some men round to collect the body. They'll be here in the hour."

Glorianna gave a little start.

"Didn't he sign the death certificate? I could call the undertakers myself."

"He couldn't make up his mind what killed Eustace." Clara gave a shrug, as if to say 'doctors, huh?', "He wants to do a post-mortem."

"Oh. Oh." Glorianna was agitated, "Then I better tidy the room, can't have it looking in such a state when strangers come in."

Glorianna hustled away and Clara watched her walk up the staircase. She was letting dark thoughts stir inside her mind, linking motives and opportunities and picturing a killer. Finally she shook herself and decided she could do no more for the moment for Eustace. Anyway she had another person to attend to.

When Clara quietly tapped on Susan's door she heard the sound of someone retching hard and panic gripped her. She burst open the door against all propriety and ran to the girl who was half stretched out of her bed being ill into an enamel bowl.

"Are you all right?" Clara took Susan's shoulders and held her while she retched one last time and then sighed, "Have you taken any tonic water?"

"What? No." Susan flopped back onto her bed as pale as the sheets, "What's the fuss Clara?"

Clara was frightened, she looked at the girl lying feebly on her bed and all her calm escaped her.

"Eustace has been found dead, perhaps food poisoning. He had been sick before he died. How do you feel Susan?" Clara rested a hand on Susan's forehead and tested its temperature.

"I'm fine Clara." Susan brushed her away.

"Clearly not! I shall call back Doctor Hogg and have him examine you, before it is too late!" Clara jumped from the bed heading for the door.

"NO!"

Clara stopped in her tracks and turned back to Susan. The girl was reaching out to her, making a 'stop' gesture with her hand, her weakness replaced by a look of pure terror.

"You can't do that Clara!"

"You are ill Susan." Clara took another pace to the door.

"Please no! I'm not ill. I don't know what happened to Eustace but I am certain it has nothing to do with me."

"How?" Clara asked suspiciously.

"Close the door and let me talk to you." Susan begged, "I have to talk to someone anyway, before I go mad."

Clara stared at Susan for a moment, then she walked and closed the door. She headed back for the bed and removed the offending bowl to the corner of the room, before sitting down beside Susan.

"How?" She repeated.

The adrenaline that had pushed Susan upright had exhausted her too, and she fell back frailly on the pillows. She wiped at her lips with a handkerchief.

"Could I have a glass of water first?" Susan pointed to a jug on a nearby chest of drawers.

Clara poured her out a glass of water, taking a very close look at the jug before she was satisfied it was clean. She returned to Susan.

"I'm going to take some convincing to prevent me calling the doctor." She said sternly.

Susan took a long sip of water.

"There's no need, I've been to a doctor."

"So you are sick. Nobody has mentioned it?"

"That's because nobody knows." Susan gave a sigh, "And I'm not exactly sick, I've just been very foolish."

Several thoughts came together in Clara's brain.

"You're pregnant."

Susan glared at her wide-eyed.

"I suppose I should have known you were sharp

enough to work that one out." She groaned, "Yes, pregnant."

"That explains the plumpness and illness." Clara nodded, "It also clarifies what happened the night before the wedding."

"You won't tell anyone?" Susan pleaded, "That was why I jumped in the river, because I couldn't bear everyone knowing. It all hit me the night before Andrew and Laura were to wed, suddenly I couldn't stand it anymore."

"I shan't tell a soul, but you best explain everything to me Susan. It will be impossible to keep this a secret forever, I'm sure you are aware of that."

Susan gave another little sigh.

"I know, it shall become obvious soon enough. Oh Clara, it was not as though I set out to be wicked I just got carried away."

"What happened?"

"It was the night we all finished school." Susan pulled a face as she remembered, "We were supposed to stay in the school until our families picked us up, but Bella Hope wanted to have a night out since we were almost all eighteen and some of us, like Katherine Hardings, were heading back to families abroad. So we would never see each other again and Bella said it would be such fun to end school with a night out. Something to remember."

"Where did you go?"

"London, it was nearest. We snuck out and caught a train. It was end of term and a lot of the teachers had already left so it wasn't so tough. Bella seemed to know what she was doing. There were twenty of us and we giggled all the way to London and made the conductor glare." Susan's eyes glimmered with amusement, "Bella knew a night-club, so we all went and had cocktails. There were these girls in indecently short skirts and they were dancing. Such dancing! It wasn't what Mrs Prince taught us in deportment class, I tell you!

"Well, we were all really following Bella's lead and

when she was asked to dance by this young man in uniform none of us blinked an eye about doing the same. I was 'picked up' by this young man in a dark green jacket and beige trousers. His name was Derek and he knew all the newest dances, he showed me them and I was soon kicking my heels. I loved it, such freedom Clara! I had never known it! I suppose that was half the problem. I drank too much and then Bella had this wild idea that we should all go to a hotel and return to school the next morning. Looking back I think Bella was out of her depth too, but she wasn't going to let anyone know that."

"I take it things became more serious after that?" Clara said carefully.

"Rather. Several of the girls didn't want to stay overnight, they said they didn't have the money. They headed back for the train station without us. Five of us were left, including Bella. She was still hanging on the arm of her soldier friend and raving about finding a hotel. Each of us girls who stayed had a man with us, I had Derek, and the fellows were all up for it too. We egged each other on, it was such a game! We found a hotel, not sure how. It was a bit down-market, but clean enough and it didn't cost us everything in our purses, which was good. Oh, you know Clara those cads let us girls pay for it all! Knowing full well what they were about!"

Clara nodded rather solemnly, she was not entirely surprised.

"We each had a room, how stupid was that?" Susan grimaced, "I asked for a double and Derek leaned over with a wink and said 'double-bed she means'. The more I think about him the more awful it seems. He looked so elegant in the night-club, but later he seemed so cheap and tawdry. I don't who he was, maybe just some street-seller who hung around clubs waiting for girls to pay for his evening out. I suppose you can imagine what happened next?"

"It isn't hard. Did he hurt you?"

Susan gave a little slant of her shoulders, a half shrug.

"No, not really. Derek was all right in that sense. I was a bit worried at first, but he was quite charming and I was rather tight after all the drinks, so things just happened. There was nothing really spectacular about it. It was over in a moment. It hurt a touch, but Derek was all kisses. Clara have you ever..."

Clara shook her head.

"No, you have more sense. Well, that was it really. Bella rounded us up about three o'clock, she had been crying. Said she couldn't stand anymore and wanted to go home. So I take it her soldier boy was not as nice as Derek. The other girls agreed. One, Cassandra, was trembling all over and looked about fit to be sick. I'm not sure if it was the alcohol or otherwise." Susan indicated what 'otherwise' meant with her eyes, "We left the men asleep in the rooms and we headed home. It was an awful journey, we had trouble catching a train and then Cassandra went all peculiar in the carriage and we thought we would have to call the conductor. We returned to the school and found our rooms. No one saw us, more is the pity. We never talked about what had happened. The next day our bags were packed and we went each to our own homes. Who would have thought that one silly night would have led to this?"

Clara patted Susan's hand reassuringly.

"It happens. You were very foolish. But it happens."

Susan visibly relaxed.

"What now?" She asked.

"As marrying Derek is out of the question, I think you will just have to be honest with everyone and brave it out. If it's any comfort I will stand by you and support you. I shan't see you cast out or anything."

"But I don't want a baby!" Susan suddenly wailed and tears burst from her eyes.

She threw herself over on her side and sobbed hard into the sheets. Clara rubbed her back, feeling a tad frustrated. Sympathy came to Clara in small doses and then she felt it necessary to be practical. Susan had behaved foolishly and sometimes there were consequences to such foolishness, but you couldn't howl about it. That was life.

"I'm afraid there really isn't an option." Clara told her.

"I know." Susan contained her tears, "Don't hate me Clara, but I looked at the alternative. I couldn't do it."

"Alternative? Surely not here?" Clara thought of the small village and wondered who on earth could be offering women pregnancy 'solutions', "Someone would have talked!"

"Oh no, it was all through Reverend Draper, he is very discreet." Susan had sat up again and was rifling under a pillow for a hanky.

Clara felt dazed by the information, she turned it over in her mind again.

"Susan, did I understand you correctly? You sought out an illegal abortion through the vicar?"

Susan went pale.

"Is it illegal?" She asked nervously.

"Yes." Clara said, "That is why you can't go to a doctor."

Susan turned and stared at the bed clothes, swallowing stiffly.

"I thought it was because it's the sort of thing wicked girls do, so it was disreputable, but I didn't know it was illegal. Will the police find out?"

"I very much doubt it." Clara reassured her, "But how is the vicar involved?"

"He knows people who do such things." Susan toyed with her hanky, screwing the corners into her fists, "One of the maids told me. She had been to him. I didn't say I was pregnant, but that a friend was in trouble. The maid told me everything. There is a little house down one of the side streets, a widow lives there and most people consider her most respectable. The vicar calls there often and that makes it all right. So you have to go to the Reverend Draper and explain and he arranges things, for a fee for the church collection box."

143

Clara realised her mouth was gaping as she listened to this revelation. She pulled herself together, it was not the first time her view of the world had been shaken, but it was still shocking.

"And you went?"

"I had to, at least I thought I had to. Reverend Draper was very nice about it, very reassuring. Said it happened to a lot of nice girls and I should not be ashamed, such was life. And he took me to the house late one night, so no one would see. I went in on my own and..." Susan sniffed back more tears, "There was this little parlour with a table and a cloth and these... these tools sitting beside it and this old woman with a face like a pig, chewing on a pipe and studying me as if... as if I was just a dog that had accidentally walked in the door. She wanted me to lie down, I only knew that because she pointed one evil thumb at the table. I stepped forward and I saw the stains on the cloth, almost washed out but not quite and I saw her spitting on her tools and rubbing them with the edge of her shawl... I couldn't do it. I ran straight back out and told Draper to take me home. He did, but he said he hoped I didn't expect the money back because it had already gone towards new hymn books for the choir and I was so flustered I said it didn't matter."

Susan finished breathlessly. Clara couldn't express how angry she was feeling at that moment, thinking of the Reverend Draper standing up in church giving his sermons. Knowing all the time he had sent girls to that rat-hole of a place to experience a travesty in the name of medical help. Susan was clearly not aware of the implications of the matter, did not know how close she had come to taking a most appalling risk with her life. Clara was well-read and not just newspapers, but the reformist journals and medical works. She liked to think herself politically aware and she had read about illegal abortion parlours and the horrors that occurred in them. Many women did not survive an abortion. Though she had never seen a victim personally she had heard stories

144

from the other nurses when she had worked in the hospital during the war. Some of them had seen girls ravaged by infection, or just bleeding to death before their eyes. It was horrible and this vicar was participating in such a crime? And taking money for it?!

"Clara, you are very quiet?"

Clara let out a long breath.

"I'm very glad you walked away Susan, so very glad." She clutched Susan's hand tightly, "I will do all I can to help you through this, but you must be honest with your father. There really is no other option."

"He'll be angry."

"Then he will get over it."

"And if he doesn't?"

Clara paused.

"You shall come and stay with me in Brighton. You shall have the baby and then we can decide on what you want to do."

"I'll have no money!" Susan started to pull at her hanky again.

But she would have money, thought Clara, because Eustace had said as much. He had made sure Susan and the other children were secure for the future. But she couldn't say that aloud.

"I'm sure we can arrange something." She said instead.

Before she could offer Susan more comfort there was a furious knock on the door and Glorianna burst in.

"There you are Clara! There is a police constable at the door saying he is to see you, why is he here?" Glorianna was frazzled, the morning was going exceptionally badly and now there was a policeman on her doorstep, "Did you ask him to come?"

Clara got up from Susan's bed and ushered Glorianna out of the room, to preserve her stepdaughter's privacy.

"It is nothing to worry over Glorianna, I told the inspector I had been thinking over the case of the unfortunate Shirley Cox and had created a list of ideas on the matter. He was too busy to listen over the phone so he said he would send a constable over to pick up my notes. I fear he is humouring me again." Clara gave a self-deprecating smile, she was becoming perturbed by how easily she lied to people these days.

"Is that all?" Glorianna was pulling at her fingers agitatedly, "Nothing to do with Eustace?"

"Eustace?" Clara put on a perplexed expression.

"Oh, listen to me, I am being so silly. The last few days have wrecked my nerves. Of course it is nothing to do with Eustace, of course. It's just with those men coming to collect his body and the room in a mess and I can't find the jug."

Clara looked innocent.

"Jug? What jug?"

"The glass pitcher Eustace had by his bedside. I was seeing that the room was tidy and the jug is gone. How can it have gone? It is always in that room. I asked the servants and none of them know anything about it."

"Perhaps someone else took it." Clara offered.

"Why? No one would take it."

"There was a little water left in it. Perhaps Hogarth needed a drink after the shock of seeing his brother that way and took the pitcher to his room?"

Glorianna's eyes looked ready to stand out from her head.

"Oh no, he wouldn't do that? Would he?" She suddenly turned and ran off to her room.

Clara headed for the stairs musing on what she had just seen and heard. A non-suspicious mind would think the shock had turned Glorianna's head and had her running about after inconsequential things. Clara did not have a non-suspicious mind. Instead she believed she had seen the fumbled panic of a guilty conscience. And that was very worrying indeed.

Chapter Eighteen

Clara found the police constable idly kicking his heels in the hall.

"Come with me." She motioned with her hand and led him towards the back of the house. For the first time she was rather relieved the family had ensconced herself and Tommy in bedrooms on the ground level. It meant they were out of sight of the main bedrooms and, for the moment at least, a safe distance from the family.

Clara unlocked the door to her room and headed inside. The constable hovered on the threshold. Clara motioned with her hand again, but he shuffled from foot to foot and glanced anxiously about. This was no time for worrying about manners. Clara grabbed his arm and dragged him into the room.

"It's not right miss!" The poor constable squeaked as she pulled him away from the door and shut and locked it behind them.

"No time for propriety now!" Clara hissed at him, listening for anyone nearby, "A murder has taken place!"

"Murder?" The constable was as perplexed as ever and wondering desperately why the sergeant had to pick him to come to the house.

"I've gathered two vital clues which I think need

examining." Clara had left the pitcher and jar on a chest of drawers, out of sight from the window, "You need to take them both back to the inspector at once."

The constable looked at the large pitcher and his face fell.

"But I came on my bicycle."

Clara resisted the urge to groan. It should not be this hard to get evidence to the police. She frowned at the policeman.

"Do you have a basket?"

"No." He was rather sheepish under her stern stare.

"Well how are you going to get these to Jennings?"

The constable gave a small shrug. Clara was just about to give in to her frustration when she heard the front bell ring again.

"Wait! Quickly, who would the doctor send to collect a body?"

"Undertakers, they have the hearse." The constable shrugged again as if it was obvious.

"Even if he wanted to conduct a post-mortem?"

The constable nodded as if to say 'who else?'

"Is the hearse motorised or horse-drawn?"

"Horses. Miss, if I can't help you…"

"But you can. We shan't send you back by bicycle."

"We shan't?" The constable felt his anxiety peaking around this strange woman who spoke fast and seemed full of odd ideas.

"You will return in the hearse, then you can carry the jug and jar."

"I shall not!" The constable was horrified, "That's for dead people!"

"Constable, a crime has been committed here, I am sure of it. You must bring this vital evidence to the inspector it is your duty and if that means riding in a hearse then I am afraid that is how it must be."

The constable grimaced and tried to make one last desperate stand.

"I have a thing about dead people."

148

"You're a policeman!" Clara gasped at him in exasperated.

"Well yes, but you don't get many dead people around here." The constable scratched at his head, "Do I really have to ride in a hearse?"

Clara looked at the unfortunate young man, she supposed he could be no more than twenty or twenty-one, very boyish still in his manners. He probably hadn't been with the police long and had spent most of his time on the thankless task of 'walking the beat'. What little crime they had around the area would be petty stuff, burglaries, fake postal orders, nothing particularly messy. The constable was green about police work and very new to the idea of murder.

"Yes, I'm afraid you do."

He gave a little sigh, but conceded defeat.

"All right miss, what should I do?"

"Go around the side of the house and come to this window. I shall pass you the jug which we must avoid being seen by the family at all costs. I shall bring the jar myself. Wait for me by the hearse."

The constable gave a nod and she let him out the door. Clara waited impatiently for him to appear at the window, wasting the time by tearing some cotton tape-ties from the edge of a pillow case and using that to secure the cloth over the glass jug. It wouldn't prevent the water leaking out if there was an accident, but it might catch the strange grains lurking at the bottom. Besides, it helped to conceal the pitcher.

Overhead she could hear thumping about in Eustace's bedroom. They were trying to negotiate his large girth onto a stretcher by the sounds of it. She wished the constable would hurry.

She was just ready to go out and look for him when the policeman gave a light rap on her window. She pulled up the sash and smiled at him.

"Take this carefully, but be quick." She handed him the pitcher and watched as he carried it gingerly back around

149

the house. Then she snatched up the jar and holding it low in her hands hurried for the door.

In the hall she was confronted with the sight of four men trying to wrestle Eustace's corpse down the staircase. The weight and height of the man was making it difficult, though they were all robust individuals themselves. Transporting the body was proving very tricky. The man clutching the bottom corner of the stretcher stepped too far to the right and Eustace thudded into a picture hanging on the wall. Glorianna was just behind the men and gave a little shriek.

"Be careful!"

Clara spotted her and made a dash for the door. She saw the hearse – unadorned for the time being, the horses without their usual gay apparel – and went around to the far side. Putting the vehicle between herself and the house. The driver was sitting on his seat at the front; an older man whose days of heavy lifting were behind him. He glanced at Clara curiously.

"Would you mind ever-so giving a policeman a lift in your hearse?" Clara asked, "It is very urgent."

The driver was about to open his mouth when the constable appeared from the side of the house.

"This constable, in fact." Clara gestured to him as he drew beside her.

The driver eyed the policeman suspiciously.

"Why?"

"Vital evidence needs to be carefully escorted to the station." The constable spoke before Clara could, making her smile, "This is police business, I hope you understand? Might I ride in the back of your hearse?"

The driver turned his head and gave a long look at the vehicle behind him, as if it might have an opinion of its own, then he turned back to the constable and gave a shrug.

Eustace had arrived at the front door, but there was apparently a problem negotiating him outside. Clara was relaxing a little as the drama of the moment seemed past.

She moved to the edge of the hearse and peered round, watching the proceedings at the door. It occurred to her, in that moment, that death was a very undignified state of affairs. There was lots of talk about respecting the dead, honouring them and doing what one could to ensure they were well looked after, but somehow it never really worked. At the end of the day a body had to be moved from a building, several stone of dead weight had to be dragged out and carried. That was awkward in itself, like man-handling a wardrobe down a flight of stairs; there was no way of doing it without it seeming something of a shambles. It seemed until you were in your coffin dignity had to lay sway to practicality.

The police constable came and stood behind her.

"Is he the one you think was murdered?" He asked.

"Yes."

"And the pitcher?"

"Full of poison, I fear."

Clara watched the men struggling with Eustace another moment and then had a thought. She glanced at the constable.

"Do you know much about Reverend Draper?"

"Not a lot. We don't go to church, not since my dad came back from the trenches." The constable answered simply.

"Have you heard anything about him?"

The constable narrowed his eyes and looked at her, curious.

"Well, he's a vicar. I hear he does, you know, reverend-things."

Clara let the matter drop. The constable was too young to yet understand the value of gossip in an investigation, nor to appreciate why a policeman never take anyone at face value.

Eustace was finally squeezed out the door and the wheezing men humped him to the hearse and slid him inside. Just as they were done Clara held up a hand for them to pause before closing the doors. The constable hesitated, then hoisted himself into the back of the hearse. The men from the undertakers were unfazed, it was a strange part of working with death day in and out that life stops surprising you. They took the introduction of a live person into their hearse as just another example of the oddities of mankind and went to find a place next to and behind the driver.

Clara handed her jar to the constable. His eyes had fallen on the corpse, considerately covered with a large bedsheet but still obviously there. Any pretence of the policeman's authority he had managed before the hearse driver was now gone, the constable was trembling slightly sat next to a dead body. Clara felt sorry for him.

"Now constable, I have entrusted you with a vital task." She said, distracting him temporarily, "A murder is one of the most serious crimes and can't be left unchallenged. You have the responsibility of bringing in the evidence that might just catch the killer. Inspector Jennings, I am sure, will be impressed and the accolade it will bring to you might even mean promotion."

A flicker of hope buoyed in the constable's eyes.

"Promotion?"

"Yes, but as we all know police-work is a business full of ups and downs. Sometimes the ups can only come after a down." Clara refrained from nodding at the corpse of Eustace, but she felt he was getting her message, "A policeman isn't made by the number of hours he marches on the beat, but by the risks and discomfits he endures to ensure a criminal is brought to justice."

The constable was listening keenly.

"Promotion." He whispered to himself again.

Clara patted his sleeve.

"I'll bring your bicycle back to the station myself." Then she stood back from the hearse and before he had too much time to think about his plight she closed the back doors with a clunk.

The driver gave her a look like the ones old and weary cattle give to a stranger in their field, deciding whether they are worth the energy to worry about. Then he clicked his reins and the horses started off, quickly rising to a fast trot, beautifully in time with one another. Clara was enjoying the sense of relief that the calamity was out of her hands (for the moment) when she turned and looked straight at Glorianna.

"Did that policeman go off in the hearse?" Glorianna snapped.

Clara wondered how astute the woman was, how much had she glimpsed?

"He came over a little queer." Clara lied quickly, "Sort of... faint."

"What was he carrying?" Glorianna pressed.

"Oh, only a bowl. The driver refused to take him unless he had one. He didn't like the idea of him being ill in the back of the hearse. I'm sure he'll be fine."

Glorianna gave Clara a hard look, it seemed she was boring into her skull and reading her thoughts. Then she turned abruptly and marched into the house. Clara let her breath out slowly. Had Glorianna rumbled her? She couldn't be sure, but she was going to be much more careful about what she ate and drank over the next few days.

Clara went and leaned against the front wall of the house, fanning herself lightly with one hand. It was a new experience having a murder occur under the very roof she, herself, was sleeping under. There was a lot to think about, perhaps too much. She glanced down at the bicycle, what a bother she had to deliver that back. She would have to cart it all the way into town, unless...

Clara stared at the bicycle a little longer. She had to go see the vicar, not a far walk if he was at the church, but then she needed to get into town as fast as possible. Perhaps as fast as if she was on a bike? Pushing herself away from the wall Clara went to find Tommy.

Within a few minutes they were both outside the gates of the Campbells' house looking at the policeman's bicycle. It was black and a little rusty in places, but Clara

153

had tried the brakes and they seemed sufficient. Tommy had a slight smirk on his face.

"A bicycle, Clara?"

"I took my cycling proficiency at school when I was thirteen." Clara answered curtly.

"You didn't pass though."

Clara glared at her brother.

"Do you intend to help me or don't you?"

"I'm not sure its right to unleash you into the world on a bicycle."

"If you won't help..."

"Oh don't be so sensitive." Tommy wheeled himself forward a bit, "Do you remember the basics?"

"Most of it." Clara gave the brakes another experimental squeeze, "It's the mounting I'm having trouble with."

"Well for a start its left foot on the left pedal, that's it. Now push off with the right foot and when you have a little momentum going swing over the right leg."

Clara gave herself a short thrust forward, testing the balance of the bike as her foot briefly left the ground. She wobbled dangerously.

"A little more speed!" Tommy called.

That was all Clara needed, she was already working out the best places to fall over should she need to. The hedge looked a good option, soft and springy, could prevent any nasty injuries. The bicycle wheeled on quite happily, going at a steady speed, but Clara was having trouble relinquishing the ground from beneath her right foot.

"Clara, get your leg over!" Tommy yelled loudly.

Clara was mortified by the shout, the phrase had so many coarse connotations and she couldn't help thinking that someone might have overheard. But oddly it also distracted her from being off-balance and, hardly giving it a thought, she lifted her right leg and mounted the bicycle. A wave of relief and delight came over her. The last time she had ridden she had been wearing a long schoolgirl's skirt and she remembered the tense moment of apprehension that she wouldn't be able to swing her leg in the confines of her clothes. But the years had moved on. Her skirt was shorter and her movement freer. Clara suddenly realised she was riding a bicycle.

"Bravo!" Tommy cheered, "Now turn around and come back to me."

Clara described a lazy circle in the wide road, feeling the smooth action of the pedals and almost laughing to herself. This was much easier than she remembered.

"All right, now all you have to do is stop. Apply the brakes gently."

Clara was listening to the instructions, but her mind had flicked back into a memory of the last time she had ridden. As her fingers found the brakes she remembered poor sergeant Blake conducting the cycling classes in her school playground. He had been signalling the children right and left and as Clara approached him on a borrowed bicycle (only one of the girls had a bike of her own) he had signalled right. She could see him now, looking sternly out from beneath his helmet, arm stretched out at 90 degrees, and there was Clara heading closer and closer, a sudden fear hitting her as she knew she would never turn in time. And then Blake was waving his arm and a frantic look was dancing in his eyes and she never understood why he didn't just move to the side, but perhaps it was already too late, for in that instant she collided with the unfortunate policeman. The front wheel had took out his knee, Clara flying over the handlebars had winded him, the final stab was when the bicycle did a graceful half-flip and clipped him across the chin. Sergeant Blake had lain groaning on the floor, rubbing at his bruised anatomy and trying to catch his breath.

It was that image that spun in Clara's mind as she reached for the brakes. She had never ridden a bicycle again for she had been so mortified by her first and only experience. Now she was on another policeman's bike and the front wheel was wobbling.

"Steady!" Tommy cried, but it was all too late.

Clara jammed on the brakes, the bicycle almost bucked beneath her and she was tipped over into the hedge. It turned out it was not as soft a landing as Clara had hoped for.

"Are you hurt?" Tommy was chuckling as he rolled over.

"Only my pride dented." Clara extracted herself from the hedge, "And the sleeve of my cardigan torn."

"You almost had it. But you pulled too hard on your brakes and you forgot to put out a leg to balance yourself."

"Put a leg out?" Clara had a vision of wobbling along a road with her leg out at one side like a wing.

"Like a stand for the bike, as you come to a halt you put out a leg on the side the bicycle leans to stop it tipping right over."

"Oh." Clara digested this, "Yes, that makes sense. Well let's try again."

Tommy wheeled away as she remounted, a little more confidently this time, and cycled off. She pushed thoughts of injured sergeant Blake from her mind and made the same turn as before, noting the slight mark in the ground from her last manoeuvre and headed back to Tommy. As she came level she gently eased the brakes on. The bicycle tipped to the right and almost unconsciously she put out a leg to stop herself falling. She found she was standing in a perfect halt.

"You've got it old girl." Tommy grinned at her.

Clara was so amazed she was almost speechless.

"So what are you planning on doing now?" Tommy asked.

Clara was glancing at the bicycle, almost disbelieving she was really sitting on it.

"Clara?"

"Oh, I'm going to see reverend Draper." Clara answered, "But I would rather not say more until a little later. I suggest a 'Council of War' in your room this evening, Annie included. I'll explain everything then."

"What about me? I haven't done anything except talk to Eustace. I'm decidedly bored."

Clara came back to herself, her mind working seriously.

"I need you to go around the house discreetly and find what supplies of arsenic they have."

Tommy didn't think he had heard her clearly at first.

"Arsenic?"

"I am certain Eustace was poisoned, I'm not sure the exact substance used but arsenic is a good bet. Big houses tend to have lots, but if they are as efficient as Annie they will keep a record of how much and what they use. People are much more worried about household poisons these days and servants like to keep themselves covered."

"So you want to know if any is missing?"

"Yes, and how much. If you can't find any gone astray I'll have to think again."

Tommy was letting this all sink in.

"Who would kill Eustace Clara?"

Clara looked up at the house, almost feeling a shiver running down her spine.

"Oh Tommy, aside from you and me, I think the better question is, who wouldn't?"

Chapter Nineteen

The church was about a mile up-hill, sitting at an angle to the vast grounds of the Campbell house. Clara pedalled up the road, the bike seeming to fight her all the way, wondering why she had ever thought borrowing the damn thing was a good idea. The church jutted up from around a corner, the biggest building for miles around with its stone tower and long nave. Clara came to an unsteady halt beside the churchyard gate and dismounted with a little embarrassment as her skirt caught around the bicycle seat. Fortunately there was no one around to see.

The church was equally empty. Clara glanced around and even poked in the vestry thinking someone might be about, but she was alone. She returned to the gate where a notice board was prominently displayed and glanced through the various details of services, choir practice, church hall luncheons and ways of leaving donations before finding an address for the vicar.

She retrieved the bicycle and decided to push it along for the next slog uphill. She wasn't entirely sure where the address was, but she suspected the rectory could not be far from the church. The road twisted around the church again, almost cutting it off on its own little island of grass, then it turned left and she was wandering among a set of three workers cottages. There were small children fudging around in the dust at the side of the road and at the far cottage a woman was sweeping at her doorstep. Clara approached her.

"Good morning, could you direct me to the vicar's house?"

The woman looked up, she had to be around 28 or 30, but she seemed very worn and tired. She wiped a strand of hair off her forehead with the back of her hand.

"Just up the lane, but he isn't in."

"Ah." Clara felt deflated, so much for her plan for the morning, "When will he be back?"

"Who knows? Probably not until the weekend, that's the usual."

Clara stared at the woman in puzzlement.

"Where has he gone?"

He woman gave a shrug.

"London."

"And he does that often?"

"Every week between Sundays."

Clara realised she had gone silent out of astonishment.

"Has he family there?"

"Who's to say?" The woman gave another shrug, "All I know is he goes off to London on a Monday morning regular as clockwork, then he turns up back here Friday teatime. Personally, it suits me just fine. Better than some of those interfering pastors, and the churchwarden keeps an eye on the church."

Clara didn't know what to say, she had never heard of anything so bizarre, a vicar who merely popped in and out of his parish on a weekend as though it was a holiday retreat! She was sure the Anglican authorities would not approve, but she supposed he was not really doing any wrong, except for neglecting his flock.

"What did you want him for?" The woman was giving Clara an appraising look, as if she was used to this sort of question and had a hunch why Clara was interested.

"I wanted to talk to him." Clara said honestly.

The woman stood her broom upright and leant on it like a tall walking stick.

"I've got the address of Mrs Patterson if you want it." She said.

"Mrs Patterson?"

"The lady who does for the vicar. Personally I wouldn't recommend it, but if you girls will get yourselves into bother." She tutted.

Clara grasped what the woman was about, so she was aware of the vicar's alternative services too?

"I take it this doesn't surprise you?"

"Women come up here all the time." The woman looked bored, "All sorts, usually with a spot of bother. Her next door even takes them in sometimes, when they get caught poorly like. I refuse, you never know what sort of business you will end up involved in. What if one of them dies? Girls can die from that sort of treatment you know."

"I do know." Clara admitted.

"Then follow my advice and don't be messing with nature. If God chose you to have a babe so be it, who are we to question him?"

"I thought you weren't much of a Christian?"

"Oh I believe in God all right." The woman pulled herself up stoutly, "I'm just not for all that religion lark. All them pompous souls telling me about my sins when I see half their daughters walking up here for a 'chat' with the vicar."

"Well, if it puts your mind at ease I am not one of them." Clara found herself smiling slightly, beginning to like the woman.

"Then what are you doing here?"

"Well, I suppose…" Actually Clara wasn't sure what she was intending to do, "I was half imagining giving that vicar a piece of my mind on account of a friend who had a 'chat' with him."

"She all right?" The woman actually seemed

concerned.

"Yes, thankfully. But I will take the address of Mrs Patterson, if you don't mind."

The woman disappeared inside briefly then re-emerged with a slip of paper.

"I don't like the woman, for what she does, but I suppose that might not make her a bad sort." She handed over the paper, "Was your friend a recent one?"

"Recent? Ah, I see what you mean. Yes she did come quite recently."

"Not that woman with the mink stole? I thought her a bit old for it really, but she didn't look half pale."

Clara almost jumped at the statement. She had to wrap her brain around it before she could reply.

"Was that on Saturday?"

The woman had to pause to think.

"I expect so, I was peeling potatoes by this window." She motioned to a small pane of glass that gave a hint of a kitchen beyond, "And I saw her walk passed."

"It was early evening?"

"Dinner time really, my husband gets in around seven so I cook for then."

"Did you see her come back?"

"No, once it gets dark I pull the curtains so no one can peep in. Was that your friend then?"

Clara hesitated about replying, she didn't want to reveal too much.

"Actually my cousin's wife."

"Then what was she doing up here then?"

Clara shook her head.

"I would very much like to know that. As far as I am aware she should have had no business here."

The woman studied her curiously for a moment, then she seemed to conclude it was not her problem and returned to sweeping. Clara trundled up the lane a little further and quickly spotted the red-brick rectory. She propped her bicycle against the garden wall and rapped the door-knocker. She really didn't expect an answer, it seemed unlikely Reverend Draper had a housekeeper when he spent so much time away. Probably he just had a lady pop in on the weekends to cook his meals and clean. She wandered along the front of the house and glanced in a window. There was a well-appointed parlour just beyond, but it was very tidy and bare. At the next window she saw an equally empty dining room, a drooping vase of flowers set upon the table.

Clara walked to the right side of the front door and peered in that window. She saw a study which at least looked a little busy. There were numerous books stacked on the shelves and the desk had papers carefully piled on it. Otherwise there was no sign of life. She took a pace back and glanced up, not sure what she thought she would see. The upper rooms had the curtains drawn.

Clara gave up, it was a house under lock and key, secure but empty. Until the vicar came back at the weekend she would have no luck here. She grabbed up the bicycle and headed away.

Going downhill was a lot pleasanter than going up, except for the odd stray dog or cat wandering into Clara's path, which caused frantic braking and swerving. Remarkably Clara avoided crashing all the way down into the town, there the ground evened out and she had to go back to pedalling. She quietly coasted to a stop outside the police station, feeling she had more than made up for her disastrous experience during cycling proficiency class.

Clara wheeled the bicycle through the front doors and greeted the sergeant behind the desk.

"I'm returning this to one of your constables."

"That would be Stan." The sergeant observed the bike morosely, "He felt right queer riding back in that hearse."

"But he made it safely?"

"He did."

"Good, could I talk to the inspector please?"

The sergeant gave her another strange look, the sort reserved for people of dubious character, and hopped off up the stairs to see the inspector. He was back in a moment to tell Clara she could see the inspector at once. Clara leaned the bicycle against the front desk, gave the sergeant a bright smile and hurried upstairs.

Jennings was haphazardly typing a draft report on the case when Clara entered his office.

"The lab won't have any results until the morning, the coroner will be even longer." He said rather shortly.

"Well that is disappointing, fortunately that is not why I came."

Jennings peered at her.

"Should I be excited or dismayed?"

"I don't know." Clara helped herself to a chair, "It is rather curious, it seems Shirley paid a call on Reverend Draper at his home on Saturday evening."

"He told you this?"

"No, he is out of the parish. But one of his neighbours saw her go up."

Jennings leaned back in his chair.

"I suppose no reason she shouldn't go to a vicar like anyone else for spiritual guidance and comfort."

"Perhaps, but I think you should know a bit more about the illustrious Draper."

Jennings eyes twinkled.

"Go on."

Clara removed the paper with Mrs Patterson's address from her purse and laid it on the table.

"If this station doesn't have something on this woman I would be surprised. She is running an abortion clinic, if you can call it that, and the good reverend is helping her."

Jennings whistled through his teeth, he stared at the slip of paper.

"Are you certain?"

"I have an impeccable witness. Even if I did not, his neighbour confirmed it. She, in fact, gave me the address."

"What is the reverend doing caught up in this business?"

"At my kindest I would suggest he is doing it out of a warped sense of Christian charity, at my worst I would suggest he was nothing more than a sleazy profiteer. He charges the girls for referring them to Mrs Patterson, of course."

"Right here, under our noses." The inspector shook his head, "Hold on a moment."

He went to his door and bellowed for the desk sergeant to come up. When the policeman appeared he looked deeply uncomfortable. Clara wondered if he thought he was in trouble.

"Sergeant, is there a file on a woman called Mrs Patterson?"

The sergeant gave a little jerk of surprise.

"Yes sir." He went to the filing cabinet in the room and started flicking through folders, "We've been keeping tabs on her for a while."

He found the file and handed it over.

"What for?" Jennings asked as he took the file.

"Well…" The sergeant's eyes fell on Clara.

"Please don't be shy on my account." Clara said sweetly, "You would be amazed at the awful things I have heard."

"Come on sergeant." Jennings pestered.

"I only know odd bits, but we believe she is running a house of dubious activities."

"Namely?"

The sergeant glanced at Clara again and shuffled uncomfortably.

"Abortions, sir. Nothing we can pin on her, no girls have come forward. We think they aren't locals anyhow, so they go home after it's all done and we never hear no more. Besides, they won't talk about it, sir."

"No, they won't." Jennings was thumbing through the file, "She has never been arrested?"

"We've never even got close to it. She is very secretive. We've raided her once or twice but haven't found anything. She has an accomplice, an unknown man."

Jennings gave Clara a significant look.

"You have nothing on him?"

"He drops the girls off, but we've never seen his face. They always do things at night. Besides, there just ain't enough of us to keep a watch all the time."

"All right sergeant, thank you for explaining that. You can go back to your desk now." Jennings shuffled the folder back together as the sergeant left, "Who told you Clara?"

"I would rather keep that private." Clara was already feeling a little over her head, breaking Susan's confidence was the last thing she needed. Murder, an illegal abortion clinic and the suspicious demise of Eustace – it was all getting out of hand.

"How does a vicar get embroiled in something like this?" Jennings was leaning back in his chair again, wondering if it was time for another cigarette, "It's not their usual territory."

"It strikes me Reverend Draper is not the usual sort of vicar. Did you know he spends most of the week in London, only returning here to hold services? That is extremely odd."

Jennings nodded.

"I wonder where he goes in London?"

"What troubles me most is why Shirley was heading towards the rectory. Why was she going to see him? We know she didn't need to arrange an abortion and I hope you are agreed that on further evidence it is unlikely she was heading for spiritual purposes."

"What does that leave?"

"I don't know." Clara sighed, "You will do something about the vicar and this Mrs Patterson, won't you? Who knows how many girls they have killed with their 'help'!"

"Leave it with me Miss Fitzgerald, I'll see if I can track down our elusive reverend in London. Then we can start thinking about what we are going to do with Mrs Patterson."

"That just leaves Eustace to consider."

"Old men die." Jennings heaved his shoulders in a

shrug, "Sad, but true."

"I think Eustace was murdered, but I see you will need more than my suspicions before agreeing with me."

"Miss Fitzgerald, you once more read me astutely. However, the very fact I am having those tests done at all should indicate to you, how seriously I take your suspicions."

It was the closest Jennings would go to giving Clara a compliment. She had to smile.

"I shall see you later inspector. Please thank the constable for the use of his bicycle."

"Yes, perhaps next time you will not send one of our policemen home in a hearse. He was shaking like a leaf when he arrived." Jennings was chuckling, "It was all we could do to get some brandy down him."

Clara rolled her eyes.

"Honestly!" She was close to laughing as she headed downstairs and went home.

Chapter Twenty

Annie presented the large Oxo tin to Clara as though it was the crown jewels. Clara opened it cautiously and looked at the bags of white powder inside.

"Any missing?"

"The cook says there should be 100oz in there."

"And?"

"We only weighed 65oz."

Clara looked at the deadly substance in her hands. It didn't take 35oz of arsenic to kill a person, not by a long shot.

"What if someone was taking it out a teaspoon at a time?"

"We thought of that." Annie smiled proudly, "We did a test, a teaspoon is about 4 or 5 grams, and we reckoned it could be done so easily. Someone says they are going into the larder for a spoonful of sugar for their cocoa and instead take some arsenic for Eustace's tonic water. That is how you think it was done, don't you Clara?"

"Yes." Clara put the lid carefully back on the tin, there was something awful seeing such a pile of poison heaped before her and knowing that almost every house in the country held a similar pile. Who needed 100oz of poison? Which druggist would dispense it so freely? There were supposed to be laws about such things, but of course a large house could give the excuse that they had a lot of mice and rats to contend with, not to mention those in the gardens.

"Could it have been taken by accident?"

"No, the cook was very good on that account. It was kept in a cupboard away from everything else."

"So no accident." Clara rested her head against the bed rest and wished she had never come to the Campbell house.

They were sitting in Tommy's bedroom, having a meeting over the events of the last few days. Clara had brought Annie up to speed on the case, then outlined her morning. Once the news of Reverend Draper and Susan's condition had sunk in, Tommy shared his and Annie's adventures of the day. Not that it had been terribly adventurous as such, the cook had been jolly co-operative, but the measuring of the arsenic had caused something of a stir.

"So who do you suspect?" Tommy asked boldly.

Clara had closed her eyes and was thinking that you never really knew people, not even your flesh and blood. She opened them cautiously.

"I suspect everyone, but top on my list is Glorianna."

"She did hate Eustace." Tommy nodded.

"And it wouldn't seem so odd, the lady of the house popping into the kitchen. A man's presence would have been remarked on." Annie suggested.

"True, but we can't rule out Peg and Susan."

"They don't seem to have much motive." Clara sighed, "Unless they learned about Eustace's will, of course. Somehow I doubt that."

"But how does this fit with the vicar and that Shirley woman?" Asked Annie.

"I'm not sure." Clara shut her eyes again, "I'm not sure any of it fits."

"Well, let's start at the top. Shirley Cox appears out of nowhere and ruins Andrew Campbell's wedding, then she turns up dead. She is seen visiting the Reverend Draper on the night of her death, who Susan visited about an abortion. That is the first connection." Tommy held up a finger to make his point, "We don't know why she visited Draper, but it seems rather odd under the circumstances. However, Andrew still seems the prime suspect for bumping Shirley off."

"It's not much of a connection. How does Eustace fit?"

"I've been rattling my brain on that one. Eustace was very open with me about his thoughts on the matter, what if he was open with someone else? Someone who deemed him dangerous?"

"I'm almost certain Glorianna had a hand in his death." Clara rubbed at her forehead, "She was so anxious about that damn jug."

"If he was poisoned." Annie pointed out, "It could all be coincidence, after all."

"Let's put Eustace on one side until we have some hard facts." Clara agreed, "Draper still worries me, how did he even come to know about this woman Mrs Patterson?"

"He is a funny one, I don't think I would like him at any wedding of mine." Annie gave a heartfelt shiver.

As they fell silent there was a tentative knock on the door.

"Come in." Tommy called.

"Is Clara there?" An uncertain voice called back without the door opening.

"That's Susan." Clara looked at the other two, wondering what was up now, "Come in Susan!"

Susan timidly opened the door. She looking woefully pale and was draped in a long, thick shawl that hung off her like a shroud. Clara jumped from the bed at the sight of her and tenderly put her arm around her shoulders, edging her into the room and shutting the door behind.

"What are you doing out of bed?"

"I want to talk to my father now, I can't bear waiting any longer." Susan looked miserably at Clara, "Will you come with me? They are all in the drawing room, Peg and

Andrew are there. I think it will be better with all of us, I'm hoping Peg will stand up for me."

"All right." Clara nodded, "If you are sure?"

"Not really. But I can't wait any longer, I lie in that bed worrying about it. At least if I get it over with I know where I stand."

"Do you have any idea how your father will react?"

Susan gave a little shrug.

"I think I'm more worried about Glorianna. She hasn't been herself today."

"Well, Glorianna doesn't count. She isn't your mother." Clara squeezed Susan reassuringly, "Come on, let's face the music."

Clara and Susan walked to the drawing room where the rest of the family had gathered. It was a morose little gathering and it wasn't about to be made any better by Susan's announcement. Glorianna looked sick to death and was walking around with a glass of sherry wedged in her hand. Hogarth was smoking, lost in his own grief. Peg was reading and looked the calmest of the lot, though she kept glancing at her father as if checking he was still there. That left Andrew by the fireplace, tapping his cigarette against the marble mantel and watching Glorianna pace impatiently. A quiver ran through Susan as she saw them all. Clara had her arm hooked through Susan's and stood stoically beside her, giving a smile to remind the girl she would stay there no matter what.

Susan was braver than a first glance suggested, she might hesitate but at this moment in time she was not about to back down. It would be worse to go back upstairs and fret then to face the wrath of her family. Still, she was extremely glad Clara was at her side.

Susan gave a polite cough.

"Could I speak to you all for a moment?"

"Susan, we are really all rather distracted." Glorianna didn't even stop her pacing for her stepdaughter.

"I think you will find it is important." Clara said, her tone causing all but Glorianna to glance at her.

"Has something else happened?" Hogarth spoke, his voice husky and tired. He seemed in a daze as he looked at his youngest daughter.

"I'm sorry father, but I've got some news that won't please you." Susan took a gulp of air.

Glorianna had stopped pacing at last and was staring at them.

"What have you done?" She snapped accusingly.

Susan ignored her, focusing all her attention on her father. She had to coil her nerve into a tight ball inside to say the words that were desperate to come out, it was a moment before her mouth seemed to function.

"I'm pregnant."

The room erupted. Glorianna shrieked and the sherry glass flew from her hand, clipping Andrew across the side of his head, so he swore at her and grasped his scalp where blood was dripping. Peg dropped her magazine, gasped in amazement, then applauded her sister with a laugh. Meanwhile Clara, seeing no one else cared to attend to Andrew, grabbed a handkerchief from her pocket and pressed it firmly against his head. Glorianna was caught between sobbing and screaming, glancing around the room as if someone could offer her a solution to her dilemma. She suddenly pointed at finger at Susan.

"You!"

But Hogarth interrupted what was to come by raising a hand and indicating his wife to be silent. He had not moved or spoken since the announcement. He simply looked at his daughter, curiously at first, then with a sad sensation of understanding.

"My poor Susan." He muttered softly, "What has happened to you?"

He stood and wrapped his arms around his daughter.

"I haven't been keeping an eye on you." He choked on a sob, "Who is the scoundrel?"

"I didn't really know him, he took advantage of me. I didn't realise…" Susan started to cry too, "He asked me to dance and I didn't know it would lead to…"

171

"All right, my darling, all right." Hogarth held her and stroked her hair, "It will be all right."

"Hogarth!" Glorianna snapped, she could not hold her tongue forever, "The girl is a disgrace! The Campbell name will be ruined."

"Oh shut up Glory!" Andrew growled, wincing as Clara held the cloth to his head, "The family name has already been ruined by me, Susan getting pregnant is rather old hat compared to me having two wives and one of them being murdered."

"Don't be so coarse!" Glorianna squealed, she was losing control of herself, "This is disgraceful, you are all disgraceful! I can't imagine worse step children. Peg dresses like a man, Andrew is a murderer and now Susan is pregnant by a man she doesn't even know! You are all so wicked!"

"Glorianna will you be quiet!" Hogarth's roar silenced everyone. His face was twisted in outrage, "You will not say such things about my children. They have made mistakes, but they are not wicked, and my son is not a murderer!"

Glorianna yelled like a banshee at her husband, grabbed up a cushion and flung it at him before racing from the room in floods of tears.

"If she thinks I am following her she is sorely mistaken." Hogarth still clung to his daughter, "Sit down Susan and let's talk about this. I'm sure we can make it right."

Hogarth sat with Susan on a sofa and Peg quickly joined them. She clutched her sister's hand and kissed her cheek tenderly.

"Silly girl, you could have told me! I'm a modern woman." She grinned.

Clara was still helping Andrew, now the situation seemed to have settled she decided to focus her attention on him.

"Right, let's get some ice on that bump and see if we can stop the bleeding." She commanded him, finding her

172

old nursing voice coming right back.

Andrew gave her a groan in response. She took his hand and, with the other still pressing the hanky to his head, led him down the hall to the kitchen.

The staff were still around and a maid gave a gasp at the sight of Andrew's head wound. It must have seemed to them that the whole family had gone mad – who would be bumped off next? The cook, fortunately, proved more pragmatic. She came over at once and asked Clara what she needed.

"Some cold, clean water and some cloth. Iodine, if you have it, and an ice pack and some bandages." Clara instructed as she set Andrew down on a chair.

"Should I be concerned you know about head wounds?" Andrew asked as the cook headed off.

"I was a nurse during the war." Clara supplied, "Let's remove that cloth and see what we have got."

The cut was more of a graze, not so deep, but head wounds were good for producing gallons of blood and sending the less hardy into a fainting fit. In fact head wounds were Clara's worst nemesis. In the hospital in Brighton she had become notorious for fainting at the sight of a bleeding scalp, so much so she had been scorned about it by the other nurses. Oddly Andrew's wound was not having the same effect; Clara wondered if she had become tougher over the years, or whether it was just because if she collapsed on the floor who was going to help him? Besides, she couldn't bear for Andrew Campbell to see her faint.

The cook arrived back with a bowl of water. Clara cleaned the wound, rinsing the worst of the blood out of Andrew's hair, before she took a closer look at the cut. She picked up the bottle of iodine.

"Is that necessary?" Andrew gave her a mournful look.

She examined the cut again, thought about it a moment and instead gave Andrew the ice pack to hold against his scalp.

"It isn't so bad and the coldness of the ice will help to

stop the bleeding." She sat down on the chair next to Andrew, "I'll keep an eye on you for a bit, if you don't mind, in case you go dizzy or faint. Head wounds, even minor ones, can be funny things."

"I know, I saw enough during the war." Andrew pressed the ice against his skull and realised he was feeling rather relieved that Clara had come to his aid, he hedged around for the right words, "It was... good of you to help."

"No one else was being very practical." Clara shrugged.

"My family aren't practical." Andrew answered, "I take it Susan had already confided in you?"

"Yes, I've been worried about her since that incident the other night. I've been keeping an eye on her."

"We should be grateful for that too. None of us have been paying much attention to poor Susan." Andrew felt a pang of queasiness, "That was a nasty blow Glory dealt me."

"I didn't expect her to have such a temper."

"You don't know her." Andrew managed a smile.

"Eustace told me exactly the same." Clara felt that familiar unease returning, "He made out that Glorianna was manipulative, controlling and an attention-seeker. I didn't care to believe him."

"Eustace was correct. Glory is all those things and more. Spiteful, cunning and with a nasty tongue when she cares to use it."

Clara gazed across the room, trying to focus her thoughts.

"I personally believe it was partly Glorianna's unkindness that drove Susan to jump in the river. She fears her."

"Not anymore, I'll watch out for Susan." Andrew said with a strange sternness, "I've been negligent of my family."

"Why is that Andrew, might I ask? Why do you distance yourself from those who care about you?" Clara waited to be told to mind her own business, she had certainly pushed her luck, but it seemed her help had had a thawing effect on Andrew.

"I don't know why it is. I just finding it easier not to talk to them much."

"I wonder what sort of people we all would have been without the war happening."

"It's not just the war."

"No?"

"You must know the story of how Glory inveigled herself on my father?" Andrew tried to shake his head and instantly regretted it as the room swam, "She was my father's secretary. I don't say they were having an affair, I think my father too decent for that. But she moved quick after my mother's death, when father was still vulnerable. Persuading him to a fast wedding, making herself indispensable, reminding him his daughters still needed a mother figure."

Andrew snorted.

"I've always hated Glory, but after that it just made everything worse."

"I don't think Eustace cared for her either." Clara said carefully, "He implied she might have aided your mother's death."

"That is always a possibility, but mother was very ill." Andrew sighed, "It just made things so much worse. I was fighting day and night in the trenches, watching my friends die and all I could think was that at home there was Glory walking through my mother's rooms, touching my mother's things. I even imagined she was turning my father against me. I was wrong about that."

"I don't think Hogarth is so gullible." Clara comforted him.

"What about you? Has Glory convinced you I am a killer?"

Clara gave a tight smile.

"I don't think you killed Shirley. I don't have proof of that, just call it instinct. But you did lie to the inspector."

"Did I?"

"You told him you hadn't seen Shirley after the wedding, but her landlady confirms a gentleman matching your description visited Shirley later that same afternoon and Shirley recorded your visit in her diary."

Andrew seemed amused rather than perturbed.

"My lies are always found out." He said.

"So now is time for the truth. Was that the last time you saw Shirley?"

"Yes, I'm sorry to say it was. Look Clara, we have gotten off very badly. I thought you an interfering gossip who liked to stick her nose into other peoples' business. I see now I was wrong."

"Oh no, you were quite right." Clara laughed, "Only, I do it for the best of reasons."

"In any case, I realise now you are not what I thought and that you do genuinely want to help, and maybe you can. Those policemen don't seem so very thorough and, despite what anyone might think, I do want Shirley's killer caught."

"Then perhaps you would be prepared to help me understand her a little better. Understanding a victim very often provides a key to the killer. Would you tell me about your last meeting with Shirley?"

Andrew grimaced. Clara was certain he was about to tell her to clear off, when he seemed to slump back in his chair and concede defeat.

"Our last meeting was unpleasant. I went to her to give her money and talk about a divorce. I have been a cad to her, I see that now. At the time I was so angry and ashamed…" The memories flooded back to Andrew bitterly, "I went in and she was so glad to see me, but I didn't want her to touch me so I became angry and showed her the money. I told her I wanted a divorce and I wanted her to leave now. She refused. I tried to shove the money into her hand but she wouldn't take it. She said all she wanted was me, not the money, it wasn't about the money. At the time I was so furious I couldn't see how important that was. For so long I had believed she had married me for one thing. But it wasn't true. I only understand that now, and now is too late. I shouted at her, she wouldn't budge. Finally I flew out of the house with my money. That was the last I saw of Shirley, crying and begging me to come back to her. I didn't want to go back. I had left all that behind me."

Clara understood. While she felt sympathy for the unfortunate Shirley, she could also feel sorry for Andrew. His marriage and his wife had become tangled in the emotions of war and left him feeling betrayed and confused. He couldn't go back to Shirley, because he couldn't face that portion of his past. Shirley would be forever mixed up with trenches, shell-fire and bloodshed. It was all very sad and not so unusual.

"After you left Shirley went out, around 4.30. I don't know what her purpose was, but she was seen walking up the lane to the rectory. After that I don't know what became of her. Do you know if she had a connection with reverend Draper?"

Andrew thought for a moment.

"No." He answered succinctly.

"It's all very confusing. Why was she headed up there?"

"Shirley wasn't religious." Andrew confirmed, "She didn't take any interest in God."

"I imagine she felt she had very little to be grateful to a Heavenly Father for. The police have her trunk, I saw the programmes from her performances on stage."

"She was a good little dancer. She was on stage from the age of two." Andrew almost smiled as he remembered the things Shirley had told him, "She performed with her mother and father at first. She always drew a good round of applause from the crowd."

"And then? Her career on stage seems to have ended?"

"Her father was an alcoholic and died when she was ten. Her mother was very ill so she continued to work to support her. The older she got the more competition for

177

roles there was, and she was not the cute little girl she had once been. Slowly the work dried up. She was lucky if she could get a part in a chorus line. The theatre is a cruel place to try and make a living. Poor Shirley was no actress, she couldn't get better parts. Gradually she had no money and the family had to eat." Andrew tailed off, the next part of Shirley's life was inevitable enough.

"I think it is safe to say Shirley's adult life was not an easy one." Clara offered tentatively.

"A thousand girls and more are in the same boat. Shirley did the best she could. She still got on stage when she had a chance. She had such a cockney accent though, she once tried for the part of Juliet with a Shakespeare company. The producer told her if he wanted Juliet to sound like a market trader he would call her."

Clara nodded, it was all making sense.

"I suppose that's what she returned to after I left." Andrew cringed over his own guilt.

"She searched for you. In her trunk was a scrapbook showing she had been tracking you for some time, but only really knew where to look after the wedding announcement."

"Another thing to thank Glory for. No, actually, I don't mean that. I needed to see Shirley, it was good she came here. I should have done more for her. But if she wouldn't take my money, what could I do?"

"I don't know." Clara answered, then she glanced at his head, "Let's have a look at that cut."

Andrew gingerly removed the ice pack, rubbing at his wrist where it had gone stiff from holding the soothing ice to his head. Clara leaned in and checked the cut.

"It looks much better, I think you will be fine."

"Thank you nurse Fitzgerald." Andrew stood woozily and shook her hand, "I'm rather glad we got to talk."

"I'm glad too. I will try my best for you Andrew."

Andrew smiled with difficulty, then, very carefully, he exited the kitchen. Clara watched him go, feeling triumphant in herself. She had not only overcome

Andrew's reticence but had banished the demons that had once haunted her at the hospital. She was rather pleased with herself as she turned to ask cook for a cup of tea. As she moved she spotted the rag still sitting in the bloody water of the basin. An image of Andrew's cut flashed into her mind vividly.

Clara's legs suddenly turned to jelly. She had enough sense of the situation to be cross with herself and blurt out,

"For Heaven's sake!"

Before the world vanished and Clara sank down in a dead faint.

Chapter Twenty-one

Tommy was grinning at her, it was most irritating.

"It wasn't at all amusing." Clara glowered at him, sitting up in her bed as Annie handed her a tray of scrambled eggs and bacon.

"I just love the fact you managed to avoid fainting until Andrew had left, do you think it was a delayed reaction or just force of will?"

Clara narrowed her eyes at him.

"I don't want to talk about this."

"It was only a little bit embarrassing Clara." Tommy continued to grin at his sister.

"The cook and all the maids were standing over me when I opened my eyes." Clara stabbed at her bacon, "I was mortified at myself. They didn't tell anyone, did they?"

"Only me, I was nearby." Annie gave Tommy a stern look, "It was just one of those things Clara, you have probably been over-working."

"So when can I get out of bed?" Clara hinted.

Annie pushed the blankets around her firmly.

"When I am satisfied you are fine." She said.

Clara sulked over her eggs.

"Look old thing, while you were collapsing in the

kitchen I had an idea. I thought to myself someone must know if Andrew, or anyone else, took a car out on the night of the murder of Shirley Cox. So I went out to the garages to ask." Tommy smiled smugly.

"And?" Clara nudged.

"And, the fellow who keeps the cars in top nick doesn't think any of them were moved from Saturday lunchtime to now. For a start he lives in a small flat over the garages and can hear any cars being moved, that is partly for security in case someone tries to steal one. Then there is the petrol. He fills the cars up on a Monday usually and he knows, roughly, how much each car consumes over the course of the week. They aren't driven far, he says, so a weekly top-up is all they need. So he checked them this Monday, as he expected out of the three cars in the garage the one used for the wedding needed filling up, the other two had full tanks since they hadn't been used that week."

"So the wedding car could have been used?"

"I suggested that, we thought over it a minute, trying to work out how we could say for sure if it had or had not been driven. Well then this fellow has an idea. Each car has a dial that tells him how many miles it has done, it isn't something you pay much attention to. But the wedding car had a once-over at the main Bentley garage just before Saturday, some concern over the spark plugs or something. Anyway, as a matter of routine they fill in the car's logbook and put down the miles it has done. Well we got out the logbook and it said that car had driven 113 miles, so we checked its dial. It still said 113 miles. It isn't a mile to the church and back, but it is to Brooklands. If that car had moved it would have more than 113 miles recorded."

Tommy sat back looking triumphant.

"None of these cars were used?" Clara mused on the information, "Two problems. One, Andrew could have used his Napier from Brooklands."

"Except no one saw the car move. Andrew can't be

always accounted for, but the car was there in plain sight, we could double-check by asking some of the other mechanics who were working that night. He couldn't have moved it without someone seeing and, besides, the car came towards Brooklands to dump the body. Why would Andrew drive away from the track and then drive back?"

"All right, problem two, we are assuming the body was dumped from the car."

"Yes, I agree that is a problem. If we take the car out of the equation everyone is back in the picture as a suspect."

Clara gave a slight sigh that turned into a groan.

"We are no further forward then."

"I wouldn't say that." Tommy disagreed, "We have a clearer picture of it all."

"Do we?"

Before Tommy could answer there was a knock on the door and Peg popped her head round.

"Clara, there is inspector Jennings in the hall wanting to see you."

"I'll get up!" Clara started to push away the bedclothes.

"You will stay put!" Annie said firmly, "The inspector can come to you."

"I am not seeing him in bed!" Clara was aghast.

"Then you shouldn't go around fainting. Send the inspector to us Miss Campbell." Annie instructed primly.

Peg was smiling as she vanished.

"I hate being in bed Annie, you know that!" Clara said grumpily.

"Sometimes we all have to do things we hate. Now behave and perhaps you'll be fit to get up by dinnertime."

"I am perfectly well!"

"It will do you no harm to sit there a bit. You gave your head a bump too, don't forget. For once do as you are told Clara."

Clara realised she was not going to win this fight. She gave a small groan and settled back against the pillow.

"At least pass me my wrap, so I look a little presentable."

Annie was passing over the embroidered wrap as there was a second knock on the door. Clara called out that the inspector could enter and Jennings bobbed into the room. He gave Clara a concerned look.

"Are you hurt, Miss Fitzgerald?"

"Not in any way that matters. I fainted last night." Clara explained quickly, "I have an aversion to head wounds and Andrew Campbell cut his scalp open. I'm afraid the sight of blood disagreed with me."

"I'm sorry to hear that." Jennings was looking at her curiously and Clara felt it necessary to elaborate.

"It is not blood as such that bothers me, but cuts to the head. I can't explain it really. I discovered the foible when I was serving as a nurse during the war."

"That must have been inconvenient." Jennings said.

"Well, it was, but I survived. Now, I take it something urgent has occurred to bring you here so early?"

Jennings gave a little nod, went to speak then paused as he remembered Tommy and Annie were in the room.

"They are 'in' on the matter." Clara assured him, "They are my partners in crime. I should introduce my brother Thomas Fitzgerald, and Annie my maid and friend. Both have been doing some sleuthing of their own with interesting results."

Jennings said hello and introduced himself to Tommy and Annie. Annie had found him a chair and he sat down facing Clara. He still was rather uncomfortable in his surroundings and glanced at the window before getting up and closing the bedroom door himself. Only then did he finally decide he could speak without being overheard.

"I've got the first results from the lab on the samples you sent in."

"That was fast." Clara was surprised.

"I pressed them for quick results, I thought it might be a good idea. They are running more tests as we speak for thoroughness but the early results are interesting on their own." Jennings pulled a slip of paper from his pocket and unfolded it, before clearing his throat to read, "The vomit sample you collected was laced with arsenic."

Clara felt her stomach drop, suddenly those eggs and bacon she had eaten with relish brought a pang of nausea.

"So he was poisoned." She said softly.

"The residue you spotted in the water was the same, white arsenic. Apparently it doesn't always completely dissolve and can leave a residue."

"Poor Eustace." Tommy muttered.

"I'm still waiting for the results of the post-mortem, I don't expect those until later. But I would be happy to wager what the coroner's conclusion on the cause of death will be. Now all I need is the 'who'." Jennings returned the slip of paper to his pocket, "Any thoughts Clara?"

"Glorianna." Clara was so dazed by it all the words came out automatically, "She was frantic when she discovered the water jug missing and she was odd all yesterday. Also Tommy and Annie discovered a large amount of arsenic missing from the kitchen store."

"How much?" Jennings asked.

"Around 35oz." Annie said.

The inspector whistled through his teeth.

"And that is only this visit, inspector. Eustace complained that he always had problems with his indigestion when he came here. He blamed the food naturally. I believe Glorianna has been poisoning him for a while." Clara shuddered at the thought, "I'm not sure she meant to kill him, it was more out of revenge or irritation. She made him feel ill each time he came, maybe hoping he would not return. Or perhaps she was just experimenting to get the right dose. Eustace was a big man and it make take more arsenic that you would expect to kill him. He only stayed a couple of days at a time, not long enough to get things right. But this time he stayed on longer."

"Strikes me that last dose was bigger by far than any other Glorianna had given." Tommy interjected, "She was poisoning him slowly, but suddenly she gives him a huge dose. I think she was worried and angry because Eustace was talking loudly and bluntly about Andrew being a murderer and had even gone as far as saying Glorianna poisoned the former Mrs Campbell. He told this all to me quite openly, so I doubt he had any problem telling others."

"There is one hitch, Eustace went to bed already feeling unwell, that was before he drunk the tonic water." Clara said.

"Then she poisoned his food as well, or the whisky he loved to drink." Tommy shrugged, "Glorianna had stolen enough to poison everything Eustace touched."

Jennings whistled again.

"And you say Eustace claimed Mrs Glorianna Campbell had poisoned the former Mrs Campbell?" He asked.

"He was of that opinion." Clara nodded, "But only because of the short timespan between Hogarth becoming a widower and Glorianna becoming the second Mrs Campbell. Andrew Campbell is less convinced; his mother was very sick anyway."

Jennings tapped his fingers on the blanket on Clara's bed.

"In my humble experience a person who has killed once is more than likely to kill again to solve a problem. Could it be that Glorianna decided to deal with the unfortunate Shirley Cox as well?" Jennings cocked his head to one side, "The coroner tells me it was something like a silk scarf that strangled her. Something soft. I'm thinking how hard would it be for a woman to pull a scarf tight enough to strangle someone? Not that hard, I imagine."

"There are still too many questions unanswered." Clara noted.

"Quite. Talking about questions, we haven't been able to track down Reverend Draper in London yet, but I'm planning on paying a call to Mrs Patterson. Would you care to come, Miss Fitzgerald?"

Clara cast a sidelong glance at Annie. The maid gave a very slight shrug.

"I'll be ready in a moment inspector if you can wait for me?"

"I can indeed."

"Then I shall meet you in the hall shortly. Tommy could you kindly show the inspector out and get him a drink while he waits?"

Tommy wheeled around the bed and Jennings joined him to leave Clara to dress. Just outside her room Jennings found himself stifling a laugh of amusement.

"How did she know?" He said to Tommy.

"Clara follows her instincts." Tommy smiled, "You get used to it after a while."

"But she has no sense of danger, does she?"

"Absolutely none." Tommy agreed.

"Keep an eye on her then, because I have a nasty feeling about this business. More and more this family is feeling like a nest of vipers."

"They're not so bad." Tommy chuckled nonchalantly, "You're forgetting, I'm one of them."

"Just be careful, that's all. I don't need another murder on my hands."

Tommy's smile evaporated with the seriousness of the inspector's tone.

Chapter Twenty-two

At first glance Mrs Patterson did not appear to be at home. At first glance...

Inspector Jennings knocked at the door repeatedly while Clara idled behind him. When no answer was forthcoming he peeped through the window.

"Maybe she is out." Clara suggested.

"There is a full cup of tea on the table." Jennings was grinning, "They always forget something."

Mrs Patterson's front door faced onto a wide alley between two houses. She occupied the back portion of a terrace house, the front, with large windows was currently occupied by an ex-sailor living on his pension. Jennings tapped at his door and it was opened almost at once.

"Aye?" Asked the sailor, peering at them with bad eyesight.

"Can I get into your backyard through your house?" Jennings asked politely.

"No you can't, anything to do with the backyard you go through that gate." The sailor eyed them cautiously, "Is it about the rats? The little buggers keep coming back you know."

"It isn't about the rats." Jennings smiled, "We wish to

talk to your neighbour Mrs Patterson."

"Her?" The sailor gave a knowing nod, "Good."

Then he slammed his door shut. Jennings winked at Clara.

"I think we'll speak with him later, but first the lady."

The gate was not bolted so Jennings held it open for Clara and then followed her into a narrow passage between the end terrace and the one next door. A low arch of bricks covered the first portion of the passage and connected the two houses. The passage was filled with rubbish, old boxes, newspapers, piles of decomposing rubbish, from food to garden clippings, all dumped in this little grotto of filth. Clara gritted her teeth as a fat rat scrabbled out of an empty tin just in front of her and raced towards the opposite wall.

"Yes, this is just the sort of person you wish to entrust with giving girls abortions." Jennings said sarcastically.

They picked their way down the passage, it opened into a barren yard, also semi-blocked with old rubbish. There was a sweet, rancid smell of decomposition all around. Clara found herself staring at the washing line straddling the yard and wondered how anyone could hang their clothes on it and expect them to smell clean afterwards. She had never seen such layers of dirt. Fresher, identifiable rubbish was sitting on oozing black piles of... who knew what? It was disgusting in a way that made Clara feel sick.

"I'll bet the back door's unlocked." Jennings was picking his way over a puddle of brown water. Clara followed, wincing as another rat, fat and wet, eased itself out of a stack of discarded beef and chicken bones.

Jennings had reached the door and was trying the handle gingerly. He gave Clara a sly smile, she was about to respond when something caught her eye. She pointed, there was no way to speak of what she had just seen. Jennings moved back from the door and looked in the direction she indicated.

Close to the house, in what might be deemed a 'clean'

corner in that pig-sty, a bloody bundle of cloth sat. For once Clara's nerve failed her. She glanced at the inspector, but even he was reluctant. Finally he stepped forward and warily nudged the rags with his food. Something pink and unformed plopped out of the cloth, along with a small rat that scurried away with unerring speed.

"Is it what I think it is?" Clara asked as calmly as she could.

"Yes. And fresh too, the rats have hardly touched it." Jennings looked back at the door, "No wonder Mrs Patterson isn't at home to strangers. She has been busy recently."

Jennings returned to the door and opened it as quietly as he could manage. Clara crept behind him as they entered Mrs Patterson's abode, surprisingly the interior was rather neat considering the grime in the yard. Though everything was rather old and tattered and there was a pervading smell of stale grease and cabbage. Jennings closed the door and wedged it shut with an old chair to prevent their suspect fleeing, then they took a pace into what proved to be a narrow passage between a tiny bedroom and a kitchen. As they reached the kitchen door there was the sound of someone moving.

Jennings jumped through the open doorway and Mrs Patterson dropped the dish she had been wiping dry onto the floor. It smashed loudly. They all stood and stared at each other in silence.

Mrs Patterson was neither plump nor thin, her clothes hung on her uneasily, as though trying to escape her presence. She wore her hair up underneath a dull, grey cap, though thick strands fell about her face. She was very ordinary in appearance, not the sort who stood out. Her surprise turned to anger as she glared at the intruders.

"Get out!" She shouted, pointing a finger violently at them.

"Not so fast Mrs Patterson, I'm inspector Jennings and I would like a little chat."

Some of Mrs Patterson's fury left her. She took a good

look at the inspector, trying to decide if she believed him. Then her eyes drifted helplessly about the small room, looking for something she had forgotten, something she had left in plain sight.

"You seem uneasy about visitors." Jennings remarked, nonchalantly pulling out a chair to sit down.

"A woman's entitled to her privacy." Mrs Patterson snapped.

"That she is, she is also entitled to a reasonable degree of medical care, especially during intrusive procedures. I think we both know why I am here, don't we?"

Mrs Patterson's eyes flitted back and forth. She licked her lips anxiously.

"I don't know what you can possibly want from a poor widower like me." She declared.

"Shall I fetch that unfortunate bundle from just outside your door?" Jennings answered blithely, "Might that help explain my presence?"

"What bundle?" Mrs Patterson was still trying to play the innocent, but her nervousness was growing by the moment.

"The bundle you left out for the rats to eat. With all the rich pickings in your yard it seems they have taken their time getting to it. When was the girl here? Last night?"

Mrs Patterson was desperate to deflect attention from herself. She turned on Clara.

"Who's she?"

"Clara Fitzgerald." Clara announced herself, taking a step forward, "I have a vested interest in seeing you put out of business."

Mrs Patterson glowered.

"Don't know you and I don't know what you are talking about. I can't help the rats, the dustmen won't come down the alley and collect the rubbish. What I am supposed to do with it? I'm just a poor widower with a bad back, who is virtually housebound." Mrs Patterson reeled out her sob story, "And don't the neighbours take advantage! I imagine it was one of them left the bundle you were talking about, they are always throwing their rubbish in my yard. They know I can't do nothing about it."

"Can we stop these games Mrs Patterson? You are an illegal abortionist."

"I never heard such unpleasant tosh!" Mrs Patterson flung her hands in the air furiously, "I'm a respectable widow, my poor husband was in the late Queen's light infantry. He fired a gun as part of the salute at her funeral. He would be horrified to hear me accused of such nasty business."

Jennings was losing his patience. Suddenly he stood and exited the kitchen, within moments he was back with the cast-out bundle in his hand. Clara turned her head away as he dumped it on the small kitchen table and exposed the contents.

"Can you deny this Mrs Patterson?" He demanded.

"Han't you ever seen a dead kitten before?" Mrs Patterson growled back, "My old tabby had it last night, poor creature weren't even formed, just this little pink blob. What was I supposed to do with it?"

"So you are claiming this is a dead kitten, not a dead baby?"

"Didn't I just say so? You policemen are ever so stupid." Mrs Patterson's anxiety was being superseded by delight at turning the tables, "Now you can get out of my house and stop upsetting a poor old widow who has done nothing wrong."

Jennings fumed for a moment, but he was snagged. It was his word against hers. She could claim the pink bundle a dead kitten, he could claim it a baby, but no layman would know which was right.

"I shall take this to the coroner and have it tested."

"You do that." Mrs Patterson said confidently, "And take this little miss with you, she is giving my place a bad stink with that look on her face. Sour-faced creature."

Clara refused to be drawn into the argument, she knew

when she was beaten. She touched the inspector's sleeve and he angrily snatched up the bundle. They could do nothing that day, but they would come back with their proof and then Mrs Patterson would be really worried. Clara consoled herself with that fact as she and Jennings exited the house.

It was a relief to leave the rubbish-filled yard and stand in the sunshine at the front of the house.

"I need to get this back to the station at once." Jennings scowled, "Will you be all right to make your way home?"

"Yes," Clara assured him, "I'm going to speak with that sailor fellow first though."

"Go ahead, perhaps he can give us some hint how to nab that old crow."

"Do you think a doctor will be able to tell if that mess was a human baby?"

Jennings shrugged.

"I have no idea, but right now I'm low on options. I'll let you know if I get any news." The inspector walked off.

Clara straightened her hat and rapped on the front door of the sailor's portion of the property. The old sailor answered and gruffly asked what she wanted.

"Would it be possible to have a word with you about your neighbour Mrs Patterson?" Clara asked.

The sailor's demeanour suddenly improved.

"Now that is something I would like to talk about." He showed Clara into his small house, which was well kept and aired regularly.

His furniture was minimal, a life at sea did not lend itself to collecting tables, chairs and sideboards. But in the small property the lack of large pieces meant the rooms felt open and bright. The old sailor offered Clara a small armchair and pulled another close so he could listen easily. Then he offered her tea or whisky. Clara declined both.

"I hope not to take up too much of your time."

"No matter, isn't often I have a pretty girl in my house

these days." The old sailor gave a lop-sided grin, "My name's Able Seaman Samuel Fairing, but you can call me Sam."

"Nice to meet you Sam, you can call me Clara." The formalities over Clara got down to business, "I presume you know a little about your neighbour's varied activities?"

Sam folded his hands in his lap.

"What business have you got with her?"

"In honesty, she has had dealings with a friend and I wish to prevent her from laying her hands on anyone else."

Sam gave a gentle nod.

"You understand, I just wanted to make sure we weren't talking at cross-purposes. I know Mrs Patterson performs abortions. These walls aren't exactly thick and I've heard the girls crying out. Not to mention some of the things I have seen in the back yard. Not that I am supposed to go down there, Mrs Patterson has made that very plain."

"How long have you lived here?"

Sam did a rough calculation in his head.

"Nine years, since I gave up the sea. My rheumaticks couldn't take it anymore."

"Was Mrs Patterson already here?"

"That she was, in fact I picked this place thinking it would be nice to have a quiet old lady living just behind me. Peaceful, I thought to myself. I'll get no bother from her. Pfft, what did I know!" Sam chuckled, "Since I've been here, aside from the comings and goings of the girls, I've had all sorts knocking on my door after my neighbour. Some of them were right thugs, scared the life out of me. I suppose they were fathers and brothers and lovers, all up in arms over the matter. Not to mention the police. I knew at once that was what that fellow you had with you was."

"That was inspector Jennings."

"Yes, well I just knew he was a policeman. They stand

out, you know."

"There must have been lots of girls over the years," Clara said, mostly to herself, thinking of so many desperate women beating a path to Mrs Patterson's home.

"I suppose once a month would be average. Occasionally there are more. I think a couple of them I've seen more than twice, but my eyes aren't so sharp, so I couldn't swear to it."

"Have you seen the person who brings them?"

"Aye, that would be Reverend Draper." Sam watched his guest's face, "You don't seem surprised."

"I'm not. Does he come always?"

"Mostly. Sometimes the girls come alone."

Clara leaned back in her chair trying to think what to ask next. Sam could be a witness, but much of what he had seen and heard was circumstantial. It was simply not enough. Sam was sensing this and was keen to be of more use.

"He came on his own the other night. I thought that was a strange thing."

"Reverend Draper?"

"That's right. He come calling on Mrs Patterson and they sat in her parlour talking. Her parlour wall is my bedroom wall." Sam indicated to another room, "I could hear almost every word. Quite a fuss that vicar was making, something about this woman turning up out of nowhere and causing a stir. He said she had ruined everything. Mrs Patterson was trying to calm him down, though she isn't really the sympathetic sort. She finally got rid of him, anyhow."

Clara was certain the reverend had been referring to Shirley Cox. He had been shaken by the wedding being interrupted. What a peculiar man to be upset in such a way, though she supposed it was not good for a church or a vicar's reputation to have gate-crashers barging into a wedding.

"I don't suppose you happened to recognise any of the girls who have come here?" Clara asked, slightly hopelessly.

Sam shook his head.

"Hardly see 'em, they only come after dark. Except for last night, of course." Sam smiled, pleased with himself, "You were after her just now for that one, weren't you?"

"We thought she had conducted a…" Clara hedged for words, "A procedure last night."

"That was Ethel Thwaite. I knew her voice, she has a bit of an impediment. She used to clean for me. She isn't married." Sam added the last as if it wasn't fairly obvious.

Clara's mind was working fast. If they could find Ethel… If she would talk to them…

"Where does she live?"

"24 Alms Street. With her widowed mother."

"Thank you." Clara was on her feet again, "Thank you so much Sam."

The sailor grinned as she hurried out.

"Glad to be of service!" He called.

Clara gave him a wave before she was across the street and hurrying in the direction of the police station.

Chapter Twenty-three

Inspector Jennings took the information calmly enough and agreed that it would be best if Clara called on the girl first. The police arriving on her doorstep would likely frighten her. She would more than likely be scared enough already as it was.

Twenty-five minutes after learning about Ethel from Sam, Clara was on the doorstep of her house and already feeling it was fortuitous she had come. For the door was open and there were sounds of distress inside. Clara didn't knock; she walked in and took a look at the scene in the front room with the practical eyes of a nurse. It had been a rough four years in that hospital, but it had taught Clara that getting upset over injury or illness was not helpful. You had to be pragmatic, keep a cool head and avoid getting emotional. Even so, Clara felt her heart sink as she saw poor Ethel helplessly lying on a sofa, blood on the floor and on rags her mother was trying desperately to press to her bleeding daughter. There was too much blood, far too much.

"How long has she been bleeding?" Clara asked sharply.

Mrs Thwaite looked up astonished that someone had entered her house unannounced. She had been the one making the weeping sounds. Her daughter was too weak to do so.

"Since this morning. It won't stop, I've never known a monthly to be this bad."

Clara did not correct Mrs Thwaite, there would be time for that later.

"I'll call an ambulance."

Clara hurried outside suddenly wondering how she was going to find help. There was unlikely to be a phone in the street from which she could call the hospital.

"Think Clara!" She glanced up and down the road, there had to be somewhere.

She picked a direction and began to walk, there was no knowing if it was the right way to go, but she moved purposefully deciding that force of will alone would have to make it the right way. Just at the end of the road she spotted a sign for a small grocery. She dashed forward and burst through the shop door.

"Do you have a phone?" She asked the man behind the counter.

He looked at her blankly, then shook his head.

With a groan Clara raced out of the shop and headed back the way she had come without even thinking to check the road. There was a loud squeal of brakes and Clara unconsciously braced herself, expecting to be struck. There was just a moment to consider how stupid she had been and then a tyre bumped her and she fell down.

"Clara!"

Clara was unhurt. The car had been almost stationary when it had nudged her over. She had run her stockings though and her hat was covered in muck. She glanced up at the driver of the vehicle and saw Timmy.

"Are you all right?" Timmy asked, reaching down to her.

"No time for that! We have to hurry!" Clara was on her feet and pushing Timmy back into the car, "There is a girl in trouble and we have to get her to the hospital!"

Timmy, baffled but used to taking orders, hopped into the driver's seat and set the car off down Alms Street at Clara's direction.

"I'm supposed to be picking up Mrs Campbell from the Town Hall." Timmy mumbled, not exactly trying to make difficulties but aware he was putting his position into peril.

"I'll explain to her." Clara reassured him, "Do you have blankets in this car?"

"Some they use for picnics in the boot."

"Right, while I go in spread them over the back seat. You are going to need them."

Timmy gave her a worried look.

"This is important Timmy, just hold your nerve and you will be fine."

24 Alms Street loomed on their right. Clara jumped out before the car was fully stopped and hurried inside.

"I have a car outside that can take Ethel to the hospital."

Mrs Thwaite was bamboozled by this stranger coming into her house, but she was too worried over her daughter to think about it deeply. She had to get her to a hospital and if this woman she didn't know was prepared to help, so be it, she would accept it if it would save Ethel.

Between them they helped Ethel to her feet. She was a dead weight in their arms, sagging forward. Clara had an awful feeling she was too late, Ethel didn't even seem to have the strength to drag her feet as they edged towards the door and there was more blood trickling down her legs. Mrs Thwaite was gulping down on her sobs, but her face spoke of her utter distress over what was happening. Clara was cursing inwardly, using all the words her parents had told her a lady never knew, let alone spoke, to silently describe her feelings for Mrs Patterson. More than ever she was determined to nab the woman.

What if this had been Susan? So easily it could have been, and what of the others over the years that had stepped into that viper's lair hoping for help? Had they lived or had they suffered the fate of Ethel?

Timmy was gobsmacked when he saw the pale, bleeding woman being brought from the house. Not least because he suddenly recognised her.

"Ethel?"

The girl's head seemed to jerk up, as though she had heard, but then the lifelessness returned.

"Help me get her into the car Timmy." Clara instructed, seeing the young man's confusion.

"She waitresses at Lyons tearooms." Timmy took Ethel around the waist and picked her up as though she was nothing but a rag doll, "What's happened to her."

"She needs a hospital." Clara said firmly, not about to discuss Ethel's condition on the street.

She bundled Mrs Thwaite into the back seat with her daughter then joined Timmy in the front with orders to drive as fast as he dared. She knew she would regret it, but right now her discomfit had to be upstaged by Ethel's dire needs. Timmy pressed down on the accelerator. Clara clenched her eyes tight shut. And they were on their way.

Later on Clara could hardly describe what had happened in that first hour at the hospital. All she remembered was the controlled panic in people's voices, the rush of nurses, the summons of a doctor and then Ethel being swept away into a room that smelt of disinfectant and bleach. Mrs Thwaite's heavy sobs rang in her ears a long time after the woman had actually stopped crying. Clara comforted her as best she could, what could be said other than it would be all right and that her daughter was in the best possible care?

She sent Timmy away. Told him to dump the blankets now covered in blood and to carry on with his original task, but once he was done, she said, she would be most grateful if he could go to the police station and explain to Inspector Jennings where she was.

So Clara sat alone with Mrs Thwaite, and lost the next few hours, burying them behind a fug of forgetfulness as there was no other way to deal with them. Someone made them a cup of tea, she couldn't remember who, and Mrs Thwaite finally cried herself out and sat trembling beside Clara asking herself over and over what had gone wrong, why was this happening to her? Sometime in the afternoon, when Clara was feeling light-headed from missing lunch and Mrs Thwaite had fallen into an uneasy doze, Inspector Jennings appeared.

Clara left Mrs Thwaite silently and walked away to one side with him.

"What exactly is happening?" Jennings asked in a low voice.

"I think Ethel Thwaite is bleeding to death. In fact, she may have already done so. We haven't seen a doctor in ages."

Jennings face fell.

"Damn!" He hissed.

"I don't know what to say to Mrs Thwaite." Clara felt a wave of emotion suddenly overwhelm her, she had been keeping it tight inside from the moment the chaos had begun, but now it started to escape her. She realised she was very close to crying, "I keep thinking this could have been Susan."

"Don't Clara, you can drive yourself mad that way."

"How many other girls have suffered like this, inspector? Mrs Patterson is a fiend."

Jennings nodded solemnly.

"I know, and I will stop her."

"When?"

Jennings had no answer. Clara wanted to scream at him, not because she was angry with him, rather she was angry at the world in general. Angry that it could be so hard to nail a woman like Mrs Patterson. Angry that nobody seemed able to do anything. It made her throat tight, until she could taste bile. She was so furious it seemed impossible that it didn't show outwardly, it felt like a fire raging within, so much so she expected to exert warmth, to burn with it. Instead she appeared calm and cool.

"Is that the doctor?" Jennings looked up.

A man in a white coat was heading for Mrs Thwaite. Clara and Jennings hurried over. The doctor gave them a curious look.

"Are you to do with Ethel Thwaite?" He asked.

"Yes," Clara said without hesitation, "Is she…"

"We've managed to stop the bleeding and we think she will pull through." The doctor said.

Clara was so relieved she felt as though her whole body sagged with the lifting of tension by about two inches. Mrs Thwaite was rousing from her sleep.

"Ethel?"

"Would you like to come this way and see your daughter?" The doctor asked kindly.

Mrs Thwaite just about managed a small nod and forced herself to her feet. Following the doctor urgently she disappeared into a side room, leaving Jennings and Clara behind. Surely Ethel would talk to them now, Clara kept thinking, surely she would agree to be a witness? Clara didn't dare contemplate the alternative.

After Mrs Thwaite had gone in to see her daughter, the doctor came back out and gave them that same curious look.

"Inspector Jennings," The inspector held out his hand to shake, "This is an associate from Brighton, Clara Fitzgerald."

The doctor remained mute.

"We are investigating a woman who deals in illegal abortions. We believe Ethel Thwaite was her latest victim."

"I would agree with that." The doctor said.

"Is there anything else you can tell us?" Jennings pushed.

"She was lucky, very lucky." The doctor replied with a shrug and then he turned and left them standing in the corridor.

It was half an hour later that Mrs Thwaite poked her head out the door and asked if Clara would enter the room. Clara agreed and came face-to-face with a much healthier looking Ethel. She was still peaky, and her skin pale, but her eyes were bright and alert. Far from the dragging, half-dead creature they had brought to the hospital.

"I think I have you to thank for saving my life." Ethel beamed at Clara, "How did you come to be there at the right moment?"

Clara took a deep breath and then revealed herself.

"I had just come from Mrs Patterson's house."

Ethel's smile didn't fade, but it did stiffen.

"Mother, why don't you go see about getting a bite to eat while I chat with this lady?" She said.

Mrs Thwaite wavered, not wanting to leave her daughter.

"I'll be all right." Ethel assured her, finally waving her off with a promise from Clara that she would not leave until Mrs Thwaite returned.

Ethel's mother left the room feeling more confused than ever.

"You understand, mother doesn't know?" Ethel said, her bright eyes digging into Clara.

"Yes."

"So who are you?"

"Clara Fitzgerald. I happened to stumble onto your situation because my cousin came very close to the same procedure. I have every intention of stopping Mrs Patterson from carrying out her filthy trade."

"Who are you to say what a person should or shouldn't do?" Ethel snapped, taking Clara by surprise.

"I presume you are aware she came very near to costing you your life?"

Ethel gave a shrug of her shoulders.

"These things happen. I took a chance, wouldn't be the first I've taken."

Clara felt it best to change tack.

"I am not fool enough to think that I can stop girls seeking out someone to rid them of their troubles." Clara said calmly, "But I can't allow a woman who has come close to, in fact probably has, killed some of those girls who have sought her help to carry on practicing her trade. I am not one of those who believe having a baby out of wedlock is a fate worse than death."

"You are a rarity then."

"Would your mother prefer you dead, than having a baby?" Clara asked pointedly.

Ethel had the dignity to look away.

"I am not about to judge women who get themselves into trouble. But I will judge a woman who 'helps' them with a knitting needle for a handful of money. Mrs Patterson is no saint coming to the aid of girls' in distress, if she was she would take a bit more care. But she doesn't give a damn if any girl she tends lives or dies. Doesn't that make you angry?"

Ethel tightened a wad of the hospital blanket that covered her into a ball in her fist, but she said nothing.

"It angers me." Clara continued, "There will always be women who think they need the help of people like Mrs Patterson. Women who are desperate. Perhaps there are even some of her sort out there who genuinely want to help the girls who come to them. Mrs Patterson is not like that, she is a common criminal. Who, after she was done with you, threw your baby out with the rubbish for the rats to eat."

It was harsh, Clara didn't like to say it. But Ethel should have no illusions about the woman she was protecting with her silence.

"Threw it out?" Ethel seemed pained by the thought.

"Did she show you any kindness at all to justify defending her?"

Ethel fudged with the blankets.

"She said the last girl she had in ran away, and she hoped I wouldn't be so silly." Ethel grimaced, "I wasn't sure I could stick it, but I had to save up a month's wages for the cost."

"How long were you in with her?"

"Ten minutes, can't have been many more. She said it was better done quick. I lay on her parlour table, like a corpse laid out. I've never been so humiliated…" The tears came, at last breaking through the cold exterior Ethel had been maintaining desperately.

She sobbed hard and Clara took her hand.

"I'm sorry."

"I would have had the baby too, if it weren't for Billy, the father, getting cold feet and up and leaving me. I thought we was to be married, I really did. I never would have got cosy with him otherwise."

"These things happen." Clara said softly.

"I just feel so empty now. I didn't think of that, I was so scared about losing my job. Mother can't work because her nerves are bad, so I support us both. And if I lost that job what then? But when it was all done and the baby gone, I felt as though I had nothing left. What was there for me except serving on people?" Ethel choked on her sorrows, "The doctor says I might not ever be able to have children, after all this. What have I done?"

"This is why Mrs Patterson has to be stopped, because she takes advantage of girls in a bad state. She doesn't care how you feel after, or whether you are scared or hurt. All that matters to her is that she is paid."

"But what can I do about it?" Ethel cried.

"There is a police inspector outside, you can talk to him and explain."

Ethel's eyes went wide in panic.

"No! Send him away!"

Clara took a deep breath before responding.

"He isn't going to arrest you. He only wants to talk. He might want you to make a statement against Mrs Patterson."

"I can't do that! Everyone will know what I done!"

"The inspector has ways around that, I am sure. But you are the only hope we have Ethel. We might wait weeks or months before we find another girl willing to speak and how many will have been to Mrs Patterson by

204

then? What if one of them dies? All I am asking is that you speak with him."

Ethel shook her head.

"What would mother say?"

"Stop thinking about what other people will do or say and think about your own conscience. Ask yourself, what is the right thing to do? There is really only one answer to that."

"I don't want to get into trouble."

"You are not in trouble Ethel."

Ethel closed her eyes and pulled a face.

"No one can know. The shame of it would be too much, my mother could never hold her head up again."

"You must discuss that with the inspector, Ethel." Clara was trying her hardest to think of other ways to persuade the girl, "In any case, I'm afraid it is already known what you have done, because someone saw you."

Ethel blanched.

"Who?"

"A neighbour. The problem is, if we don't have a statement from you, he is our only witness and he will have to explain how he came to know what Mrs Patterson was about. On the other hand, if you were to give a statement we might persuade Mrs Patterson to make a confession and you will never have to speak."

Ethel considered this for a long time.

"That neighbour, knew who I was?"

"Yes. He recognised your voice."

Ethel cursed herself.

"I don't say my Rs and Ts right." She shook her head, "So what am I to do? I don't want all this commotion and fuss, but I reckon you aren't going to let this be."

"No." Clara said softly, "Too much is at stake."

Ethel gave a soft moan and closed her eyes.

"Send in the inspector then."

Clara left the room and told Jennings he could go in and talk with Ethel. She remained outside, waiting for the return of Mrs Thwaite so she did not interrupt the discussion. Of course, how she was to explain Ethel talking to a police inspector was another matter entirely.

It wasn't long before the clumsy shape of Mrs Thwaite appeared, balancing a cup of tea in one hand and a sandwich in the other. She stopped before Clara and it seemed as though it was the first time she had really seen her.

"Ethel is just having a chat with Inspector Jennings, because he thought she might have witnessed something to do with that murder the other day." It was a reasonable lie, full of snippets of truth.

Mrs Thwaite ran this through her memory.

"Oh, that girl at the race track?"

"Yes, you see a Lyons girl sees a lot of people during the course of the day. She might have seen her with someone."

"Couldn't that wait until Ethel is better?" Mrs Thwaite glanced suspiciously at the door.

"I'm afraid the inspector is in a dreadful hurry, for he can only be in town a short time." Clara elaborated with only a slight glimmer of remorse.

"Still…"

"Now you must sit down Mrs Thwaite, it has been such a day for you. Sit here and eat that sandwich." Clara smiled brightly as she ushered the woman into a seat, "Ethel is very hearty now, I think she will be perfectly fine."

"Yes, she does seem over the worst." Mrs Thwaite took a bite from her sandwich, "She hasn't been quite right since that Billy left. That shook her right up, they had been walking out over a year. I didn't like him though, not really. Bit on the worldly side, if you ask me."

"I'm afraid it seems to me most trouble that befalls a woman starts with a man." Clara said glumly, thinking of the present drama she was caught in.

"Isn't that true? Why, I got married and thought all would be well and then he ups and dies before Ethel is twelve and I'm left trying to look after the house and a girl. And me with my bad nerves. It was almost more than I could take."

"At least you have Ethel."

"Oh yes, and I can't tell you how grateful I am you came past and helped us when you did. I don't know where I would be without my girl. You have my endless thanks for coming to our aid."

"Sometimes we just happen to be in the right place at the right time." Clara smiled.

The inspector emerged from the room and gave a polite smile to Mrs Thwaite.

"Sorry to take up your time."

Mrs Thwaite gave him a long look, clearly disapproving and then bustled off to see her daughter. Clara and Jennings walked down the corridor a little way before they spoke.

"She told me everything. We have Mrs Patterson."

"Good." Clara felt a strange relief come over her, "What about the…erm… baby?"

"Took it to the doctor, he's not sure he can tell if it was human or not. Too small, you see. Apparently up until a certain point a foetus from different animals can be rather similar. But he will see what he can do. I have got something else for you, though." Jennings pulled a folded slip of paper from his pocket and gave it to Clara, "Uncle Eustace's post-mortem report."

Clara unfolded the paper and read the typed report very carefully.

"What do you want to do about it?" Jennings asked, "I don't think I can make a murder charge and even with manslaughter it's going to be iffy. Besides, who do I accuse?"

"No, your job is done." Clara agreed, "Now it's my turn. A guilty conscience can be punishment enough, in some cases. Anyway, I have no intention of letting the culprit remain anonymous."

"Be careful." Jennings insisted, "Need I add that I would prefer you to keep our other case separate from this?"

"Of course, I won't jeopardise that."

"Well, I have a woman to arrest, and I doubt it will be pleasant."

"You could take that young constable with you, for the experience." Clara added mischievously.

"He's only just recovered from his encounter with you." Jennings looked grave but he was close to laughing, "I imagine the Brighton constabulary are terrified of you."

Clara gave a little shrug.

"It is not as though I am the one committing murders."

Chapter Twenty-four

"What are we all doing here?" Peg surveyed the room, "This gathering of all of us is rather sinister Clara, what are you about?"

Clara had gathered the Campbell family, along with Tommy and Annie, into the drawing room without giving an explanation for her actions. There had been grumbling from various parties about being interrupted in the middle of the afternoon, except for Andrew who had turned a corner with his appreciation of Clara. He had been the only one really willing to participate.

"I thought it was rather important I got you together since I have just learned some news about Eustace's death." Clara said.

Gloriana seemed to spasm a little in her chair.

"News?" She asked nervously, "From the coroner?"

"Yes, the inspector asked me to relay the information." Clara paused to examine the room, all were waiting for her pronouncement with varying degrees of interest. Glorianna was clearly the most anxious, "The doctor found that Eustace died from a heart attack."

Glorianna gave a fluttering gasp.

"Oh… oh, well… oh…" She glanced at the family, "He was a big man, his heart was surely under strain."

"The arsenic someone was feeding him hardly helped." Clara added coolly.

The room fell silent. Hogarth suddenly spluttered and began to cough, but it was Glorianna with her mad trembling that was drawing everyone's attention.

"Arsenic." Hissed Peg, "How?"

"His tonic water was laced with it. They found some in his vomit and more in his stomach. The only saving grace for the poisoner is that the heart attack killed him before the arsenic could. Though a case could be made that perhaps the poison induced the heart attack."

"You took the jug!" Glorianna scowled at Clara, "It was you!"

"Yes, I was concerned Eustace's death wasn't accidental."

"A spy in my own household!" Glorianna reared up from her chair and pointed at Clara, "Watching us all, spying on us! Telling tales to the police!"

"Shut up Glory." Andrew put a hand on her shoulder and firmly placed her back in the chair, "Clara has been watching out for us. If there is a poisoner I would rather he or she were caught before another of us comes in for their attention."

"Do you know who?" Susan asked quietly.

"I only suspect." Clara began, "And, I have to state, because of the nature of Eustace's death the police cannot make a case for murder on the matter. Not without being able to prove that the heart attack was directly caused by the arsenic poisoning, which they can't. But I am sorry to say one of the Campbell family is a cold-blooded poisoner and we should all be aware of that."

"But who" Susan repeated, looking anxiously from one family member to another.

"My initial thought was that Glorianna was the culprit."

Glorianna gave a stilted laugh.

"Me? Why me?"

"Little things. You were so worried about the jug

going missing and you had a natural antipathy towards Eustace. He drove you insane." Clara said, "You really detested him. Besides he had already placed the thought into my head that you had murdered the first Mrs Campbell."

Glorianna hissed through her teeth.

"I did not!"

"No, I am certain you didn't. For a few reasons, not least that Mrs Campbell took years to die, years when you were waiting impatiently. I think if you were a poisoner things would have moved along quicker. For that matter I had to ask myself what opportunities would you have had for poisoning her? You were Hogarth's secretary, not her nurse. She ate the same food as everyone else, you would have had great difficulty planting the poison regularly in her drink, just from the point of view of access. In fact, the more I thought on it, the more unlikely it seemed. Then there was one last piece of the puzzle. I was at the hospital earlier today and that gave me an idea. I decided to make a discreet inquiry. No one had bothered to tell me that the first Mrs Campbell spent the last month of her life in the hospital, in a place you could not reach her with poison."

Glorianna tried to speak, but the words failed her.

"Eustace liked to goad you Glorianna, telling tales about you was part of that. Once I dismissed the notion that you had already poisoned one person, other questions came into my mind. The most obvious one, and the one which it is shocking I didn't pick up before, was when was Eustace poisoned. It was natural to assume the tonic water was the only source of poison, but then I recalled Hogarth saying Eustace went to bed with a bilious attack on the night of his death. That was before he had touched the tonic water. The jug was a red herring, or perhaps insurance. Eustace had consumed arsenic earlier in the evening. So, I asked myself, why was Glorianna so worried about that water pitcher?"

Clara looked straight at Glorianna. The woman

twitched in her chair, fumbling with her dress.

"The jug? It… I…"

"You knew the water was poisoned." Clara continued, "My only mistake was thinking that meant you were the poisoner, when in fact you were covering for someone else."

Glorianna appeared to being having trouble breathing.

"You are very conscious of reputation, the way only a person from poor stock who has risen up beyond her expectations can be." Clara was speaking quite calmly and the room was focused on her, "Reputation means everything to you. When Shirley Cox turned up in the church your concern was for the reputation of the Campbell name. The same when Susan revealed her secret. All the time you are constantly guarding this family from any hint of shame."

"And what is wrong with that?" Glorianna snapped, "No one else seems to bother! But your reputation is the one thing in this life you keep forever, good or bad. I do worry about it, I admit that. I would hate to be known as 'that woman from the dreadful Campbell family'. I've worked hard all my life to be in this position. I won't see it spoiled now!"

"This is nonsense Glorianna." Hogarth spoke, offended by his wife's ramblings, "No one is threatening the family's reputation."

"No? Can't you see it? Can't you see how you all harm yourselves? You care so little for your actions, but everyone is watching. I hate that everyone is watching us, waiting for us to fall. Laughing because you were raised up above your position in life and so was I, and all they want is to see us come tumbling down." Glorianna started to sob, they were deep, heartfelt sobs, dredged from a place they had been hidden in too long, "Don't you see?"

No one answered her except Clara.

"Who were you covering for, Glorianna? Who did you fear would disgrace the family this time?"

Glorianna dabbed at her eyes, the sobs almost

uncontrollable as she hiccupped out her words.

"Since none of you seem to care, I don't suppose it matters if I tell the truth? Well Clara, I was covering for someone else, because I saw them in the act of poisoning the water."

"Who Glorianna?"

"But Eustace didn't die from poisoning." Susan said sharply, "What's the point of this?"

"The point is that someone had the intention of murdering him. That they failed doesn't make them any less guilty of the attempt. I would prefer to know who is so free with arsenic about this house." Clara said angrily, "Personally."

Glorianna was calming herself and looking sternly at her family.

"I might not have liked Eustace much, but at least I tried to get along with him."

"So who are you accusing?" Andrew interrupted, "I hope it's not me again, I have one murder on my plate already."

"I'm sorry Hogarth." Glorianna spoke very quietly, but perfectly clearly, "It was Peg who poisoned your brother."

If there was such a thing as a collective gasp of air, the crowd in the room took it. Peg was sitting opposite Clara and had not said anything for some time. She was smoking, one leg crossed over the other, wearing men's slacks and shirt.

"I saw her add the arsenic to his water jug." Glorianna persisted as no one had responded to her announcement, "It was by chance, I had gone to the kitchen to see if cook would make up a mustard plaster for the blisters on my feet. Those damn wedding shoes were too tight. It was after dinner, about nine o'clock. The maid had just set down the pitcher with Eustace's tonic water on the table. I knew what it was because the bottle of water was nearby. She had gone to fetch a lemon to cut up and put a slice in the water; that was always how she did it. I was just in the doorway. The lights were off so it was dark. I saw Peg come out of the pantry with the Oxo tin. She took a spoonful of white powder from it and dropped it in the water. Then she stirred it hastily and retreated back to the pantry as the maid returned. I didn't know at the time what that powder was, honestly Clara else I would have stopped the maid taking the water to Eustace.

"I was going to say something. I thought maybe Peg had added salt to the water, I never thought... but then cook appeared from her room behind me and I mentioned the plaster and she said she had some made up in her room, better than the ones from the pharmacist. So I went into her room and I was completely distracted. I have had such things on my mind since the weekend. The jug was forgotten, until the next day...

"When I saw Eustace I knew something awful had happened. The look on his face was just... I went to the kitchen when I called for the doctor and I asked cook what did she keep in the Oxo tin, was it salt? She was horrified, 'oh no Mrs Campbell, don't go thinking that is salt that is arsenic for the mice and rats'. So then I knew and I went to fetch that jug with every intention of pouring away the contents. But it was already gone."

"It wouldn't have really matter if you had Glorianna, Eustace was full of arsenic." Clara said, "It would have made knowing the exact cause more complicated, but otherwise things would not have changed. Besides, Eustace was poisoned before he drank the tonic water, that was just for insurance, wasn't it Peg?"

Peg tapped out her cigarette without haste. She smirked at Clara.

"Why would I kill Eustace?"

"I could suggest a few reasons, but I think what really did it, what sealed his fate, were the snide comments he made about you. I can only postulate, but noting Eustace's character I wonder if he could resist a few unpleasant, or rather, in his mind, too honest, remarks about the man you loved and lost." Clara replied.

Peg gave a sort of snort, as if she found this all

amusing, yet at the same time rather dull.

"Could it be that simple?" She said.

"Yes." Clara answered, "Murders are committed usually for very simple, uncomplicated reasons. Hate being one of the strongest."

"Peg, is there any truth in this?" Hogarth was torn between his wife and his daughter. Glorianna appeared truthful, but she could be lying, she could be trying to cover herself.

Peg gave a long sigh.

"What does it matter now anyway?" She drawled, "Everyone in this room wanted to kill him at some point, well maybe not quite everyone. Clara hardly knew him, but he had this way about him. Somehow he always knew your weakest spot."

"So you did attempt to kill him?" Hogarth asked wearily, tired of the lies and secrets within his family, "Did you poison his food?"

"It was his evening drink." Clara enlightened them, "That was the reason I began to suspect someone other than Glorianna. The meal was too difficult without poisoning everyone. He was ill before the tonic water, so that left his after dinner drinks. And who nearly always made them?"

Peg ran her finger around the edge of the ashtray and smiled.

"I thought I was being rather clever. I've been working on it for years, you know, no one has suspected me until now."

"A man the size of Eustace with an appetite for rich food and drink? It was natural to assume he was a regular victim of dyspepsia. No one was really listening when he said he was always worse when he stayed here."

"Except you." Peg gave a respectful nod to her cousin, "What it must be like to be suspicious all the time."

"In general it appears to be quite a healthy state of mind." Clara said pointedly, "After all, who else were you planning on poisoning?"

Glorianna paled, but Peg was not looking at her. Her stepmother was a nuisance but not anything worth more than disdain.

"Shall I tell you why?" Peg asked.

"Please." Hogarth said stiffly.

"He was rude about… Johnny. My fiancé. Johnny was killed in No-Man's-Land, he took a bullet in the back, there was some trouble concerning exactly how it had happened. No one was quite sure why Johnny was out there." Peg's voice began to tremble, "Eustace made comments about maybe Johnny being a coward, that he was running away when he was shot."

"It was only said in jest." Glorianna interjected.

"He knew it hurt!" Peg threw the ashtray to one side and her calm evaporated, "I loved Johnny more than anyone can ever know. I'll never love anyone else. He was brave and loyal, he had been in the trenches over a year. He had had some trouble with shell-shock, but he stayed on the front all the same. He never would have run away. Eustace insisted on disgracing his name, insisted. Until I was so sick of it, so sick of him, that I wanted nothing better than to see him dead. But he didn't die, he just kept coming here."

"When did you start poisoning him?" Clara asked.

"Three years ago, approximately." Peg couldn't meet anyone's eyes now, "I learned what was in the Oxo tin and I had the idea. In fact, all I wanted at first was just for him to stay away. I wasn't thinking of killing him, not until later. Because no matter how I poisoned him, he always came to stay again and again and again. This time was the last straw. The things he was saying about Andrew…"

Peg screwed up her eyes. Tight shut. She had not really meant to kill him, at least she hoped that was the case. She had been so angry it was hard to say exactly what was on her mind when she took the arsenic from the pantry. Maybe she had meant to fatally harm him, but surely not? Surely this was not Penelope Campbell? She pressed her face into her hands, wanting to scream and let it all out; the spite, the anger, the bitterness, the grief. Instead it lodged, as it always did, in her throat.

"I... need to go think about this for a while." Hogarth stood, an unearthly look on his face, as though he was seeing something unreal in the room. He slumped away and shortly they heard the sound of his study door.

No one else moved. Finally Clara spoke.

"Peg, there is nothing the police can do about what you have done. In my opinion your guilt will be enough punishment. I'm just sorry you ever thought murder was a solution to your problems."

"Have you never hated someone Clara? So badly you wished them dead?" Peg briefly pulled down her hands.

"Yes." Clara said without hesitation, "But I only wished it. I did not act."

Peg hid back in her hands.

"What now?" She asked.

That was not Clara's question to answer; only the Campbell family could decide on Peg's fate. Whatever it was, whether estrangement or forgiveness, Clara knew one secret that would ensure Peg had a safe future. Eustace had left her some of his money, a fair chunk by all accounts. Since Peg did not actually murder him, there was nothing excluding her from inheriting the money, however ethically wrong it may seem. In short, Clara knew Peg was safe whatever happened. She just wasn't about to say that. Nothing would induce her to tell a would-be murderess she was to become a wealthy woman in her own right.

More than ever Clara wished she could get out of the Campbell home. There was nothing she wanted more than to be out of the house and heading home.

Chapter Twenty-five

It was late in the evening when Clara received the message to go to the police station. She finished a sandwich Annie had kindly made her – she had not been inclined towards dinner with the family – and asked Timmy if he would run her into town. He was quite happy to, as long as she told him all that had gone on with Ethel along the way. Clara could not avoid the truth since Timmy had two eyes in his head and a brain that he occasionally used, and he had noticed just exactly how Ethel was bleeding to death.

He extracted the final details, as much as they were, under a strict oath of secrecy. Clara made no mention of Mrs Patterson and suggested she had just been passing when she noticed something was amiss at 24 Alms Street. Timmy didn't entirely believe her, but he was satisfied with everything else she told him, including that Ethel was doing well.

"Tell a soul and I will skin you alive Timmy." Clara informed him as they pulled up outside the police station.

"I won't say anything. Though a fine thing it was explaining to cook what had happened to those blankets."

Clara left the car, saying she would call the house when she needed a ride home, and went to discover why inspector Jennings had summoned her.

Jennings was not in his office, but in a small room at the back of the police station, once perhaps a scullery. He was smoking and making a cup of tea. Clara discovered him in the cubby-hole and asked what was the matter with a look rather than words.

"We got Mrs Patterson. Thought you would like to see her."

Clara gave a sigh of relief.

"I imagine she is delighted to be here."

"She gave me a piece of her mind. I was waiting for you before I spoke to her further. She hasn't confessed as such yet, but she knows we have a witness to her actions."

"Inspector if she knows anything about Shirley Cox I would like to hear it."

"So would I. Shall we see her now?"

The inspector took them across the hall and through to another back room. It was sparsely appointed with a table and chairs. One window, with bars, looked onto the back yard of the station. Mrs Patterson was sat at the table, glaring at them.

"So you brought that tart again?" She snapped.

"Mind your tongue!" The inspector barked, "Aren't you already in enough trouble?"

Mrs Patterson folded her arms over her chest and gave Clara the 'evil eye'. Clara was unmoved.

"We have a witness Mrs Patterson. One of the girls you, ahem, helped. Also the doctor believes he can prove the bundle we found in your yard was a human baby."

"Nothing to do with me, the neighbours dumped it there. Threw it over the wall." Mrs Patterson said quickly.

"Amazing how it landed so close to your door." The inspector replied blandly, "Do you suppose a jury will believe that? In my experience juries are very biased against abortionists."

Mrs Patterson grimaced. She wasn't stupid. She had survived many years in her illegal trade just because she was smart enough to cover herself. On this occasion she had been sloppy. Why had she not taken more care? Well, she knew the answer. She had been feeling queer, had been for weeks, there was this constant lump in her throat making it hard to swallow and her chest was not so good. She just hadn't had the strength to do more than dump the body outside her door – sloppy, sloppy! But she had gotten away with it for so long…

"A confession would make things easier for everyone." Jennings continued, "If you were to co-operate, it would look favourable in the eyes of the judge, especially if you were to name your accomplice."

Mrs Patterson started to shake her head, but then wondered why she was bothering. It was all over, wasn't it? They had her, a witness and a body, they had never come so close before. So what was the point in protecting that bloody vicar? In any case what had he ever done for her? When she had started this sickness and asked for a little consideration had he come? Had he dropped by to check on her? No! He had continued his trips to London and brought her girls at all hours of the night, even after she said she was through with the whole business.

And hadn't she been feeling just a touch anxious over her immortal soul these last weeks? Funny how the thought of dying had crept into her mind and with it worries about her actions in the eyes of God. What did He make of her? Sometimes, when the pain was bad in the middle of the night, she started to think of all the things her mother had told her about God as a child and it had made her a little scared about the way she had lived. Soon, she feared, soon she would be meeting her maker and what would He say?

Draper had been no help when she had asked. For a man of the cloth his concept of God was flimsy at best. He had smiled his watery smile and changed the subject. So what help was he? No, she didn't owe him anything. It was time Millicent Patterson thought of herself and herself alone. She resolved her mind to the truth, maybe it would ease a little of that fear she had grown accustomed to. In any case, the police had a doctor, which was more than could be said for Mrs Patterson. Maybe she could get some medicine and not die after all.

"So if I confess, what then?" Mrs Patterson asked.

"That depends on the magistrates, not me." Jennings took out some plain paper and a pencil, "But they usually take these things into consideration."

"And my age, they got to consider that. And me health, that ain't so good."

"You have still committed a crime, you can't escape that."

"So you say, I was only helping those girls, but I see I will be judged for it."

Jennings gave her an unimpressed look.

"Does that mean you will make a confession?"

"What do you want?"

"We can keep this quite simple, how about 'I, Mrs...'"

"Millicent." Mrs Patterson said as the inspector looked to her to fill in the gap.

"I, Mrs Millicent Patterson, hereby swear in front of Inspector Jennings of the Surrey constabulary, that I have been conducting illegal abortions within my premises at King Street for the last..."

"Twelve."

"...twelve years. During which time I have worked in association with..."

"Reverend Irving Draper."

"...Reverend Irving Draper, to perform these illegal actions. I am aware my deeds were a crime and have made this confession with my full co-operation." Jennings finished off the paper, "If you are happy I will have this typed up for you to sign?"

Mrs Patterson nodded solemnly.

"Back in a moment." The inspector disappeared briefly, giving Clara and Mrs Patterson a chance to glare at each other with mutual dislike, before he returned.

"Now to our next business," The inspector sat down

contentedly in his chair, very pleased with his evening's work, "Tell me all you know about the Reverend Draper."

"What don't I know?" Mrs Patterson snorted, "I always smile when someone calls him vicar, what sort of a vicar is he?"

"I don't know, you tell me."

Mrs Patterson was suddenly rather pleased to be the centre of attention, especially as it was no longer concerned with her. She puffed herself up, proud to have something useful to tell the police and began her revelations with gusto.

"Reverend Draper came knocking on my door back when I was in London. Those were grand days, I was rolling in it because the city Madams sent all their girls to me. I was the best then and they paid me well. I hardly ever lost a girl in my charge and if I did it was usually the strumpet's fault for not following my advice."

Clara bit hard on her tongue, silence was not easy at that moment.

"One day, a few years before the war I has a knock on my door and there is this man, dressed all in black. I think he's an undertaker, but no he has this little white collar on." Mrs Patterson mimed with her fingers a collar around someone's neck, "He were a clergyman, on my doorstep! I was beside myself, what could he want? I half told him where to go, when he said I need use of your talents. Well, I could see it weren't for him so I ask the usual questions, who, when, how far gone is she? Well he has a cab waiting down the road and he goes back and he fetches this girl. A regular doxy as far as I could tell, I wasn't sure what he was about. But he says, she's his mistress and she's pregnant, and he says he can't be having that, what with the church and all. So I sorts her out all right and off they go.

"Well blow me if he don't come back a few months later and now he has another girl in tow! I've done it again Mrs Patterson, he says, I just can't resist a pretty face. Well, this next girl is a slip of a thing and it's a nasty job and she comes over a bit funny. So I set her in my back room and keep an eye and the vicar hangs around and he is talk, talk, talk. Quite a business this, he says. How much you paid? Not enough, I laugh, well he laughs too and says he knows a few girls could use me, not just the regular doxies, but decent girls who've got themselves in trouble and don't know where to go. Girls from good families who have got money to pay well. He hears things in the church, he says, he can spread the word that he can help them. Well I think he is full of bull, but he says we should try it anyhow, and I suppose he persuades me.

"Anyway he takes his girl away and within a week he is back again. I've got one Mrs Patterson, he says, daughter of local squire, been busy with a farmhand, needs some help. Came to me through a friend of a friend. She'll pay well for the service and us keeping quiet. Then he tells me how much she will pay and my eyes almost fall out my head. So I say yes and I kept saying yes for the next twelve years."

Mrs Patterson puffed out her cheeks as she paused for breath. For a moment she was quite carried away with herself.

"Twelve years." She repeated.

"All this time Reverend Draper has been an agent for you?" Jennings asked.

"If you like." Agreed Mrs Patterson, "He seems to find the girls all right and he keeps quiet. He still spends most of his time in London. I dare say some of them he brings are really girls he has gotten into trouble. Just lately it's become a bit of a nuisance."

Jennings nodded and duly wrote down what she had said. There was a tap on the door and the constable Clara had stuffed in the back of a hearse appeared with a typed copy of Mrs Patterson's statement. Jennings offered her a pen to sign it.

Meanwhile Clara was thinking hard, she had a question she was burning to ask. A question that possibly only Mrs Patterson and the good vicar Draper could answer. She glanced at Jennings, trying to sense if it was alright to butt in. He was making notes and not looking up. Finally Clara could not resist anymore.

"Mrs Patterson what do you know about a woman named Shirley Cox?"

Jennings' head shot up. Mrs Patterson gave Clara a look of low regard.

"Can she ask me a question?" She demanded in imperial tones.

Jennings stared at Clara a moment.

"She can." He answered.

Mrs Patterson huffed to herself and fussed with her paper statement before her.

"Don't seem like she has the authority."

"Please answer Miss Fitzgerald." Jennings said more sternly.

Mrs Patterson focused again on Clara.

"Miss? Yes, you look like one of these lasses who abhor men."

Clara refused to be offended.

"Mrs Patterson, you may insult me as you please, it does not change my question. Nor will it change the fact that once this short interview is over I will leave this room quite freely. Bear all this in mind as you level comments at me, since they may just go against you in court." Clara wasn't sure if all that was true, but Mrs Patterson believed her and it flustered her into talking.

"Now, now, I wasn't trying to cause trouble." Mrs Patterson gave a little smile, "I can tell you what I know about Shirley Cox, which isn't a lot I might add."

"Anything would be good. I am aware she was connected to Reverend Draper."

"Connected?" Mrs Patterson gave a tight laugh, "You could say that, all right. She was his mistress for more years than I know. At least until 1915 or 1916."

Clara's heart missed a beat.

"His mistress?"

"One of a handful he always has on the go. He brought her to me a few times for my services. I think the last was in 1915. That may have been when he was through with her too. She was getting on, you know. He likes them young. I can't say a lot about her. She was quiet, sullen. Professional, I thought to myself, like the doxies. Probably she was one of them normally. It was all business between her and me. Some of the other girls, the non-professionals, want a chat as it happens. Not this one, not a word slipped through her lips."

"Are you saying the last time you saw her was in 1915?"

"Saw her, yes. Heard about her… that's another matter." Mrs Patterson's eyes crinkled with pleasure as she saw the way the conversation was heading, "Will anything I say about this matter go into consideration for me? I mean, am I helping to solve her murder or some such?"

"I'll put it all before the judge." Jennings said noncommittally, "I will inform him how useful you have been. If your information proves correct, of course."

"Oh it's correct!" Mrs Patterson said firmly, "Now what can I tell you about that girl?"

"Did she visit Reverend Draper in the last few days?" Clara asked.

"Last Saturday. She upset Draper a lot. He said she was after money, blackmailed him, said she would tell the bishop all about him if he didn't pay up. He was shaking in his boots thinking about it." Mrs Patterson grinned, "He came to me wanting to know what he could do. Said she was ruining everything he had built for himself. Well, what did I care? Silly old fool. I sent him away and said he would have to sort himself out, I had no more time for him. Does that help you?"

Jennings was eyeing Clara, trying to keep a smile off his face.

"Thank you Mrs Patterson." Clara said, "That helps considerably."

"Perhaps you could say that to the judge." Mrs Patterson piped up hopefully.

Clara met her eyes, her expression implacable, her temper barely checked.

"I don't think so Mrs Patterson." She said coldly, "It's too late to ask me for help."

Chapter Twenty-six

It was over a week before any more could be done. Reverend Draper had apparently vanished, no sign of him could be found in London and his rectory remained empty and quiet. Clara passed the time uneasily at the Campbell house. She was itching to get back to Brighton and to her usual work. The Campbells were morose now, hardly talking to one another. Clara felt like the person who had brought this curse upon them. Not to mention her exposure of Peg's poisonous intentions, which were enough to make her very careful of everything she ate and drank.

Inspector Jennings set the young constable to monitor the rectory and report the return of the vicar. Clara came to know the time he cycled up the hill towards the house each morning and would wait by the gate to ask him for any news. She repeated the process in the early evening as he cycled home. Three long days of this dull waiting with only a negative response was very trying on her nerves and she began to wonder if Reverend Draper had proved more canny than they thought and had fled the country.

Then Saturday came and the constable cycled down the hill rather fast just after lunch as though he was pursued by the Devil himself. Clara spotted him out of a window and turned to Tommy.

"He's back. Quickly!"

They hurried up the hill, they could hardly expect to make it much before the police, for Inspector Jennings had a car that he could use for important business, and catching Reverend Draper at home seemed pretty important. Even so Clara was determined to be there first. She puffed up the hill pushing Tommy's wheelchair.

"He can't know what we have been about." Tommy spoke excitedly, "Else he would not have been fool enough to come back. Oh Clara, just supposing, just supposing..?"

Clara couldn't answer him due to her exertions, but she was equally eager. Since her conversation with Mrs Patterson several facts had played on her mind and had brought her into deep consternation concerning the good vicar. In particular she was playing out Reverend Draper's words in her mind "I never expected that. To see her walk in like that!" Oh at the time it had made such simple sense to assume he was referring abstractedly to the ruined wedding but what he had really meant was that he had recognised Shirley Cox, his one-time mistress! The shock Clara had perceived in him that day and nothing to do with the interruption of a sacred ceremony and everything to do with Draper seeing his ex-mistress standing in his church!

Clara grimaced up the last leg of the hill, she was just reaching the gate of the rectory when they both heard the roar of an engine. Jennings was coming full of questions no doubt. Clara brought the wheelchair to a stop and leaned with exhaustion against the rectory wall. She had to catch her breath before Jennings arrived, but there was the car already sweeping around the corner.

Jennings pulled up on the opposite side of the road and jumped out eagerly. The sergeant and constable were with him and tumbled out the car.

"I thought I was the first to know?" Jennings said, mildly amused to see an out-of-breath Clara leaning against a suspect's front wall.

"I spotted the constable riding downhill." Clara muttered in-between gasps.

"And you came to one of your usual, spot-on, conclusions. Well, are you ready to meet the man himself?"

Clara gave her assent and Jennings led the way to the door. The constable and sergeant flanked him, Clara and Tommy were just behind. Jennings rang the bell by the side of the door and they all stood waiting impatiently. Everyone seemed nervous and twitchy, as if something horrible might at any second erupt from the door. Clara reflected it was somewhat of a disappointment instead to see a humble-looking vicar open the door in carpet slippers.

"Hello?" Draper asked curiously.

"Inspector Jennings, might I come in and speak with you a moment?"

Draper glanced at the small crowd on his doorstep.

"I suppose." He said, more bemused than worried.

Jennings stepped into the house and Clara followed, but when she tried to help Tommy in the inspector stopped her.

"Just you, Miss Fitzgerald. You're the one I have an agreement with."

Clara glanced at Tommy, but he just gave a shrug.

"Best I stick here and make sure he doesn't leave." He grinned.

Clara gave him an apologetic look and followed Jennings indoors. The front door was left ajar so the constable and sergeant outside could be aware of anyone trying to leave unexpectedly. Clara followed Jennings through the tidy, but rather barren, rectory, he, in turn, behind Draper. They entered a small front room where a fire had just been started in the grate to try and take the dampness out of the air. Draper pointed to a pair of chairs one side of the hearth and then took a seat opposite. He studied them with benign, grey eyes.

229

Reverend Draper was a compact man, without his clerical clothes he looked like a clerk or some similar very ordinary person. He had a weak smile and watery eyes, his hair was thinning on top and receding at the temples, emphasising rather prominent ears. But all in all Clara felt it seemed an honest enough face, and that of course was the real danger. Draper did not give the impression of a man embroiled in a nefarious life of mistresses and illegal abortions, he seemed a perfectly studious and non-threatening vicar.

"Sorry to disturb you reverend, but we have been needing to speak with you. I believe you have been away in London?" Jennings began.

Reverend Draper smiled politely.

"That's right."

"You have only just returned?"

"About an hour ago. I came from the opposite road to avoid going through town." Draper persisted with his wincing smile, "As a vicar, one gets waylaid a lot, so one tries to avoid town if possible."

"That is quite all right reverend, I was merely curious if you could tell us anything about the girl who died here last week? You may recall her name was Shirley Cox?"

Draper gave a little shrug.

"We have a witness who saw her pay a call here on the night of her death. As far as we are aware that is the last time she was seen alive. Perhaps you could help us by explaining why she came to you?"

"No one came to me." Draper smiled blithely, "Would you care for a cup of tea?"

"Reverend, you don't appear to grasp the seriousness of this." Jennings continued, "We know she came here. We know that you know Shirley Cox. Mrs Patterson has told us everything."

"Who?" Draper asked without blinking.

"Mrs Patterson has explained her working relationship with you and has told us how you came to know Shirley Cox."

Draper gently shook his head.

"I can't say I know this Mrs Patterson. She doesn't sound like a regular at the church. I'm afraid she must be mistaken."

Jennings contained the sigh that threatened to escape his lips. He didn't look at Clara but he knew she was thinking what he was. What evidence did they have of the connection between Draper and Shirley? The confession of a woman who conducted abortions? What jury would believe that over the word of a vicar?

Jennings decided to make himself comfortable, since this was going to be a long job, and settled back in his chair.

"Let's start again, tell me about last Saturday, every detail you can remember…"

Outside Tommy watched a pigeon flutter onto the road and peck jerkily at the ground.

"What does Inspector Jennings want with a vicar?" The constable was asking.

"I imagine he is a witness to something. He was there at the wedding, right." The sergeant answered him.

"I thought we were going for that Andrew Campbell on that one?"

"No evidence. I mean, he probably did it, but we can't prove it can we?"

"Oh, but maybe the vicar can?"

"This is the joy of police work, constable. Repeatedly banging your head against a brick wall."

Tommy smirked to himself. They were silent a moment, then the constable started again.

"I thought it was funny being posted here. Just staring at this house."

"That is another joy of police work. Waiting."

"I mean, the lady down the road kept on watching me and this morning she asked me to help with her washing line which had snapped. That was all right, wasn't it sergeant? I'm supposed to help people?"

The sergeant pursed his lips.

"You were supposed to be watching this house."

"Yes, but the line snapped and all her washing had fallen down, and she couldn't reach up to re-tie the line. I was only gone a few minutes, I was hardly expecting him to turn up after three days of watching for nothing. Certainly not in a car."

"What did you say?" Tommy interrupted.

"I was hardly expecting him to come." The constable dutifully repeated.

"No, the other part, about the car. The reverend arrived in a car?"

"From the wrong direction too. I was expecting him to come up the hill, instead he came from the other road. No one mentioned that."

"You have to be alert to such possibilities." The sergeant commented with a roll of his eyes.

"Well, it all took me by surprise."

"What became of the car?" Tommy pressed.

The constable looked at him perplexed then pointed to a workshop structure at the back of the house.

"Push me over there constable." Tommy insisted.

The constable looked to his sergeant for what to do, his sergeant gave a vague nod and so Tommy was pushed to the workshop doors. He tried them. Locked.

"I need you to break open this door constable."

"I can't do that." The poor constable was having memories of being press-ganged into a hearse by Clara. It seemed all the Fitzgeralds were adept at getting him into trouble.

Tommy had his fingers in the crack of the door and was trying to lever them open.

"Constable, vital clues could be inside here. You must open it!"

The constable shuffled his feet. He tried the doors rather half-heartedly to see if they were really locked. They were. He looked at the lock for a bit, poked at it with a pencil from his pocket.

"Constable, find a lever of some sort." Tommy

instructed.

The police constable flapped his arms at him.

"This is breaking and entering!"

"Can you pick locks?"

"No!"

"Then do as I say and find a lever. I want to see this car."

The constable huffed and hesitated. He paced back and forth, gave the door a little nudge with his foot just in case. But nothing was working. Tommy was glaring at him with the sort of look Clara had perfected for neglectful tradesmen. The constable felt stuck, he turned back to his sergeant, but he was annoyed with him for having left his post to help with a washing line and wasn't taking any notice. Supposing this car was important? Should the constable really ignore it? Would it not redeem him for his earlier failings? With another sigh the constable made a decision and picked up a sturdy piece of wood from the pile of lumber beside the workshop. He wedged the narrow end in the gap of the door and gave a tentative push. The door resisted him admirably.

"You would be better off with that." Tommy was pointing to a forgotten gardening trowel sitting upright in a flowerbed where it had once been left.

The constable picked it up and stared at it as if it were a meteor from Mars.

"Try wedging that in the door and giving it a good jerk."

Once again the constable gave Tommy an odd look, then he did as he said. The end of the trowel slid into the gap of the doors easily enough, the constable gave a tentative push on the other end.

"Harder." Tommy commanded, one eye watching the door of the house. The sergeant was watching them curiously, but from his angle he couldn't quite see the door operation.

The constable pushed at the trowel a little harder. Still not enough. Tommy looked at him irritably, grabbed the trowel and wedged it in around the height of the door lock, which was just above his shoulder height. Then, half falling out of his chair, he pressed against it with all his might and the door groaned. He pulled back then jerked forward again. His wheelchair spun out beneath him at the same time the door popped open with a rattle and creak.

"Oi!" The sergeant was running forward.

"Get me in my chair." Tommy snapped at the constable who was standing indecisively between him and the sergeant. Abruptly he bent down and hoisted Tommy into his wheelchair.

"What do you think you are doing?" The sergeant yelled as he reached the workshop.

Tommy ignored him and left the constable to fend him off, while he pushed at the wheels of his chair and made his way into the workshop. The car was there all right, bright and shiny, new red and black paint, wheels sparkling clean, leather interior smelling of saddle soap and polish. Tommy peered over the side of the door, the soft roof was pulled back and it was easy to see the entire interior of the car. It was clean and neat, very much like the vicar's house. Not even a road map cluttering the floor space or seat. Tommy moved a folded travel rug, but there was nothing beneath it. If this was the car Shirley Cox had been transported to Brooklands in, there was no sign of it. Tommy felt he had hit a dead end. Here was the car, but any evidence was gone.

"You can't just go breaking open doors!" The sergeant was yelling at his constable.

Tommy tried to block out the row. If I had a body to move what would I do with it, he asked himself. Put it on the back seat, cover it with the travel blanket, but there would still be a visible lump. Anyone could see it, really. Anyone might notice. Tommy pulled back from the car.

Reverend Draper was a cautious man, he had spent years keeping multiple mistresses secret, living two lives. Surely he was not fool enough to travel around with a body in the back seat of his car. Even at midnight you could stumble across someone…

Tommy's eyes wandered to the boot of the car. It was reasonably big, the sort advertised for being capacious enough for a luggage trunk or a picnic basket. Maybe even a body…

Tommy rolled himself around the back of the car. The sergeant was still shouting at his constable, clearly feeling the need to make a very elaborate point over the matter. Tommy fingered the boot. There was a spare wheel fixed to it and a shiny oval handle in chrome just below. Tommy took it in his hand and turned it. The handle moved easily and a click followed indicating the boot had popped open. Tommy knew he was holding his breath, but couldn't help it because beneath the lid of that boot could be the clue they needed or nothing at all. Tommy lifted the boot; the space below was dark and empty except for another travel blanket.

Tommy sighed. It had been a nice hope while it lasted. For the sake of thoroughness he moved the neatly folded blanket. There was nothing behind it. Tommy went to put down the blanket and paused. The bundle of cloth felt oddly bulky, as though something was tucked inside and causing the blanket to bulge in the centre. Tommy unfolded the blanket, he was just pulling it open when the sergeant appeared.

"And what do you think you are doing?" Demanded the policeman.

Tommy looked up at him and grinned.

"I think you better go fetch Inspector Jennings." He held up a folded mink stole.

Inspector Jennings glanced up at the sergeant hovering in the doorway. He was feeling more than a little frustrated and the last thing he wanted to see was his sergeant standing anxiously to one side.

"What is it sergeant?" He demanded.

The sergeant gnawed at his lip a moment and then

held out his arms. The mink stole was draped over them.

"We found it in the Reverend's car boot."

Draper's eyes flashed.

"H…how did you get into my car?"

Clara ignored him. She stood up and fetched the stole. She studied it for a while.

"This is Shirley Cox's mink stole, the one she was last seen wearing on Saturday. The one that was missing when her body was found." Clara said softly.

Draper glanced between her and the inspector.

"I…I…I…"

"I believe you said you did not know Shirley Cox?" Jennings said coolly.

Draper's calm was leaving him. He was beginning to tremble.

"Wait, I do recall a lady visiting me. She was distressed, I never did quite catch her name. I gave her a lift in my car, she must have dropped the stole."

"It was folded in a blanket in the boot of your car." Tommy announced from the doorway. The constable had helped him up the steps into the house.

Draper stared around at them all, his mouth working but no words coming out.

"How…" He finally settled his attention on Jennings, "You can't do this to me, my reputation is everything."

"You murdered Shirley Cox." Jennings said calmly, "You ruined yourself. I have witnesses to place her here and the mink stole that we were certain had been taken by her killer. With all that against you, do you still deny knowing Shirley Cox?"

Draper hesitated for a long time. There was really little he could do. Denying the evidence was not going to help. He whirled his thumbs together in his lap, slowly making up his mind. He gave a little sigh at last.

"I don't suppose I really thought I could carry on forever." He said sadly, "Someone was going to spot it eventually."

"I think your bishop will be very curious to know how

236

you could afford a car on a Reverend's living." Jennings hinted, planting the last nail in the coffin.

"Need I explain that? You have Mrs Patterson after all. I presume she has explained our association."

"She has and it was clearly a profitable one for you at least." Answered Jennings, "Now, will you tell us about Shirley?"

Draper sighed again, he eyed his audience warily. He was not a tough man, not really, and he knew when the game was up.

"I never meant to kill her." He said quietly, hoping to draw some sympathy from at least Clara, but she remained silent, "She came here on Saturday night. I dreaded she would, I hadn't seen her in years. The last we spoke she was planning on marrying this young soldier, that was what finished our affair. Not that I really worried, I'm not the jealous type. I wished her luck and off I went. Normally when I finish with a girl I give them a little something to set them on their way, but Shirley finished with me, so I didn't. Then she comes on Saturday with all these ideas that I owe her."

Draper shook his head.

"I didn't owe her anything, but she wanted money. She was completely broke and the old life had worn her down. How was I to know that soldier had been Andrew Campbell or that he had left her like that? She was aggressive. She shouted. I hate shouting. I wanted to leave but she wouldn't let me go. I tried to make her leave and she turned into a banshee yelling abuse. I…I don't really know what happened. She was making me so angry and afraid. What if the neighbours heard? What if she told somebody about me? I wanted her to be quiet and I grabbed at her, I only meant to make her stop yelling but my hands fell on that damn stole and I hauled it tight. At first I hardly knew why I was doing it, only it made her quieter. Then I couldn't let go and then…" Draper fell into silence.

"Why did you leave the body at the racetrack?" Clara

asked.

"I thought it might throw the blame onto Andrew Campbell." Draper rubbed at his arms as if he was cold, "Are you going to arrest me?"

"Yes." Jennings nodded.

Draper resigned himself to the situation.

"They don't hang men of the cloth, usually." He said, almost to himself, "I imagine they will be lenient."

Clara wanted to kick him. His amiable expression was back as if he had not just confessed to murdering someone. He was so complacent, assuming his dog-collar would spare him the worst the courts had to offer. She hoped he came upon a very mean jury and a judge who wasn't swayed by the façade a man wore.

"Shouldn't you rather be worrying about God's leniency?" She said.

Draper looked at her, his expression genuinely puzzled.

"Why?" He asked.

And Clara realised he meant it.

Chapter Twenty-seven

Bags packed, Clara was only too glad to be leaving the Campbell house. Timmy was loading the car with their belongings. Their train would be leaving at 11.15am, taking them back to Brighton, back home.

Hogarth stood on the porch of the house and watched the proceedings. He was a quieter man than when she had first arrived, a man with a lot of challenges ahead of him. Clara went to say her farewells.

"I hope you will come down for a visit at Christmas." She told him, "Brighton does a good show at Christmas, the shops are beautiful."

Hogarth gave her a smile and embraced her.

"Thank you for everything Clara." He said in her ear.

She knew he didn't just mean finding Shirley's murderer and saving Andrew, his thoughts were on Susan and Peg too.

"I was just being my usual nosy self." Clara shrugged at him, "I would do it for anyone."

Hogarth patted her shoulder, his eyes growing tearful.

"Just like your father. I miss him dreadfully."

"Oh now Hogarth." Glorianna fussed at her husband, "Clara doesn't need tears to see her off. Where is everyone?"

Andrew, Peg and Susan were holding back in the shadows of the hallway. Glorianna ushered them forward, her final duty as hostess to see her guests off in style. Andrew took Clara's hand and shook it, a gesture she appreciated.

"Thanks. I mean, for sorting out my mess. Can't say if Laura will ever forgive me, but if we do finally have that wedding you will be first on the list of guests."

Clara smiled brightly, but hoped to Heaven she was never invited to another Campbell wedding.

"I was rather mean with you at first. I'm sorry about that." Andrew continued, "If you ever need anything."

"Thank you." Clara answered.

Peg was next on the farewells. She couldn't meet Clara's eyes.

"Safe journey." She said rather stiffly.

"Keep strong Peg." Clara winked at her, "You know you are a decent soul at heart."

Susan interrupted them by wrapping her arms around Clara and hugging her.

"Come back whenever you can!" She said with a smile, "If I have a girl I'll call her Clara."

"Oh no, the poor child!" Clara laughed, "Don't burden her with my name!"

"Without you there would not be a child, I'm very glad you were here. Sorry about how awful we all were, but I hope you can forgive us and come back soon."

Clara promised she would, then she disengaged herself from Susan and stood before the whole family. She started to speak but words were rather difficult. Should she say thank you for a lovely stay? Of course not, that would be silly, but saying nothing would be awkward too. As it was Tommy came to her aid.

"Well there is a train to catch folks!" He cried, "So Cheerio, Pip, Pip! Come on Clara."

Clara stumbled into the car, waving at the family. They waved back, their farewell not ending until the car was out of sight. Clara sat back in her seat and closed her eyes.

"I'm never attending another wedding." She said firmly.

Tommy laughed loudly.

"Not all of them involve murder!"

"No, just the ones in our family!" Clara hissed a sigh out through her teeth, "Tell me we aren't as peculiar as that lot?"

"Don't worry Clara." Tommy grinned at her, "We are far worse."

He chuckled all the way down the hill as Clara groaned at him.

Printed in Great Britain
by Amazon